IMMORTALITY AT ANY PRICE

by the same author

NOVELS (*as* H. S. HOFF):

Three Girls: a trilogy:
Trina
Rhéa
Lisa
Three Marriages

(*as* WILLIAM COOPER):

Scenes from Life: a trilogy:
Scenes From Provincial Life (with an introduction by Malcolm Bradbury)
Scenes From Metropolitan Life
Scenes From Married Life
Scenes From Later Life (a companion volume to the trilogy)
The Struggles of Albert Woods
The Ever-Interesting Topic
Disquiet And Peace
Young People
Memoirs Of A New Man
You Want The Right Frame of Reference
Love On The Coast
You're Not Alone
From Early Life (autobiographical reminiscences)

PLAY

Prince Genji (adapted from *The Tales of Genji* by Lady Murasaki)

DOCUMENTARY

Shall We Ever Know? (an account of the trial of the Hosein brothers for the murder of Mrs McKay)

PAMPHLET

C. P. Snow (British Council Series: *Writers and their work:* No. 113)

IMMORTALITY
AT ANY
PRICE

 a novel by

William Cooper

SINCLAIR-STEVENSON

FOR A.S.B.
A WONDERFUL WRITER

First published in Great Britain by
Sinclair-Stevenson Limited
7/8 Kendrick Mews
London SW7 3HG, England

British Library Cataloguing in Publication Data
A CIP catalogue record for this book is available from the British Library.

ISBN 1 85619 063 3

Photoset by Rowland Phototypesetting Limited
Bury St Edmunds, Suffolk
Printed and bound in Great Britain by
Clays Limited, St Ives plc

1

❦ *A Wildean Truth* ❦

'There's nothing like the animosity of old friends.'

While she was saying it, Randa was giving me her characteristic smile – sleepy-looking and slightly venomous . . .

'Sounds like Oscar Wilde.'

Her eyelids flicked. 'So far as I know, it's original.'

'Then congratulations!'

She turned her head aside, her neck seeming to lengthen, her profile showing smoothly. She didn't speak.

'The animosity of old friends . . . It's a revelation of truth, Randa!'

I saw no response to the irony in my remark – in all probability she didn't notice it. She went on weightily:

'I think you *could* find it rewarding.' Pause. 'You know? . . .'

We had been talking about people who figured in *Private Eye*.

Just to be sure I was on the same wavelength, I repeated –

'The Horsfall Circus.' (The *Eye*'s term for them – Horsfall and his old friends Gotham and Protheroe, all three Men of Fame and Distinction; well, some Fame and some Distinction . . . enough to catch the *Eye*'s attention.)

She made a movement of the head appropriate to someone who doesn't demean herself by noticing someone
else's concern about whether he's on the same wavelength
or not.

'*Three* old friends,' I said.

'Enough for your purpose?' She smiled.

Enough for my next biography, she meant. My first
essay in the *genre*, published a little over six months ago,
had met with considerable success. She was right. I definitely ought to be settling on the subject for my second –
actually more desirably from my point of view a subject in
the plural, i.e. subjects; and for my preference, a *circle* of
them.

During a pause in the conversation I made a start on
eating my plateful of cold cherry soup. Randa was giving
me lunch at The Gay Hussar, a small Hungarian restaurant
in Soho, first opened (I had asked the manager) in 1954,
and even now – we were in 1982 – still keeping up a sort
of reputation for left-wing chic, not totally 'In' but not
totally 'Out'. Randa was very fond of their cold cherry
soup, especially on a warm summer's day: it was not for me
to say I was rather un-fond of it, for my taste a somewhat
wishy-washy red liquid. A dissentient view on my part
was not the thing. Why not? Because I had a hunch that
her invitation sprang from having it in mind to offer me
something to my advantage.

The Horsfall Circus as a subject for me – Was this that
something? Thinking that she had been Horsfall's lawyer
for the best part of his lifetime, and that Gotham was still
with her, I presumed that she must know what she was
talking about.

I kept my head down for a while, more to give myself a
chance to think than to concentrate on consuming this
ruby-red liquid.

My stock of ideas about the Horsfall Circus flurried
through my mind. A little group of men, from the same
school somewhere on the Welsh borders, who made a

mark when they fetched up at Oxford, all of fifty years ago. Their ringmaster, so designated by the *Eye* for his superlative combination of Celtic ambition and guile, was Cledwyn Horsfall, famous economist, famous writer and finally famous publicist – well, famous up to a point. He had died some time in the New Year, leaving quite a large fortune. (The other two old friends were very much alive.)

The *Eye* had made the occasion of Horsfall's death an opportunity for reviving their scandalous account of Celtic ambition and guile getting him into a top stratum of the Honours List under a previous Government – that notorious Resignation Honours List, inscribed on a certain lady's shell-pink writing-paper, which (so it was said) led the Queen, when she was shown the List, to ask:

'Are you *sure* it's the Prime Minister's?'

It *was* the Prime Minister's. Thereafter Horsfall, a big rotund fellow singularly gifted with intelligence and *hwyl*, had been in a position to give full rein to that intelligence and *hwyl* from the eminence of the House of Lords.

Randa was concentrating on her cold cherry soup. I exerted myself to give the impression that I was doing likewise.

I remembered scanning Horsfall's obituary in *The Times* through interest in him as writer rather than as economist or publicist. Unfortunately I hadn't studied it; so my present knowledge of his career and its chronology was somewhat patchy. The story was that while at Oxford he first sighted fame and distinction for a major contribution he claimed to have made to something called *The Beveridge Report*, which had come out in the middle of the War, been turned into a couple of White Papers towards the end of it, and then widely received with such acclaim that the post-War Labour Government declared its intention of implementing it. (A national health service was one of its assumptions.)

When the implementation of the Report was firmly under way, Horsfall was thought to be an obvious man to be drawn into the Civil Service to work on it. I hadn't noted which department he went into; but from College gossip in my own time I knew that he had ended up in an influential, if rather mysterious, post in the Cabinet Office. So far so good.

However, after a long and arduous – and successful – stint in the Civil Service, Horsfall had caused no surprise by announcing that he'd had enough. He wanted to return to academic life. The College welcomed his return, of course. But it lasted for an unexpectedly short time. In less than a year he'd been tempted back to official life. By the offer of an appointment – what man of ambition (or guile!) could have refused it? – as Economic Adviser to the Prime Minister; housed in No 10 Downing Street.

At No 10 Horsfall had stayed – apart from four years' tactful retirement to Oxford while a different Government was in power – till the next impressive step forward in his eventful history. 1976, and that Resignation Honours List. Reading the obituary I couldn't help feeling that elevation must nevertheless have foreshadowed an end to his effective life in high economics. In 1976 there was a new Prime Minister, for one thing. For another, high economics was now in a state of high turmoil over the conflict in theoretical circles between neo-Keynesianism and Friedmanite monetarism. High economics was in a state of high turmoil and as a consequence high politics as well. The new Prime Minister was said to be moving towards monetarism. Horsfall was at heart a Keynesian. *Ergo* . . . 1976 must have seen for him a summary switch from the frenzied activity of No 10 to the subdued existing of the House of Lords.

In compensation, though, the subdued existing of the House of Lords must have offered him prospects of time to devote to other things. For Horsfall, I understood, there were plenty of other things, well ahead of all of them being writing. Throughout the length of his career, it seemed, he had sustained an overriding desire to write novels – he had even published a first novel while he was still completing his D Phil in Economics. That novel, at least, I'd already read: it was about intrigues and conflicts, in a small Welsh town, between Methodists (very powerful) and those whom they called 'the big people' (also very powerful). I had liked it well enough to read two or three more – I imagined, now, that I could face reading the whole of his *oeuvre*, if necessary. Since his death I'd heard animated discussions among the other dons at High Table about whether he was a major novelist – *he* had apparently thought he was. Needless to say *they* didn't concur!

Lastly as a publicist. I'd noticed his activities as a public figure reported with increasing frequency in the media – if only, I thought now, I'd paid more attention! Independent, freelance activities in the cause of world peace. I did remember having seen him on television making a powerful speech in favour of what amounted to universal détente, and saying what he himself was in the process of doing about it. (Quite impressive – was there more to him than mere Celtic ambition and guile?) By the time he died it was clear that had got himself an international reputation.

Plenty of work ahead of me if I took the assignment on. Plenty of varied work, in much of which I should be starting from Square 1.

Meanwhile not much more work was required of me on the cold cherry soup – not many spoonsful still lay in my plate. I lifted my head to find Randa watching me. Not that that was anything new: Randa had been keeping an eye on me, in the metaphorical sense, for years.

The situation was this. Randa's firm, currently recognised as the foremost libel lawyers in London, was called Goslett & Goslett; and Randa (short for Miranda) and her sister, Jess (short for Jessica), were two of its three senior partners. The third, their matriarchal mother, Mabel, known as Mabsie, was the boss, punctiliously given credit in public for ruling the firm, although she didn't – Randa and Jess did. I was a cousin of Miranda and Jessica, my paternal grandfather having married one of Mabsie's sisters; so Randa and Jess were a generation older than me – they were in their early fifties, I in my early thirties. Superficially we were all on good terms with each other. *Au fond* I never felt at ease with them. Randa's metaphorical keeping an eye on me had consisted of recurrently taking steps since I was adolescent to 'keep me in the family'. At that time I hadn't understood why. It was when I was an undergraduate reading English Literature that she started to ask my literary advice – free of charge – on manuscripts of new books that had come in to be vetted for libel. In return she was ready to vouchsafe me – free of charge – her moral advice. Nowadays she was paying me for my professional advice, of course; and in my opinion she was getting value for money. I didn't know what she thought of my attitude towards her moral advice: since I was getting it free of charge I didn't feel any obligation to take it.

Randa had finished her soup. While attacking the last of mine, I reactivated the conversation.

'The animosity of old friends . . .' I murmured reflectively.

'You *could* find it rewarding.' Pause. '*Very* rewarding.' Another pause. 'You know? . . .'

'It's an intriguing thought . . .' I looked her in the eye. 'As you act for two out of the three, *you* should know.'

Instantly Randa's eyelids half-closed. She lifted her shoulders a little and said softly:

'What can I say to that, James?'

Professional discretion! A beautifully bogus spectacle. (Here I must remark that as well as being clever and literate, Randa was a beautiful woman.) I said facetiously:

'Randa, you're a temptress!'

Instantly her eyelids lifted again and her tone of voice changed from the seductive to the imperative.

'*No*, James!'

Randa was a strong feminist.

Discovered as a male chauvinist, I dived my spoon into the last ruby-red shallows. Unease in her presence was no excuse for such a *gaffe*; and protesting that I had not intended it would only discover me in her eyes as the more abject a male chauvinist.

Randa was the strongest feminist in my acquaintance, where she was closely followed by Jess, with dear old Mabsie, as in most other things, some distance behind both of them. In *Private Eye* the firm of Goslett & Goslett was routinely referred to as 'the Virago Sisters' (not to be confused with the Virago Press, of course), but that was the least of the *Eye*'s offences. 'So-and-So firm of publishers,' it would say, 'are presently being mis-advised by the Virago Sisters.' Routinely it cast its typical aspersions on their competence: that passed. Then last year it had cast its typical aspersions on their probity. That did not pass! Not for a moment. The *Eye* had had to pay up – out of court to the tune of £20,000, it was rumoured.

'*No*, James!' This time even more emphatically if anything. 'Never let me hear you make that kind of remark again!'

I didn't lift my glance. Had she thought the temptress I had in mind was Eve? Actually it was the third party in the Garden of Eden . . .

'OK,' I said. Refusing to give up the good fight for undergraduate facetiousness, I added: 'If I make it to any other woman, I'll try to be sure you're out of earshot.'

Randa made it clear that she didn't find the remark in the least funny, which didn't surprise me. Even my relatively short Life's Experience had taught me that people who were in the grip of an 'ism' – Feminism, Monetarism, Communism, Leavisism, to name just a few – never found jokes about it in the least funny. If they let themselves laugh, I thought, the grip might slip? . . .

A waiter took the soup-plates away and brought a dish made with goose, a sort of Hungarian *cassoulet*. I saw a chance to pull myself together, to retrieve my reputation for maturity. I spoke un-facetiously, very thoughtfully:

'Reverting to your idea about my having a look at the

three old friends . . . It really is an intriguing thought, Randa.'

'You *are* looking for a fresh subject?' She couldn't resist giving me the sort of look an older woman gives when preparing to vouchsafe a younger man free moral advice.

'I'm not thinking of throwing in my hand, you know.'

Putting down her knife and fork, she said:

'James, you must learn not to take offence so readily.'

'I *am* looking for a fresh subject,' I said placatingly. I was chewing a morsel of goose which was definitely not tender.

'What does All Souls think of *Edith Wharton and Her Circle*?' Said in a yielding tone of voice.

'Praise. It's rather nice.' Then I added, 'I think they don't entirely regret giving me a Fellowship.' Irony again – what a mistake!

Randa came back weightily. 'That is to their credit.' Then her tone of voice lightened and surprisingly she smiled. 'That élitist enclave in patriarchal society!'

I'd heard the 'patriarchal society' bit before. I smiled back.

'Do they appreciate the book for what it is?'

'What's that?' I realised that I'd laid myself open. I got what I'd asked for.

'A due tribute to a woman writer.'

I didn't give in. 'I thought I was paying tribute to a *writer*. You know. A writer *tout court.*'

I meant what I said. Mrs Wharton had been brought to my attention through her name being included – unlike that of Horsfall! – by my university teachers on a supplementary vacation reading-list. (I'd discovered Horsfall for myself in the course of giving *un*-recommended writers a chance.) They were right to include her on their list. I was bowled over by the first novel of hers that I read. A marvellous writer – opening me to a refinement and strength of moral sensibility well beyond anything I had known in myself. A marvellous writer – living in a society of which all I knew was what I had picked up from Henry

James, high society at the turn of the century in Boston, New York, Paris, London, the South of France . . . The *moeurs* of this society were entirely outside my experience, yet the members of it she was writing about became as recognisable to me as living individuals – they might have been people I met in my daily life.

Then there was the circle of writers round her, collected as she became richer and more famous.

And when I came to look into her private life, a startling and moving *dénouement*, special to me . . . She didn't experience profound sexual joy till she was forty-five years old. And then she experienced it in the biggest possible way – celebrated by a beautiful passage of erotic writing not for publication. Why was it so special to me? Why did it affect me so powerfully? Because at nearly thirty-five years old I regarded my own sexual life as a dead loss. I had another ten years to forty-five – Mrs Wharton was an example to me!

'I was glad to see' – Randa, too, was having some difficulty with the texture of the goose – 'you give due credit to the influence she had on male writers.'

Instead of saying Why on earth shouldn't I? I said:

'So am I.'

'Scott Fitzgerald . . . Ernest Hemingway . . . Henry James . . .' She took a sip from her glass of Bull's Blood and there was a gleam in her eye. 'Henry James,' she repeated. She loved Henry James.

I didn't know where she got Hemingway from, but I was willing to concede Fitzgerald. And if one were prepared to call it influence, I conceded that poor old Henry James had come in for more than his share of being whirled round the countryside of England and France in her succession of (mostly open-topped) motor-cars. 'The Angel of Devastation' he called her. I drank a sip from my own glass of Bull's Blood as a cover for not allowing a syllable to cross my lips.

We were both eating steadily, and I found myself

reflecting on the strange tension that always arose between us when I was with Randa. What was its cause? My unreconstructed response to a personality which combined a sort of doctrinaire feminism with unusual attractiveness as a woman?

The goose was going to keep us occupied for some time. Randa paused, then continued expatiating on the importance of Mrs Wharton. As most of her knowledge was picked up from the book I'd written myself – actually another book on Mrs Wharton had come out just after mine, but I doubted if Randa had read it – I didn't feel that I was learning much more about Mrs Wharton, though what Randa was saying was intelligent and perspicacious enough. What I might have been learning more about was herself, Randa: I might have been, had I not been inhibited by feeling that in some senses I knew enough already – for instance, the way she had got control of Goslett & Goslett. That was enough to give anyone a very comprehensive lead.

Goslett & Goslett had originally been founded by Randa's father, his wife Mabsie, and his younger brother. They had all possessed literary talent as well as legal talent. (Literary talent *despite* literary legal talent – the language of literature and the language of the law, it usually seemed to me, were mutually exclusive.) So the firm came to have a special interest in literary libel, and was now, as I have observed, the foremost of its kind in London. First of all Randa's father died, leaving his share in the firm to Miranda and Jessica. (Mabsie's future had already been taken care of.) Then the younger brother died, leaving his share to his son Christopher, more than ten years younger than Miranda and Jessica.

Dear old Mabsie, relatively good-natured and not all that clever, her daughters had relegated her within a couple of years of her being widowed. Their next move was to relegate Christopher. How? From office-gossip still in circulation, it appeared that they set about treating

Christopher in the way they believed, after their doctrinaire fashion, that senior male partners in a firm treated a junior female partner. With the calculated result: according to office-gossip, Christopher ended most day's work spitting with frustration and rage. It just showed they were right. The break had come some six years ago, shortly after I came back from Yale to Oxford and Randa took me up in earnest. Goslett & Goslett lost an important action through egregious incompetence. In the preparation of their case a vital previous judgement had been overlooked.

I vividly remembered Randa's half-closed eyelids and seductive tone of voice as she explained to me how in the eyes of the world they must all three, herself, Jessica and Christopher, share the responsibility. But within the firm, 'Someone's got to carry the can, James. And there's no doubt where the responsibility for that lies. We're terribly sorry for Christopher and all that. If only we could do something to help him out.' A poignant pause. 'You do see how we feel?'

Anyone could see with half an eye.

Christopher had been handed the can and had resigned his partnership in Goslett & Goslett forthwith. (Actually he'd got a job in the chambers of another firm a bit further along the same building, and had married a pretty girl.) Meanwhile a minor field-day had begun for *Private Eye*, inventing scurrilous inside details of the story. Goslett & Goslett became the Virago Sisters, renowned for misadvising their clients. With less effect than might have been expected. Among their most important clients Cledwyn Horsfall, for instance, had continued to rely on their services just as much as before, so they said – and it appeared to be the case. With his Celtic ambition and guile? Something to be looked into, there . . . Mabsie had ceased to appear in public other than on most ceremonial occasions. And the sisters had taken on a new partner, a youngish woman, very bright – with the *Eye* hinting that she was closer than a close friend of Jess . . .

Randa appeared to have been unaffected. She continued to look beautiful, tall and slender, skinny as a model with a model's elegance. An oval symmetrical face, dark grey hair strained back into a knot accentuating the fragility of her head, a long slender neck. And those remarkable narrow eyes which glinted between hooded lids. It was no surprise to me when I saw men sexually attracted to her: I was attracted to her myself. She was married to Roger Masson, Executive Chairman of J Arthur Masson, the advertising agents, and they had two sons.

Looking at me across the table in The Gay Hussar, characteristically her gaze was unblinking for a long period – then suddenly the eyelids flicked . . . I was chewing steadily again.

Irrelevantly, inexplicably, I was visited by an apprehension of *strangeness* . . . The strangeness of the two of us sitting here . . . Who were we? What were we? Why were we? It only lasted moments – my ruminations were interrupted. 'Are you finding this goose too much, James?'

'Yes, rather.'

'I don't think I can eat any more.' She looked at her watch.

'Just coffee?' I wanted her to go on about the three old friends . . .

She ordered coffee and while we were waiting she seemed disinclined to converse. People who were leaving the restaurant passed beside our table, among them a member of the Shadow Cabinet and a TV personality – reliable indicators of The Gay Hussar's not being totally Out. The TV personality was all TV smiles, dazzlingly dishonest and ingratiating. The Shadow Minister, elderly and noted for not being quite on the ball, was glumly preoccupied – possibly by the Labour Party's *débâcle* in last May's General Election; more likely by the prospect, when the Party came to choose its new Leader in October, of finding himself as Minister transformed from Shadow to Ghost-from-the-Past.

'There's nothing like the animosity of old friends . . .' I tried prompting her yet again.

Randa merely smiled distantly and repeated, 'You *could* find it rewarding.'

The waiter delivered our coffee.

'I *could* find it. Where's the best place to start looking?'

She drank some of her coffee, showing no sign that she'd heard the question. She picked up her handbag, took out a compact and opened it. Looking at herself in the mirror, she said:

'There's going to be a Memorial Service for Cledwyn Horsfall some time in September. Gotham will be giving the Address. Protheroe will be reading one of the readings.' She touched her lips with a lipstick.

'You'll be there?'

'I expect so.'

'Getting your name in *The Times*?' (Meant of course as a joke.)

'How *naïf* you are! The list of names in *The Times* is not to be read as a list of people actually present. It's mainly the list of those who are invited to the service in reply to their letters of condolence.' She gave her lips a final touch. Her lips were thin but shapely.

'Are you thinking I could go, not having written a letter of condolence?'

'I expect the service will be publicly announced. If it's by invitation I'll get you a card.'

'I see.'

Her eyes glinted. 'Why not?'

I said, 'Why not?'

Taking a Diner's Club card out of her bag, she called the waiter. 'This is *my* lunch, James.'

I thought, Why not?

Outside the restaurant we had to wait a minute or two for a taxi. I caught a quizzical glance from her, but I said nothing. I was thinking.

I was thinking I didn't like animosity. (I was ashamed of the sort of animosity I felt towards *her*.)

'You know, Randa . . . Animosity is *not nice*.'

A taxi! As I helped her into it she smiled at me over her shoulder –

'Not nice, perhaps. But *amusing!*'

That smile, now super sleepy-looking and more than slightly venomous, seemed to hover in the air over Greek Street like the smile of the Cheshire Cat.

Feeling disturbed, excited, I realised that my feet were taking me slowly down the street while I went on thinking.

Randa approved of my book about Edith Wharton and her circle because I was 'paying due tribute to a *woman* writer'. What could she be looking to me for in a book about the three old friends?

A possible answer occurred to me just as I turned into Old Compton Street. A book that would do the three men friends *down!* (From what *Private Eye* said about them it might be surmised that they were all three eminently do-downable.)

Suddenly I felt an impulse, animosity or no animosity, to discard the whole proposition, to decide here and now not to go to the Memorial Service, not to take the idea an inch further.

Of course I was casting around for a subject for my next book. I had some other ideas already but I was far from committed to any of them, and was in no hurry to be – a state of affairs I was naturally concealing from my publisher, who was like practically every other publisher in London in wanting his authors to produce a stream of successful books as fast as possible. He and my agent, with an eye to attracting the feminist bandwaggon, were in cahoots to lure me into writing a biography of Ada Leverson – an attractive idea, I admit, but I was not going to be railroaded into it. I countered with the suggestion of Anthony Hope.

I knew that Anthony Hope was not to be found on any

undergraduate's vacation reading-list, nor likely to find favour with any publisher looking for block-busting biographies – he didn't fulfil the first requirement of being 'a household name'. But he might be no less interesting as a subject without being 'a household name'. I was not thinking only of his two best-sellers of earlier days, *The Prisoner of Zenda* and *Rupert of Hentzau*: it happened that a little while ago I'd picked up a copy of *Tristram of Blent* by chance in a second-hand bookshop and had been surprisingly impressed. Since then I had located some more of his novels in the London Library. Probably worth looking into. And there weren't already fifty-five so-called definitive biographies of him already in existence. (I intended to keep well away from the standard subjects aimed at huge campus sales – *not* another Jane Austen, *not* another Charlotte Brontë, *not*, above all, another Charles Dickens.)

I could afford to take this high line because for the time being sales didn't have to be my prime concern. One's relieved of the necessity to earn money if one has recently inherited some. I had recently inherited family money, indirectly through Grandfather Cole, who had married Mabsie's sister. (So Randa knew about it.) Consequently I could consider myself a man of means while those means lasted. And that was lucky for me, as I surmised that I should earn no more than a couple of thousand pounds from *Edith Wharton* in England; hopefully, but far from certainly, a bit more than that in the USA. (The current disastrous daily fall in the rate of exchange of the pound sterling troubled me less than it was troubling the Chancellor of the Exchequer – my American royalties happened to be paid in dollars. There were paperback editions in the pipeline and my agent thought I might pick up, with one of the lesser literary prizes, another thousand or so. (The grand total of these sums accrued from no less than six years' work.) I could earn additional sums from literary chores such as reviewing, writing articles, reading for a publisher; but I was not compelled to, thank God! Or rather thank Grandfather Cole! I didn't intend to do any more teaching in Oxford, either. I was free. That was the crux of my situation as I saw it. I was *free*! . . .

Randa was presenting me with a potential subject of a different order from Ada Leverson and Anthony Hope, because to begin with it was in the plural – three men who formed a circle. That had been one of the things which drew me more deeply into thinking about Mrs Wharton, into looking on her less concentratedly as a single individual than as she was, a whole human being, set in 'the web of relationships'. The same would go for the Horsfall Circus. That must have been a web and a half!

More ideas sprang to mind while I strolled. As well as interesting me, the Horsfall Circus would attract any publisher, not on account of the merits of their works but on account of their being, at least in the case of Horsfall, well-known 'names' (vide *Private Eye*). And still more important to me, if less important to a publisher: nobody else had so far written about them as a circle. (Incidentally the appearance of another book about Mrs Wharton so swiftly on the heels of mine had taught me a lesson: if I were going to write about Horsfall and his circle I'd better get down to work right away.)

So much for my ideas. Suddenly I was aware of an afternoon which earlier had seemed overcast and now seemed warm – the sky was lightening. The stale scents of Soho, of coffee, cheese, continental cigarettes, human bodies, shimmered in the air. The horn of a car turning into Dean Street sounded as plangent . . . as plangent as what? . . . A line from Cavafy. (How far can one go for a simile, even if one *is* coming out of Greek Street?) The car was a magnificent Rolls-Royce with brown glass windows – the shadowy figure inside could only be a pop star or his manager.

Which reminded me, that I was due to have tea with my agent. (Though there was no Roller, as they called it around these parts, for the likes of us!)

My thoughts turned back to the animosity of old friends. Animosity is not nice: in fact it's *nasty*.

Yet there was no denying the fascination that the nasty seemed to exercise over the public in general – how else to explain the widespread allure of *Private Eye*, for instance?

'Not nice perhaps . . . But *amusing!*'

Stopping the next taxi I told the driver to take me to the London Library, where I could consult copies of *Who's Who*; and read what Horsfall, Gotham and Protheroe had said about themselves if not about each other.

2

❧ Coincidence in the ❧ Country

I was not the sort of man to impute meaning or significance to coincidences, let Arthur Koestler et al say what
they liked about 'synchronicity'. And I had even less use
for omens and the like. What happened next was to put
me on my metaphysical mettle – I got a letter from old
Professor X Y inviting me to spend a weekend with him
at his cottage in Hampshire. There was no coincidence in
that, since he usually invited me at least once a term. He
was an ancient Fellow of the College, in the habit of
keeping up with youngish recently-elected Fellows, in
particular those who were presentable and unmarried. (I
was counted among the unmarrieds.)

A medievalist of world-wide academic reputation, the
old man was given not improperly to a touch of megalo-
mania, and not culpably at his age to a few bees in the
bonnet. He was sprightly, original and amusing. I enjoyed
a weekend in his company. We didn't talk overmuch about
the Middle Ages. He was lonely.

Then I got a second letter from him, this to say he was
ordering a taxi from the local railway station for me, as my
car was in dock, and going on –

Since I wrote to you Frank Protheroe has invited himself for the weekend. He is so busy that he cannot manage any other. I was looking forward to having you to myself, dear James, but I fear it cannot be. I hope you don't mind. Frank is a Friend.

Frank Protheroe! It didn't convert me to imputing significance to coincidences or believing in omens, but it did impress me as a very odd stroke of luck.

In early autumnal sunshine on a Saturday morning the cottage looked most attractive. The little front garden had recently been tidied up, and beside the path a rose tree was still in bloom. As I stooped to smell the last, velvety, Papa Meilland of summer, the door opened and there stood X, his face sparkling with welcome. He was very small, like a child.

'Xavier, how well you look!'

'You, James, look perfectly splendid!' He held out his hand. 'Come in!'

The interior of the cottage had definitely not been tidied up. The old man lived alone, with only a daily woman, apart from a perfunctory jobbing gardener, to do for him; a local woman, well over sixty, whose service to him was unquestionably faithful though questionably effective. All of us Fellows who were invited down for a weekend were agreed that the place was so much of a shambles that it was hard to resist doing something about it for him. To get on Xavier's roster of youngish Fellows it was obvious you had to be unmarried and presentable: it subsequently became obvious that you had to be willing to do a stint of housework. Most of us spent Sunday morning going the rounds with an antique Hoover.

On the other hand one had to say in fairness to the daily woman that when he had visitors she came in and cooked an excellent country supper. And age was no bar to X himself keeping a fine cellar. There was good reason for staying the weekend with X.

It was an Elizabethan thatched cottage, with oak-beamed ceilings whose lowness happened to be of no grave consequence to the present owner, who was not much over five feet high; but of bruising consequence to a visitor who happened to be somewhere round six feet high and who forgot to stoop when he came to a doorway.

In recent years X had begun to look very frail, yet it would have been very difficult to guess his age. He had kept all his hair and it was crystalline white. More striking, especially in contrast with his hair, was his complexion, whose dryness, fineness and uniform bright vermilion might have been mistaken for the dryness, fineness and uniform bright vermilion of face-powder, which it was not. He was aged eighty.

'I usually drink a glass of sherry before luncheon,' he said, according to a formula he uttered every time one arrived, forgetting that one had heard it goodness knows how many times before. 'Would you care to join me?'

'Thank you.' The luncheon would consist of a granary loaf, a big piece of Stilton, and lettuce-leaves already laid out by X on the kitchen table.

'Would you be good enough to pour it, James?' He pointed to the decanter and glasses. 'Your hands are so much steadier than mine.' Looking at my hands – 'And so much *stronger* . . .'

I poured glasses of sherry for us while he looked on through funny old-fashioned spectacles. We carried glasses to the doorway, where we could drink our sherry in the sun.

'You're not disturbed by Frank Protheroe's joining us?'

'Not in the least.'

'He says he knows you.'

'He's met me. My American editor was giving me lunch at the Century one day in New York and Protheroe came in.' I smiled at the recollection. 'I remember he told us he had a pad in the Chelsea Hotel.'

'A pad! That sounds like Frank. He's so amusing.'

Laughing mischievously he went on. 'And so busy. He's making such a lot of money, my dear. As well as writing those splendid best-selling biographies of kings and queens and princes, he's doing all manner of other things. Editing series, consulting, advising on films and even on *television*. He's always going to America. You can't imagine!' Pause. 'He even goes to *Australia*!' (As a renowned scholar X himself had been invited to universities and learned societies all over the world, naturally including Australia.)

'I shall be happy to meet him again. I'm sure it will be rewarding.' I smiled to myself at a double private joke. The first was at 'rewarding'. The second was at Protheroe's success as a practitioner of the same craft as myself. A Royal biographer – so much higher up the social scale than the rest of us. He had recently published the biography of a deceased monarch which had sold enormously in the USA as well as in this country, setting him that much higher up the professional scale as well. I'd just read it. He had a knack, a remarkable gift as a matter of fact, for combining the scholarly and the popular to a degree that ensured his being treated seriously by fellow-academics and being swallowed happily by a wide reading-public. X's view that he'd made a lot of money sounded entirely plausible. He was reputed to be on terms with members of the Royal Family. And since the previous January's Honours List, he'd been Sir Frank Protheroe.

'I haven't seen Frank since poor Cledwyn Horsfall died,' X said. 'He must be very upset. The three of them were *such* friends . . . And now there are only two of them left.'

I said 'Yes' gravely – and then I noticed that X's expression when contemplating Horsfall's death was less immediately grave than distantly triumphant – he had out-lived him.

'Cledwyn Horsfall, Ellis Gotham, Frank Protheroe . . . Friends since they were at school together.'

'The same school, X, but not exactly contemporaneously.' My first spell of research in the London Library was paying off. 'They all went up to Oxford from the same school. But Horsfall was the only one who overlapped at Oxford with the other two.'

My notes for the pre-War period showed – *Horsfall b 1907 Oxford 1926– . Gotham b 1912 Oxford 1930–34. Protheroe b 1914 Oxford 1932–39.*

For 1934–39 Gotham's entry gave Advertising – could the advertising firm by coincidence be none other than J Arthur Masson Ltd?

'As I was saying, James –'

'Yes?' My historical research had gone for nothing. I sensed the first hum of bees in a bonnet.

'As I was saying. What was I saying?' Momentary pause. Then he remembered. 'I was thinking of those three boys from a grammar-school in the provinces.'

I was going to say 'At Newport, Gwent', but it was not the moment to supply him with information when he was in full flow.

'At Oxford surrounded by boys from the public schools.' The bees came into full buzz. 'Outsiders – they were bound to feel they were outsiders. You know?' Suddenly his voice came out with great force. 'That's the situation I found *myself* in, James. Did you know? *I'm* a grammar-school boy!'

Everyone who knew him knew this. As for me, he had told me on at least one out of my every three visits. It was incredible to think of this bee going on buzzing in his bonnet, despite steadily growing academic fame, over a period of sixty years.

I drank some of my sherry. He seemed to have forgotten his. His forgetfulness and his splintered thinking suddenly reminded me of how old he was, how very old.

'Social outsiders.' He looked at me sharply. 'Do you think this made them literary outsiders? Would you call them literary outsiders, James?'

Irrelevantly something recalled to me a literary journalistic piece which Horsfall once wrote, accusing the academic establishment's critical techniques of – this is what raised a stir – being unable to cope with *his* novels 'as well as those of Dickens'. (I hadn't seen the piece myself, but someone in All Souls was bound to bring it up whenever he appeared on the scene.)

'*I* shouldn't,' I said.

'Why not?' He was not pleased with me.

I said mildly, 'I doubt if it's a very useful concept. And anyway, isn't it rather dated? It belongs to the Fifties, doesn't it?'

'Don't you agree that they haven't taken up all those fashions invented by the *in*-siders? Modernism and all that, don't you know.' The sparkle in his eyes was stormy. 'Imagine *The Cluniac Ethos* written in the style of *Ulysses*!'

I had heard all this before, several times. The first time I'd made the mistake of pointing out to him that *Ulysses* was generally regarded as Post-Modernist; and thence of trying to induct him – how wooden-headed could I be? – into the difference between Modernism and Post-Modernism; when he was too wilful to listen to a word about either.

This time I took the easy way out. *The Cluniac Ethos* was considered to be a classic. (So, for that matter, was *Ulysses*.) Laughing at him, I rested my hand on his shoulder and simply said:

'I can't imagine it, X. We all know *The Cluniac Ethos* is a classic, and it couldn't have been written in any other style. And it couldn't have been written by anyone but you!'

My hope of quietening some of the bees seemed to have come off. He now gave me a glance that sparkled like champagne. I was encouraged to persist in the good work.

'As for your outsiders, Horsfall and Gotham, I think they've each done pretty well all the same.'

'I think so, too. What a wise young man you are, my dear!'

I glanced with some urgency down the garden path for

signs of Protheroe. None. Thinking I might lead him on to reminisce about the three old friends, I said:

'I'm sure all three of them gave each other great moral support.'

'Indeed they did! Moral support, and practical support, James. Practical support . . . Cledwyn Horsfall used his influence in Oxford to support Frank Protheroe in getting his first assistant lectureship. And after the War was over Cledwyn took Ellis Gotham to work with him in the Ministry. That's practical comradeship, James. I admire it. They helped each other, James.' (I knew what was coming next.) 'I wish *I* had been fortunate enough to enjoy something like that, myself. *I* had to make my way alone. Always alone! . . .'

'All the same, you've got there, Xavier.' I gave the remark an emphasis that I hoped would make it final. It really was time Protheroe showed up. I drank some more sherry.

'Yes.' Xavier spoke simply. 'All the same, I've "got there", as you call it. That's right. I've got there.' The bees seemed to have given their last buzz for the time being.

'I should like you to reminisce about them, X. I'm interested. The three old friends.'

'I remember their comradeship very well in the early days, when they were struggling. I can't say how it has stood up to their achieving success.' He looked at me shrewdly. 'The real test of comradeship, James, is not whether it stands up to failure, but whether it stands up to success.'

'What a wise *old* man you are, X!'

We laughed at each other. At that moment, just when I wanted him to go on, sounds came from the gate. A silver BMW rolled to a standstill. And out climbed Frank Protheroe, wearing countrified grey trousers and tweed jacket. Sir Frank Protheroe.

At the Century Club in New York Protheroe had kept reminding me of someone, of someone I couldn't place yet felt sure of having seen frequently: it was some weeks afterwards when I realised it was not in the flesh that I'd seen this man frequently, but on television. Who was he? As Protheroe came towards me now, I knew who he was. The Trade Union boss, Clive Jenkins. (Also a Welshman.) Protheroe was a good deal older: he must once have had a head of dark wavy hair, like the other man's, but it was now wearing very thin on top though it curled luxuriantly in the nape of his neck. Like the other man he was of medium height and heavily built, carrying a handsome embonpoint before him: he might have been walking with Clive Jenkins's small-stepping galleon-like progress were it not for a pronounced limp. (Result of a stroke?) He was wearing the same type of thick-lensed, horn-rimmed spectacles. Bright, light grey eyes.

But what above all clinched the resemblance was the crowning glory of a supremely pleased-with-himself expression on his face.

'X!' Protheroe took the old man's hand warmly. 'It's so good of you to have me today.' He was looking intimately at Xavier; and copying the old man's courtesy, he said, 'I do hope it hasn't discommoded you in any way? . . . I had to re-jig – I should say re-order – all my plans. To fit in a trip to Balmoral.' He sent a fleeting glance in my direction to make sure I hadn't missed Balmoral.

'No, my dear Frank. It's perfectly all right. Perfectly.'

'Then I'm reassured. That's lovely.' Then Protheroe turned directly to me and held out his hand. 'How delightful to meet you again, James!'

I didn't recall his having called me by my Christian name at the Century. X said:

'James and I are having our customary glass of sherry before luncheon, Frank. Will you care to join us?'

'If you please. Thank you.'

I offered to pour it. X said, 'And fill your own glass, James, dear fellow!'

The preliminaries to luncheon were launched. And

when they were over we sat down in the kitchen to bread and cheese and butter and leaves of lettuce – and a bottle of Haut-Brion.

'I eat very little at mid-day,' said Protheroe, the supremely pleased-with-himself smile giving his face the look of a man who was authoritatively laying down for the rest of the world, which included X and me, the best possible regime for luncheon. Judged by his embonpoint he must have had a different regime for dinner.

During the meal he gave all his attention to the old man, enabling me to give all my attention to observing him. A strong nose, muscular rounded cheeks, a succession of pointed double chins. His manner was naturally imposing, yet the intonations of his voice, the gestures of his body were not without a certain delicacy – a Welsh lilt, almost a touch of the sing-song, in his speech: grandiloquent, yet nevertheless delicate sweeps of his small well-kept hands to illustrate his meaning.

During the last few weeks I had met men who disliked or envied him, saying he was obsequious. (A help in getting on with Royalty?) What struck me in his presence, in private as we were, was a sort of boldness. (I was to see more of that later.)

A second bottle of wine had made the old man slightly tipsy. He said out of the blue:

'Whose novels do you prefer? Uncle Cledwyn's or Brother Ellis's?' He looked round the table, his old-fashioned spectacles slightly askew, his face brighter vermilion.

My spirits sank: I foresaw a literary discussion which was not only very old-fashioned but intrinsically very boring. I looked down at my plate.

'To which of us,' said Protheroe, 'are you addressing the question, X?'

'Both of you. Each of you.'

'Then I'll answer first, if I may.' Protheroe paused. 'I should have to say I think the more highly of Horsfall's.'

He glanced from X to me and back again. 'They have greater depth of characterisation, a greater knowledge of individual human beings. You know?' (I was amused by the weight with which he delivered this oration.) 'And indeed a greater knowledge of how society works.' He paused to see how we were responding, then went on. 'They just happen to be rather boringly written. Just happen, you know. He's no stylist, but it's of no consequence, because one *believes* what he's saying. You know? . . .' (The sing-song had become noticeable.)

X nodded his head in agreement with him. Protheroe was nodding his head in agreement with himself. Apparently satisfied with our response, Protheroe went on.

'I can think of only one serious flaw in his work.' He made one of his grandiloquent sweeps through the air – a gold signet ring flashed. He delivered his next comment as a separate speech –

'Unfortunately, and it is unfortunate, Cledwyn can't portray *women*.'

Through his thick-lensed spectacles he flashed X and me a knowing look. Really! . . . (Over the criticism itself I disagreed.)

X turned to me. 'And you, James?'

I hesitated. This sort of amateur discussion was not my line – they didn't seem to know that since their day literary criticism had been 100% professionalised. And anyway, this sort of question I wouldn't attempt to answer without having read all the novels.

'The same as Sir Frank,' I mumbled. 'I think the more highly of Horsfall's.' It looked as if we were going to be stuck on Horsfall's career as writer, ignoring his career as economist and now as prime mover for world peace.

'I didn't ask you which you think the more highly of.' The old man sat forward suddenly and took charge of the proceedings. 'I asked which you prefer. I differ from you. I prefer Brother Ellis's. They're so true, so believable, so well-written, so *funny* – especially that delicious series of university novels . . . If they weren't so horribly hetero, they'd be *perfect!'*

He was definitely tipsy. I glanced at Protheroe. A Friend. His smile was serene – if one were utterly pleased with oneself, one was likely to be serene. He said to Xavier:

'My dear X, isn't it time we moved from the table and let you toddle upstairs for your afternoon nap?' He smiled even more serenely. 'Don't you think?'

X was not pleased but he bowed to superior weight. 'As you will.'

Protheroe took out of his pocket a little Georgian silver box, swallowed a couple of pills from it, and finished his wine.

'As I've got to leave first thing in the morning,' he said, 'I think it would be most agreeable if James and I were to go for a walk together – after a due pause for digestion, of course. You have some beautiful walks round here.' He gave me a glossy smile.

The due pause would allow time for me to stack away the dishes in the washing-up machine.

X had disappeared. Protheroe was standing relaxedly in the open doorway: it suddenly seemed to me that he was *looming* in the open doorway. He had taken off his spectacles and was unconcernedly polishing the lenses with a pocket handkerchief. I had an extraordinary sensation. Here was I, by a coincidence which offered me a fate-sent opportunity to pump Protheroe about the three old friends, feeling in my stomach the exact sensation with which I went into the *viva* for my D Phil.

Protheroe put on his spectacles and looked towards me.

'Are you ready, James?'

3

❧ *A Walk in the Forest* ❧

At the gate Protheroe paused for us to survey his car. A BMW Sapphire with a Y registration – this year's. It must have cost him over £20,000. Thinking of my own clapped-out old Citroën, I said:

'Very nice.'

We set off along a footpath which rambled through gaps in the forest. Sunlight was shining through the upper branches of the trees, while the leaves they had shed scuffed gently under our shoes. Sometimes a bird, disturbed, fluttered away from us. In the air there was a damp smell, strangely both musty and fresh.

'How very pleasant this is, James!'

I gauged his pace: in spite of the limp he moved powerfully. The feeling in my stomach had not subsided. After a little while he opened the conversation.

'It's a most welcome bonus to find *you* here this weekend, James. It enables me to tell you directly how highly I think of your book about Edith Wharton and her circle. It's a remarkable achievement.' He paused. 'All the more remarkable for being a first book.'

'One has to start somewhere . . .'

'Ah yes . . . My own start was so long ago.'

'Do you remember it well?' Would that draw him out?

'It's *your* book I want to talk about.'

He began to talk about Mrs Wharton and her friends. He knew her novels, or so it seemed: and he made it clear to me that he had read my book with professional attention and care. Our walk, for all the beauty of the forest, began to pass without my noticing for the time being anything but his praise. The qualms in my stomach began to obtrude less.

'In my opinion, James, you handled with consummate tact – consummate tact, I mean it – her sexual awakening, at the age of forty-five. Awakened by the remarkable Morton Fullerton.' Pause. 'He was bisexual, of course.'

I registered the 'of course' but had no intention of catching on to the deeper drift of it. 'Of course' indeed! Serenely pleased with himself, he suddenly struck me as absurd.

'A strange story,' I said. 'Extraordinary, really.'

'But heart-warming, James. Heart-warming, yes indeed . . .' I caught the lilt in his voice and glanced sideways at him, to find him looking fixedly at me while he sailed limping powerfully forward, his embonpoint swaying before him. (Swaying like the embonpoint of the Baron de Charlus?)

'I suppose it is,' I said non-committally.

'It *is* heart-warming and you put it across with great skill. And great understanding.' Stopping for a moment, so that we could look at each other directly, he said: 'I'm sure you're aware of that.'

For the moment I was too busy wondering what he was up to to reply. I had my suspicions of what he was up to. He was trying, somehow, from no matter what distance, to probe *my* sexual life? Really! . . . I wondered if it was being over-sensitive in supposing he might have heard that while I was in America, at Yale, I had been briefly married. The fact was little known in All Souls, where I passed as a bachelor, one of those donnish bachelors who seem to exist, who actually do exist, stably without any sexual life at all. That happened to be my own case: stably apart from recrudescences of bitterness and pain which mercifully were diminishing as time passed. And surprisingly, other recrudescences which didn't diminish, such as relief at not having to cope with the sexual life, at being free from it. *Free! . . .*

'That's a difficult sort of question,' I replied. 'When one's writing, I don't . . .' I wasn't too sure that he hadn't heard something, though I couldn't see how he had done it.

'The awareness will come to you, James. I can promise you that.' A grandiloquent sweep of the hand accompanied his promise. The ring flashed.

With over a decade to go, I thought, before *I* was forty-five . . . I gave him a smile of hopeful acquiescence. I had succeeded in heading him off intimate topics, for he said:

'By the way, isn't there an American book about Edith Wharton somewhere in the offing, if it hasn't come out already?'

'It's out now.' I grinned. 'But I got in first.'

'Ah, you are lucky.'

'The other is a very different sort of book.'

'No matter. You have been fortunate. It can be *un*fortunate when that sort of thing happens.' He paused. 'I discovered that someone else had his eye on my present Royal Highness. I wasn't having *that*. I warned him off.' He turned towards me.

I thought, I bet you did!

'Do you know, James, he had the effrontery to base a pre-empting claim on his being connected with the aristocracy.'

'And you weren't having that, either?'

'I should think not! It's common knowledge that I sprang from the backstreets of a small town, as did Cledwyn Horsfall and Ellis Gotham. But I've attached myself to the upper classes and I'm damned if I'm going to be shaken loose!'

I admitted to myself that I found this speech amusing and not unendearing – which must have been his intention. I laughed.

'Also, my dear James,' Protheroe went on, 'this individual hadn't made sure first of all of *his* Royal Highness. *Mine* wants *me* to do it – we're rather buddies . . .' He corrected himself. 'That's an exaggeration, but justified in the circumstances. You know?' He was smiling. 'But –'

He stopped to look at his watch – Was it time to turn back? We had been walking quite fast. I thought I was letting him set the pace; nevertheless I wondered if it had been too much for him. He was breathing hard.

'And who,' he asked as we started off again, 'are *you* going to write about next?'

'I haven't decided. I've got two or three ideas.' Weighing up whether to tell him what the ideas were and perhaps get his advice, I was suddenly deterred by an instinctive warning that to confide anything in Frank Protheroe would be to run a risk . . .

As artless as I could make it sound, I said:

'Actually it has occurred to me just now that there must be a lot of material in the life of Cledwyn Horsfall.'

'You can say that again, dear boy!'

'I wonder how you'd react to it?'

'Depends on what you say about *me*.' I realised that he was giving me another fixed sideways look, and that there was a momentary diminution of pleased-with-himselfness in his smile. 'I've lived my life under a shadow, James. Under a shadow . . . You know?' He paused. 'But you'd better know that I've got a damned good libel lawyer, a damned sight better than those Goslett women.' He stopped. 'Of course you're related to them.'

'Correct. I'm a first cousin once removed – my paternal grandfather was a sister of Mabsie's.'

'There goes the English upper-class obsession with degrees of cousinhood!' The returned serene smile incorporated an air of I-told-you-so. We started off again. I said:

'It has a sound raison d'être when there's something to inherit.'

He was not missing a trick. 'Are you in line to inherit?'

'Not that I know.'

'Do you see much of the Virago Sisters?'

Obviously it was I, not Protheroe, who was being quizzed on this walk, which was turning into a *viva* after all – so far not a frightening one, though I couldn't ignore signs of something hypnotising in his manner, *compelling* confidences . . .

'I had lunch with Randa a little while ago.'

'Do you like her?'

It was my turn to try a sweeping gesture with my hands – 'Yes and No.'

'That shows sense, anyway. She's a snake. She looks like a snake. Those glittering slits for eyes and that long neck . . . Ugh!'

Anything I might say was going to sound superfluous and Protheroe clearly took it as such. He plunged on, his original delicacy of manner wearing off by the minute.

'Didn't she tell you, if she knows you're thinking of writing about Horsfall, that someone else *has* got in first this time? She must know all about it.'

'No,' I stammered. 'Who?' The *viva* had taken a very bad turn.

'An Australian professor.' The ring flashed elegantly. 'Of no great distinction – I've never met him.'

'Oh.'

'Of no great distinction – just on the make.'

Even while failing my *viva* I couldn't miss the charm of Frank Protheroe's dismissing another biographer for being on the make.

Straight away he took the wind out of those sails –

'All men are on the make, James. Thank God they *are* – that's what makes the world go round to our comfort and satisfaction.' Pause. (I smelt the scent of Thatcherism in the air.) 'I'm on the make with very considerable success.' Another pause. '*You* are on the make, I trust, my dear James. Some of us' – the smile of a man untouchably pleased with himself came to me obliquely over his shoulder – 'are more properly on the make than others; those of us with better brains, more talent, and a deeper understanding of human nature and its necessities.'

The over-riding virtue of being on the make – all the best men were entrepreneurs. It was to Mrs Thatcher that he owed being made Sir Frank.

'Do you think,' I asked, 'the Australian professor has worse brains, less talent, and a shallower understanding of human nature and its necessities than I have?'

Protheroe went on smiling but I could tell he wasn't pleased with me.

'I'm not convinced of your understanding of human nature's necessities,' he said.

If by 'human nature's necessities' he meant the Thatcherite obsession with making money, he was right – and I was glad of it. Greed was my least favourite of human vices.

'I trust your judgement, Sir Frank,' I said. I was not going to have a row with him.

'I have no doubt of our Australian friend's understanding of human nature's necessities,' he said with a brutal laugh. 'You're right to trust to my judgement. He's a very typical specimen, you know.'

'Can he write?' I was hoping to divert the drift of this conversation.

'I've read one of his compilations. It's an attempt to jump on the Dickens bandwaggon. Some of my fellow-biographers jump from one bandwaggon to the next like those hobos you see in early American films, jumping from one coach to the next on trains going West.'

I laughed.

Protheroe was smiling. 'I have a copy of his Dickens compilation somewhere. I'll lend it to you if I can find it, then you can judge for yourself.'

'Thank you.'

We had come to a deeper patch of leaves on the ground and had to walk more slowly. We fell silent. His silence came, I presumed, from fatigue. Mine came, I knew, from a sudden mood of depression brought on by his news of my Australian rival: he had effectively destroyed my peace of mind.

When we began to talk again he said:

'If you decide to write about Horsfall, there's one thing you must never forget.'

'What's that?'

'His stature as a writer. As an economist, as a publicist, admirable, I'm sure. As a novelist in a class of his own. *Very good*.' Protheroe made a splendid gesture with both hands, making *'very good'* sound like a final unanimous statement from all the cohorts of critics in academe – which it was *not*, nor ever could be.

'You're very convincing,' I said – an elegant untruth.

In a class of his own, as a novelist – despite being unable to portray women, i.e. half the range of human beings! . . . As for my own opinion, I had to disagree. In the novels of Horsfall's I'd read so far – they were late novels, apart from his first – there were portraits of women quite the equal, in being persuading, of any of his portraits of men; and in the one which was my first choice among them, the women out-numbered the men.

'In a class of his own,' Protheroe repeated with even greater weight. Protesting too much? . . .

'But not in a class of his own,' I said, 'as economist or publicist?'

'So you want to pump me on that territory, do you, James?' He turned to look at me while he strode on. A gust of wind rustled the trees on either side of us.

Taking courage, I said, 'Why not? Whom better to pump?'

'I'm glad you acknowledge that.' Joking and being pleased with himself at one and the same time made him loom larger.

His limp, I noticed, had become more pronounced. I waited for him to reply.

'As a Keynesian don he made a brilliant mark in the

early years of his career.' He looked at me again. 'And something of a fortune, too.'

'Really?' I looked back at him. We stopped for a moment.

'You didn't know that?' He paused. 'Cledwyn took a leaf out of Keynes's book in more ways than one. Keynes played the stockmarkets: Cledwyn followed his example. He didn't make a fortune as large as Keynes's, but large enough.' Through the thick lenses came a particularly bright gleam. The thought of *Money*! . . .

The walk was beginning to pay dividends.

'Cledwyn's grasp on the worlds of money and economics was one of the things which helped to make his contribution to *The Beveridge Report* so vital.'

So Protheroe had taken on board the story of Cledwyn's contribution being genuinely massive. Perhaps my intuitions were wrong, too suspicious.

'And then?' I asked.

'One has to grant him a certain degree of success in his final years in the Civil Service.' I noticed a diminution of music in the sing-song.

'Is there some doubt?'

'There's always some doubt about economics!' A very musical Welsh laugh. 'Economists can rarely be said to come off in the end – they always seem to get their sums wrong, don't they?' He was slightly out of breath. 'That's taking a historian's long-term view.' The gold ring flashed. 'You know?'

'It's an interesting view.' The historian's!

'Nevertheless he went back to Oxford with a high reputation. A big fish in a small pool – the big neo-Keynesianism pool being in Cambridge, as I'm sure you know. He was wise not to go to Cambridge.'

'Yes.' After a moment's pause I said, 'From Oxford he went back to affairs. Economic Adviser to the Prime Minister.'

'That's right. After a slight hitch – from which he recovered – he was confirmed as Head of a rather talented think-tank, very small but very talented, actually.' He turned to me – we had to stop again. 'Which ended in failure, James, if not disaster.' Having delivered this blow he went on again, talking to me over his shoulder. 'Cledwyn found his neo-Keynesian advice *not* being taken. It was the 1970s, you know? Neo-classicism, Friedmanism, monetarism, whichever you prefer, was in the process of carrying all before it. His advice was not being taken, so what did Cledwyn do then? He misguidedly began to play politics . . . You know? As an economist he had his gifts. As a politician – everyone agrees on this, James – he had *no* gifts.' He paused with an unconcealed triumphant expression. 'I'm afraid the only mark for success you can chalk up to him from then on was getting on to the Resignation Honours List. I take it you know about that?'

'I've been told.' I was not going to give away that I'd gleaned it from *Private Eye*.

'He had to put up with a certain amount of gibing from fellow Peers on that score. It was to expiate the shame that he switched to the cross-benches as soon as he decently could. I don't blame him. I *can't* blame him . . .'

I was touched by this show of sympathy towards an old friend.

'Anyway,' he went on, 'neo-classicism was manifestly winning the day. And now with Mrs Thatcher, herself, a passionate convert to it, I imagine the only future he could see for himself, as a neo-Keynesian, was superannuation.'

It was on the tip of my tongue to say, Unless he was prepared to convert to Friedmanism himself. I didn't say it. Reflecting that as close friend of Horsfall's, Protheroe must have started off as a Keynesian, while it was under Mrs Thatcher's Premiership that he had become Sir Frank, I appreciated the wisdom of *his* political judgement and my own self-restraint.

Feeling that he had done a pretty fair job on his old friend's reputation as economist and as politician, I said:

'How do you evaluate the final phase?'

It happened that we had come to a small clearing where there was a felled tree across our path. Protheroe stopped decisively. 'Do you mind if I sit down for a few minutes, James?'

'Please do!' I glanced at him apprehensively.

We sat down on the tree-trunk. He was breathing very hard indeed and holding his hand to his chest. His complexion had changed colour. I hoped to God he was not going to have another stroke – if it was a first stroke that had caused his limp. We were miles away from anywhere; at least it would seem miles if I had to run for help. He rested for several minutes, and then said:

'So you would like to know what I think of the final phase?' He was smiling again. 'As a figure on the world-stage?' His eyes were very bright – suddenly I saw him as something of an actor, himself.

'As a figure on the world-stage.' He repeated the remark with satisfaction. 'An astonishing turn of fate, James. Or perhaps better to say, an astonishing throw of the dice.'

I nodded my head in order to avoid arbitrating between the metaphors. I said:

'Yes. But wouldn't you say that what he was aiming at was *good*?' I was echoing Horsfall's most frequent comment on his own line of thought – a source of great amusement in the College.

'Of course it was. Trying to reconcile East and West, if only on grounds combining an element of economics and an element of literature . . . *is* good.' He smiled sarcastically. 'I won't quote "We must love each other or die."'

'Is that what he said to *them*?' I asked, avoiding any reference to Auden and paying no attention to his misquoting the poem.

'Of course not. Direct exhortation is something they get every day of the week. Cledwyn was more artful and more realistic, you know. In each country he went to on one side of the divide, he teased out things that he thought, as an economist or as a man of letters, were good – and there are things that *are* good, I suppose, on both sides. Then he reported those things in the next country on the other side. And vice versa. You know? *Vice versa* was the point of the operation.'

'He found people to listen to him?'

'You could say he was extraordinarily lucky. The dice fell in his favour. He had enthusiasm – Cledwyn had a great gift for expressing enthusiasm.'

I thought of all that *hwyl* . . .

'He used enthusiasm to persuade people who were not disposed to listen to him as a man of letters to take him seriously as an economist. And people who were not disposed to listen to him as an economist to take him seriously as a man of letters. That is to say, of course, if they took him seriously as either. Some of them didn't! . . . But if they did, that was fine. His most recent triumph – I don't know if you know this? – was to persuade Mrs Gandhi to listen to him.'

'I didn't know he'd got as far afield as India.'

'You can't fault Cledwyn for being cramped in body or spirit. A comprehensive case of "Wider still and wider". He was convinced that God had made him mighty and would make him mightier yet!' He burst into laughter.

I couldn't help joining in his laughter, though I felt slightly ashamed of it. He had drawn me into a sort of complicity, a complicity in meanness of spirit.

'Tell me the truth, James. Don't you agree there was something . . . overweening about it?'

I had no idea. I gave him a smile which I hoped was non-committal.

'Something overweening.' He made a comical, wide-encompassing gesture in the air with both hands. 'Something . . . *monstrous.*'

Suddenly I visualised the metaphorical monster in reality – I saw an elephant!

Protheroe was looking at me triumphantly.

'So monstrous,' he said, 'that it made him look ridiculous. Don't you agree? I'm sure you do.'

He was confident that he had drawn me into complicity: I didn't like it. Changing tone he said, 'Such a pity!' His sing-song came back invested with a sad note. 'Such a pity he took on a hopeless task, ultimately hopeless . . . We might almost say he died just in time.'

I'd had enough for the moment. Surreptitiously I glanced at my watch – our time was running out. He noticed of course and stood up immediately.

His breathing had improved with the short rest. But his limp seemed worse when he started to walk. How old was he? 1982 minus 1912 – seventy. I made as if to support him but he fended me off. We walked some distance in silence, at a pace little faster than ambling. The sunlight was beginning to disappear from between the trees: the strange smell, fresh and musty, had become less fresh and more musty as the dusk began to fall. No longer did birds flutter out as we approached – they must have retired for the night. It had been a beautiful day.

A beautiful day but I still had something else to take up. My destroyed peace of mind compelled me to say:

'I suppose I must find out more about this Australian professor.'

'His name is Barry M'Gann. Cousin Randa concealed him from you. I suggest you ask Ellis Gotham about him. Gotham's a literary executor.'

'Will you introduce me to Gotham?'

'Our ex-Professor . . .' The faintest touch of a sneer in his smile. 'We've scarcely exchanged a word in private for forty years, but I suppose it might be arranged.'

'*Forty years!* Why not?'

Protheroe didn't answer. I peered round to look into his face but saw merely the supremely pleased-with-himself smile focused enigmatically ahead. Actually in looking ahead we saw that the path had widened and I realised that we were nearer to home than I'd thought. I didn't let the conversation lapse at this crucial point –

'If it *can* be managed, Sir Frank, I should be grateful to you.'

'I feel some diffidence in introducing you to poor Ellis. I don't quite know what you're expecting, James, but I fear you may be disappointed. He has never been the man he was since he resigned his part-time Chair at that civic University.' His lips curled on the words 'part-time' and 'civic'. 'Not the man he was. A wreck of his former self.' Protheroe shook his head from side to side. 'Sadly decayed . . . One has to admit it. Sadly decayed indeed.'

I asked if there was any specific medical cause.

Protheroe shrugged his shoulders heavily. 'It's supposed to be a rheumatic condition, basically.' He gave me a particularly sage, knowing look. 'But I should have thought . . .'

'What would you have thought, Sir Frank?'

'I should have thought that whether there's a specific medical cause or not, he's no longer what the insurance companies call "a good life", you know? Not in any sense of the term. *Not* a good life, I'm afraid.'

Another, longer pause in our conversation was ended by our rounding a corner and suddenly coming upon the cottage.

X, fresh from his nap, was standing by the gate, waiting for us. A woman's bicycle was propped against the fence.

'I've enjoyed our walk very much,' Protheroe was saying to me, 'very much . . .' To my surprise he then shook hands with me. 'Thank you, James. Thank you.'

'You're late for tea!' X was faintly put out. 'Mrs Biggs is already here, preparing our supper.' He beckoned us peremptorily. 'Come in, come in!'

To Protheroe I said:

'And I've enjoyed our conversation very much. More than I can say, really. Thank you, Frank.'

I couldn't wait to get home to my word-processor at the earliest moment.

4

❧ *No Mark Antony* ❧

'Did you see Cledwyn Horsfall's Memorial Service announced in this morning's *Times*?' Randa was on the telephone – keeping up the pressure.

Actually I had seen it. I said:

'No.'

'Well, it's there.'

'I'll look for it.'

'I think you should go, James.'

I imagined the fragile head poised on the long neck. 'Yes, Randa.'

'I shall be there. I'll introduce you to his widow. You must meet *her*. She's Iris Blackmore, you know.'

'I do know.'

'She's a descendant of R D Blackmore.'

'I didn't know that.' (I must check.)

'I hope you've read some of *her* novels.'

'Some.'

'With appreciation?'

'Yes, of course.' I was telling the truth.

'The time will come when she's given her due as a writer as important as Cledwyn.' Pause. 'She has made an exemplary contribution over the last thirty years to women's fiction.'

'Good!'

'And she was very important in Cledwyn's life.'

I wondered what kind of importance. When two writers married each other one naturally wondered if it was for *practical* help, as old X might call it. On the other hand –

'The marriage lasted,' I said.

'That's right.'

There was a pause.

'And they both got on in the literary world,' I said. 'Sort of gave each other a leg-up?' Immediately I wished I hadn't said it – or thought it, which was more serious. To write about them open-mindedly and sympathetically, one had to avoid thinking this kind of thing about them.

Randa appeared not to have heard me. 'If you're going to write about Horsfall and Gotham and Protheroe,' she said, 'you must *not* overlook Iris Blackmore as well.'

'That makes four . . . Squares the circle!'

'It does if you accept Iris on an equal footing with the three men.'

'What makes you think I mightn't, Randa?' (I prided myself on being imperturbable – but I wished the footing on which Randa and I accepted each other weren't so unstable.)

'I suspend my judgement on that, James, till I see what you write.'

'Haven't I proved myself on Mrs Wharton?'

'Yes, one might say you have. I have no complaints.' I imagined her smiling.

'There now . . .'

'If you write about Horsfall, Gotham and Protheroe, you surely must include Iris.' Randa was not afraid of repetition for emphasis.

'Exactly. Never fear!'

The conversation ended – but not my train of thought. If I wrote about Horsfall, Gotham and Protheroe, those three old friends. *If* . . .

I was going through a spell of seeing more and more

snags in the project, quite apart from my feeling about animosity as an emotion.

Getting mixed up with living persons the trouble was that they'd be around to make demands on one; and if it turned out that there was no love lost between them, they'd undoubtedly try to get one to take sides. I didn't like the idea of that. One couldn't see people truthfully if one's vision were skewed by taking sides.

At the same time I should be lacking, in presenting my gallery of living persons, the impact in the flesh of its centrepiece, Horsfall himself. That would create a discrepancy that couldn't, by definition, be compensated for.

If I wrote about them . . .

I stared at the telephone receiver which I'd just replaced, as I tried to recall what I actually knew of Horsfall in the flesh.

The impact of Horsfall in the flesh was powerful. In the first place there was a vast amount of strong, heavy, energetic flesh. (He had died suddenly of a first, massive heart attack.)

'That Big Whale of a Welshman' one of my friends at All Souls called him.

Horsfall had occasionally been invited to dine with us in College. That was how I came at least to have set eyes on him in the flesh, if not to know him as a man. He was indeed a big whale of a fellow: he had the sort of powerful limbs which set up currents of air as he passed by, much as one imagines the passage of a whale sets up currents of water.

A large round head, almost bald. A large egg-shaped face with exopthalmic blue eyes, baby-blue irises ringed with brilliant whites; above them very fine arched eyebrows. His cheeks were long and so well-filled that they shone; his mouth was shapely with a jutting lower lip. Most remarkable, though, was that while so much of the hair had disappeared from the top of his head, he wore long sideboards, currently fashionable, so huge and woolly that he looked like a veteran of the Crimean War.

His voice was clear and loud and musical, with an occasional intrusion of a Welsh vowel-sound ('ridicoolous', for example) and a Welsh consonant (as in 'to-tal' lilting upwards on the second sybllable).

Theoretically Horsfall had not been all that much of a Welshman, said the College. It was thought that his mother was more-or-less Welsh; but his father was English, born and bred in the English small town where Horsfall himself had been born, and had been bred until his father moved to the Welsh Borders when Cledwyn was about eight years old. It was a subject for amusement and sarcasm among us that his Welshness could not be missed – his mother's genes predominated to the full.

Horsfall was hardly a popular guest in the College. Small academic communities, even All Souls where there were a fair number of politicians around all the time, tended to be short on love for outside pundits from whom an apparently quite small inflow of alcohol produced an absolutely unstoppable outflow of punditry. Horsfall manifestly enjoyed the drama of punditry as delivered by himself. Intelligence and *hwyl*. The light of shrewdness and command shone in his big, baby-blue eyes; while he radiated an avuncular bonhomie that I, though not most of the Fellows present, would probably not have been able to resist had I been sitting next to him, an avuncular and guileful bonhomie.

Again, on those occasions I recognised that he was generating an overflow of original ideas. If only they had not been delivered on that stream of euphoria, boozily confidential, boozily statesman-like and self-congratulatory! After adumbrating each such he would exclaim, 'This is *good*, eh?' Emphasising the vowel – 'This is *goo-ood*, eh?' For a few weeks afterwards it was a sarcastic catch-phrase among us round the dining-table – 'This is *goo-ood*, eh?'

Such recollections could scarcely be said to constitute a proper basis for going to a man's memorial service, let alone taking up the idea of writing a book about him. However my morning's post brought an admission-card from Randa. Pressure decided it.

I had never been to a memorial service before, nor had I ever heard of this particular church in north London. I telephoned Randa.

'It's Iris's choice.'

'Seems pretty eccentric to me. You'd have thought' – this was a joke – 'she'd try for the Abbey.'

'It's a very big church, very suitable. And it happens to be the church where she and Cledwyn were married, and which she has attended ever since.'

'Has Cledwyn attended it?'

'I think not.'

'So it will be a case of coming full-circle for him.'

Silence from Randa.

'Well, it will be *my* first time. I hope there's space for parking.'

'Iris would not have chosen it otherwise.'

We arranged to meet outside the church.

The service was to be at noon, so I was there ten minutes early to be sure of a parking place. Crowds of other people were already arriving early.

As Randa remarked, it really was a very big church. Built of pale grey stone it towered up from the street in handsome Victorian Gothic solidity. Betjeman must have loved it. The morning sparkled on it – the pale grey steeple carried one's spirit upwards to a pale blue sky. The entrance, direct from the pavement, was crammed with people stopping to greet acquaintances before they went in. Most of them appeared to know everybody else – friends of Horsfall, middle-aged to elderly, politicians, peers, writers. I was acquainted with a few of the writers, myself, but I couldn't go into the church with them because I had to wait for Randa.

Randa did not appear.

I didn't see Iris Blackmore or Ellis Gotham, whom I

should recognise from photographs: presumably they were inside already.

The crowd was beginning to diminish. Where on earth was Randa?

Suddenly a large chauffeur-driven car rolled up. Out of it stepped Frank Protheroe and the Minister for the Arts. That made my waiting worthwhile. As befitted members of the chauffeur-driven classes, neither of them wore a top-coat. Protheroe looked plump and sleek, the Minister just a shade careless round the collar and tie. Protheroe, exceptionally pleased with himself, gave me an elegant wave of the hand in passing: I hoped it meant that, noticing my presence, he would not forget to fulfil his promise to introduce me to his old friend, Ellis Gotham. (I was relying on Randa to introduce me to Iris Blackmore.)

Where *was* Randa?

I held my admission card in my hand, at the ready.

'James!'

At last. Randa came down the street from behind me.

'I'm terribly sorry,' she said breathlessly. 'Jess has gone down with 'flu and I had to stay and see one of her clients. And then the only spot I could park was miles away. I've had to *walk*.'

I took hold of her elbow. 'You look very elegant all the same.' (She did look elegant, tall and slim in suavely cut dark-green.)

'Never mind about that! Let's go inside at once!' We made for the entrance. 'We want to avoid sitting at the back. I've been told the acoustics of this place leave a lot to be desired.'

'OK.'

We entered the huge church. The proceedings had not yet begun, but all the seats appeared to be full, apart from a couple in the back row, where we had no alternative but to dispose ourselves. It was clear that we were not going to be able to see very much, whatever the extent to which the acoustics affected our hearing very much. The organ was playing.

'I'm sorry,' Randa whispered to me.

'Don't worry!' I patted her arm.

She smiled. 'Do you want me to take off my hat?'

It was a beautiful hat with a brim that was too wide for the limited space availed us by small wooden chairs pushed close together. When she turned her head towards my ear the brim just missed the side of my face.

Laughing I whispered back: 'You ought to have worn a pill-box.'

'Or a cloche.' The idea made her giggle. A memorial service seemed to be bringing out the best in her – or was it that arriving at a disadvantage had humanised her? Whichever, it was all to the good.

We both hitched ourselves up a little so as to have a brief look round. A huge church; pale grey stone, and clear glass in all the windows apart from the east window; very impressive and yet – I could see why Iris Blackmore had chosen it – *not* over-awing. (Not over-awing to me. My father was a clergyman, and I had resisted being over-awed from the age of ten.) Masses of flowers on the altar, below the high-up pulpit, and beside the brass-eagle lectern. Between the pulpit and the lectern, at the top of the steps leading to the sanctuary another small lectern (presumably for the reader of the Address), with a microphone clipped to it. More interesting, on the south side, a small dais on which were assembled a string quartet and a male singer: more interesting still, on the north side –

'Do you see what *I* see?' I whispered to Randa.

'You do,' she whispered back, holding the brim of her hat.

What we were both seeing was a long trestle-table covered with a white tablecloth, on it bottles of wine and glasses.

'I'm looking forward to this.'

'Iris knows how to arrange things.'

We each took a card, giving the Order of the Service, out of the little rack on the back of the chair in front. It listed the persons who were going to give readings. I recognised all their names but from where we were sitting it was impossible to see them: they must be lined up in a pew at the front, as must Iris Blackmore too, with close friends and family. (According to *Who's Who*, Iris and Cledwyn had one *d.*; Ellis Gotham, *m* twice, had two *d.*; Protheroe was neither *m* nor had *ch.*)

The organ-playing ceased, and a clergyman, whom I took to be the Vicar, went up to the pulpit. Two or three brief sentences of welcome to us all, followed by a short sequence of sympathetic remarks about Iris and Cledwyn, with a special pat on the head – 'faithful member of our congregation' – for Iris. All very amiable and appropriate. I noticed to my surprise that there was no microphone in the pulpit. We could hear him well enough: he had a good voice. (My father was averse to wiring God's House for sound. A good preaching voice, he said, needed no electronic aid. Perhaps this Vicar said the same.) In this church, though, unlike my father's church, there was a tremendous echo.

The Vicar was followed by the string quartet. A piece by Vaughan Williams, entirely appropriate for a Welshman, even if a slightly bogus Welshman. And very well-played, though the members of the quartet looked as if they were still students. I found it moving and glanced at Randa: she caught my glance and nodded her head. Iris knew how to arrange things.

Next came the readings. There were four readers, three men and one woman, the latter not just a token woman at that – she was Roz Curtis, Iris's and Cledwyn's publisher, now famous for having graduated from running a smallish feminist publishing-house to becoming boss of a major publishing-house hitherto entirely the preserve of men. Iris did know how to arrange things!

The passages for reading were impeccably chosen. Tol-

stoi (the Arts Minister); Proust (the Editor of *The* ———);
Keynes (Protheroe's very ingenious choice); Dickens (Roz
Curtis's choice, made, I hoped, in provocative memory of
Horsfall's dictum about the techniques of contemporary
academic criticism being unable to cope with *his* novels 'as
well as Dickens's').

Each reader rose from one end of the front pew and
returned to the other end: to accommodate that, each of
his colleagues must have wriggled up – though we couldn't
see it – one space in the meantime. They read from the
small temporary lectern at the top of the sanctuary steps.
This lectern did have a microphone clipped to its side, but
the microphone was far from satisfactory: in the huge
space it amplified the sound at the expense of creating a
deeply confusing echo.

When the readings were over I whispered to Randa:

'Could *you* hear properly?'

She shook her head. Our glances met and each of us
saw the other suppressing a giggle. 'Impossible!' she whispered.

There followed more music. A piece of Herbert Howells,
the Order of Service told us: this was where the male singer
came in. Randa and I looked at each other, as if to say Do
you know what this is? I don't! By the time it ended
we were shown up for our ignorance. Below eye-level I
clapped my hands soundlessly. Randa smiled in agreement
with me. We really were getting on well together this
morning.

Now came the moment we were waiting for. Over
the heads of the people in front of us, in the distance, we
saw a scrawny little man, with a head of hair and a
beard, awkwardly beginning to climb up the sanctuary
steps to the small lectern. I'd known from photographs
that Gotham affected a fair degree of hairiness: what I
was not prepared for was his affecting a startlingly light
blue suit. I glanced at Randa: she was taking it in her
stride. I wondered if Gotham were playing some sort of

mischievous trick on us – his novels didn't put that out of the question.

By now Gotham had struggled up to the top step and suddenly had to take hold of the lectern to steady himself. I remembered his supposed rheumatic condition, his old friend Protheroe's diagnosis, ending 'Not a good life! . . .' The light from the east window shone down behind his head and lent a faint glow of colour to his thick grey hair, which was cut to stand up quite long all over his head and was trimmed to impressive length all round his jaw. (The ecclesiastical lighting-effect was more provocative than saintly.) We waited for him to begin.

Gotham first took some folded sheets of paper from the inside breast-pocket of his pale-blue jacket, then put them on the lectern for a moment while he adjusted his spectacles, then opened the sheets preparatory to spreading them on the lectern. They immediately began to slide off it: with a sideways grab he just managed to catch them – and in so doing knocked the clipped-on microphone askew. Quick, awkward gestures . . . Randa touched my arm: 'Lesson in body-language,' she whispered. Gotham was restoring the microphone to position.

Randa knew him well, of course – like Cledwyn he had been a client of hers for years, so she must be used to him. I was puzzled by his performance, body-language or not. A former professor, he must be thoroughly experienced in giving lectures at universities; and nowadays, like all authors, he must be invited to address literary conferences, seminars, tea-parties all over the place. (I had even had a couple of approaches myself on the strength of Mrs Wharton.) His body-language was clearly the opposite to his writing-language, that quick flow of entertaining words, 'So believable, so true, so *funny* . . .' (I didn't complete X Y's quotation.)

Gotham gave a series of darting glances in all directions at the audience before he began. Then, raising his voice, he declaimed to us:

'Friends, writers, memorialisers . . . I come to praise Cledwyn, not to bury him!'

A good start. Everyone must be able to hear it perfectly. I liked it; I saw that Randa liked it. It ought to have raised a faint chuckle here and there in a literate congregation. It did not. It got a uniformly pudding-like response.

Gotham stood his ground. It would have been difficult for him, marooned up there, to do anything else. He looked very small and jumpy (with that degree of hirsuteness, slightly simian, I thought). He picked up his notes and flustered through the pages. Then he put the notes down again and went on with his Address without them: he must have learnt it off by heart. Yet the ring of declamation had faded from his voice: so had the ring of effectiveness from the microphone. The new timbre of his speech was swamped by the echo.

'Don't worry!' whispered Randa. 'You can ask for a printout.' (Convinced that I meant to write about the Circus?)

Gotham began with reminiscences of early days when he and Cledwyn were not at school together, but when – so far as I could hear what he was saying – Cledwyn's brilliant performance at Oxford was floated as an inspiration above the heads of the present schoolboys, Gotham and others – who, in their turn, floated myths about Cledwyn when *he* was a schoolboy, about how he tormented the Headmaster, who had taken it upon himself to teach the senior boys Economics, by showing off that he knew more about the subject than the Head, constantly quoting Ricardo and suchlike worthies.

'This might be fun if we could hear it,' Randa whispered. 'No mention of Protheroe . . .'

She stared at me, and then deliberately gave her sudden evil blink. I laughed; she laughed. We were indeed getting on superlatively well together today.

Gotham came to their Oxford days: no mention of Horsfall's manipulating College affairs so as to get Protheroe appointed to an assistant lectureship. I wondered if Horsfall had had any hand in getting Gotham his job with J Arthur Masson – if J Arthur Masson it was. Then Cledwyn's coming to the fore in Oxford as spokesman for the Cambridge school of Keynesianism. Incidentally the microphone and the echo vouchsafed a surprising bit of information I didn't already have: Cledwyn had borrowed a substantial sum of money with which to play the stockmarket. (An odd revelation to make at a memorial service!) Then came a plug for Cledwyn's first novel, about the Methodists and the 'big people' in the small Welsh town.

Whether we could hear him or not, it was already apparent that, surprisingly, Gotham was nothing like as good a speaker as he was a novelist. I glanced at my watch and was just in time to see Randa glancing at hers. Caught, she looked as if she would giggle again if we were not in church.

On to Wartime, *The Beveridge Report* and Horsfall drawn into the Civil Service. Gotham seemed to be assuming we knew that Cledwyn had drawn him, Gotham, into the Civil Service after him. ('Really *practical* help!') Anecdotes about their experiences. By the manner in which he was telling them, I judged them to be amusing; but not, repeat not, by the pudding-like manner in which the congregation listened to him.

'If only we could hear!' I whispered to Randa.

'The print-out.'

In the echoing confusion we seemed now to be going through Horsfall's return to Oxford, then his return to affairs as Economic Adviser to the Prime Minister – the latter with its background of change during the 1970s in the country's economic and political orientation from Keynesianism to monetarism, the change which resulted, as Protheroe had explaned so authoritatively during our walk in the woods, in Cledwyn's concluding that the only future he could see for himself as a neo-Keynesian was superannuation.

Here Gotham's declamatory tones revived a little, and we actually heard what he was saying –

'Cledwyn Horsfall stood by his convictions. It would have been to his advantage to drop his convictions and set himself up as a reconstructed monetarist. No! Cledwyn Horsfall stood by his original convictions, unlike *certain other persons*. Who were prepared to change to any other convictions that would be to their personal advantage.'

Randa and I exchanged glances. There was triumph in that sleepy-looking smile of hers, as much as to say 'What did I tell you?'

Randa was right, but I was more preoccupied with thinking that Gotham had made a false move. There was a stir of attention in the audience. Puddings don't respond to humour, but they do respond to animus. Gotham had let his animus towards Protheroe get out of control.

Through the echoing buzz of electronic communication, I tried to figure out what Gotham was now saying about Horsfall's final years, spent in promoting détente 'worldwide'. Peace. Flying constantly from one country to another, just as described by Protheroe. Momentarily a window opened in the communication buzz-out and Gotham was miraculously audible –

'And there *are* things that are good. In *every* country!'

The voice was the resounding voice of Cledwyn Horsfall, of Ellis Gotham, and also of Frank Protheroe – and I would have been prepared to join my own voice with them. But it was definitely not the voice of all those devotees of the Cold War in the congregation. *Every* country was patently meant to include the Soviet Union.

'I'm afraid,' Gotham went on, still with ringing clarity, 'that he had to bear the pain of ill-disposed people calling him "a self-appointed shuttle diplomat".' (Randa and I exchanged glances, this time of surprise. *Had* he come to praise Cledwyn?) 'What more,' Gotham asked, 'could a single independent man of goodwill do, in his position?'

Good question!

'It was living a life of shuttling between East and West, between America, Russia, India – and it was to have included China as well! – that Cledwyn Horsfall killed himself.' Dramatic pause. 'One asks, Why did he choose to do it?' Another pause. 'The mainspring of his choosing to do it was – *hope!*'

It was impossible to tell how this was going down. Up to now the atmosphere had been one of lethargy if not boredom. (It had been a somewhat boring speech.) But it felt to me as if the congregation had come awake, unfavourably awake . . .

'Let *us* hope, all of us friends of Cledwyn, that the day may come when we see this hope to have been justified! Cledwyn was convinced that all is not lost. *Perhaps it isn't!* . . . Perhaps the day may come when we shall judge Cledwyn Horsfall not to have worn away his life in vain!'

Crushing his notes together and trying to stuff them back into his pocket – one of the sheets slipped out of his rheumatic grasp and fluttered down over the steps to the aisle below – Gotham left the lectern. Obviously in a state of high emotion. Staggering slightly on the steps, he disappeared to his seat in the front pew.

In the silence Randa and I exchanged glances for the last time. She shrugged her shoulders.

On cue the Vicar appeared on the scene again and blessed us in farewell. Then the organ started up and everyone rose as the procession came down the centre aisle, the Vicar and his Curate, the widow with her close friends and family; the readers, first the Minister for the Arts with Protheroe attending him, next Roz Curtis, then the Editor of The ———; lastly Gotham. (It *was* very light-blue corduroy he was dressed in.)

The arrival of the procession at the back of the church brought its members into close proximity with Randa and me.

'Come along, James,' she said, and led me up to Iris

Blackmore in advance of everyone else who had the same intention as ours.

The widow was wearing a white suit – Chinese mourning? Nobody could have looked less Oriental than Iris Blackmore. She was fair-haired and blue-eyed. Her hair was cut and waved in a short bob which made her resemble a lady-writer of the Katherine Mansfield period. She was wearing practically no make-up, and one couldn't help noticing the signs of wear – she was over sixty – in the large orbits of her eyes. She was fairly tall, almost wiry in build; most noticeably her shoulders were high and hunched . . . She appeared to have difficulty in breathing.

Randa had taken off her beautiful wide-brimmed hat so as to be able to kiss Iris on both cheeks safely.

'Lovely to see you,' they said to each other.

'Iris, this is James Cole.'

The round blue eyes looked up, wide-open. She said:

'Mrs Wharton.'

'That's me.'

'It's good, you know. Your book's so good!'

Though she seemed to have difficulty in breathing her voice was quite loud and not without a touch of harshness.

'Thank you.'

She began to laugh. 'I hear you want to write a book about Cledwyn next.'

I was taken aback. I glanced round to see how many people in the crowd could overhear. It was useless to embark on explaining that (a) I hadn't said I wanted to write the book, and (b) if I did write it it was to be about Cledwyn and Gotham and Protheroe. And if she liked to put two and two together, about her as well.

She said: 'You do know how to *write*, Mr Cole.'

Yet again, 'Thank you.'

'We can't talk about it now.' People were crowding in to greet her. 'Come round to my house! Randa will tell you where I live. Just off Curzon Street. Will you drop in for a cup of tea one afternoon? And a drink afterwards –

I'm not allowed to have one, but I'll give you one.' Smiling she stretched out her hand – to someone else who had just barged in beside me.

I was dismissed but not dissatisfied.

Iris called round the body of the interloper –

'Do go and have a glass of wine!'

I grinned at Randa. 'I hadn't forgotten the wine, had you?'

'I'm sorry, James. I've got to get back as soon as possible. Because of Jess not being there.' She glanced over her shoulder. 'Anyway, I see Frank Protheroe coming for you.'

So we parted, and Protheroe came sailing through the crowd.

'I take it you still want to meet Ellis Gotham, despite that exceedingly poor performance?'

'Of course.'

'Follow me!' Protheroe might not be particularly tall, but he had particular weight and power. He thrust his way through the throng. (I heard the alliteration in my head.) I followed. I had caught a glimpse of light-blue corduroy.

Ellis Gotham was standing near the drinks-table, holding a glass of red wine in his hand and talking animatedly to three youngish women. They were aged, I should say, around thirty. Two were holding glasses of white wine, the third a glass of red; and they were talking animatedly to him – he was at home with them.

I said to Protheroe: 'Ought we to interrupt them?'

'Why not? They're only his womenfolk.'

'Two of them must be his daughters. Who's the third?'

'His wife.'

'His wife? She's no older than his daughters.'

'He did a year as Writer-in-Residence at Indiana Falls University.' Smoothly. 'Does that explain everything?'

'Scarcely.'

'She was one of his students. He supervised her Master's thesis.' Protheroe leered. 'And that wasn't all he supervised.'

m twice. 2 *d*. by the first m. Three young women.

I kept quiet.

'I take it that you agree with me about Ellis's Address?'

I still kept quiet.

'He's no Mark Antony.'

I made a gesture not signifying one way or the other.

'A somewhat boring disquisition.'

'I don't know that I should say that, actually.'

'I'll introduce you to him and bring you a glass of wine to keep you going.'

Protheroe introduced me to Gotham, and in the moment when the two men stood opposite each other I was struck by the contrast between them. Gotham was not quite as small and scrawny as I'd thought, yet beside Protheroe's burgeoning robustness he looked it. While Protheroe's expensive suit hugged his body sleekly, especially round the embonpoint, Gotham's light-blue corduroy number, obviously off-the-peg, hung loosely from his shoulders and over his concave stomach. Protheroe's face was glowing with satisfaction; Gotham's face-hair did not conceal the fact that his face was not.

Protheroe went away and I was able to look at Gotham attentively.

From its frame of hair Gotham's face looked out, sharp-featured, with unusually high, prominent cheek-bones which made his eyes remarkably narrow. His complexion was parchment-coloured and his eyes were a bright brown. (Even in the present freedom from strain, he was still throwing darting glances around him all the while. Was it a simple nervous tic of no great significance, or was he constantly suspicious of other people's response to him? Time would no doubt tell me. Meanwhile I found it off-putting.) An odd thing, though, was that despite the constantly darting glance, the rest of his face kept a remarkably unchanging expression – impossible to tell from it what he was thinking. A strange sort of man, I thought.

Protheroe came back with my glass of wine. (Protheroe

was a bastard, I thought, but *not* a strange sort of man!) When he had gone away again, Gotham introduced me to his three women.

Gotham's daughters were prettier than the young woman he had married, the young woman for whom I presumed he must have decided while he was at Indiana Falls to divorce his wife. Which is not to say she was not attractive. The daughters had beautiful fine complexions and hazel eyes: their noses, like their father's, were fine-cut and well-shaped, their mouths, unlike his, full-lipped and rosy. In manner they were shy and retiring – perhaps like their divorced mother? Gotham's present wife, on the other hand, was very lively and confident – I thought she must be fun. She was dark-haired and slightly beaky, her complexion showing signs of coarsening, thanks, I supposed, to the harsh climate of the Mid-West. All in all, it seemed to me, Gotham might have done pretty well for himself.

Introductions over. A moment's pause. Awkward. I drank some of my wine, red wine. Gotham drank some of his and glanced at me:

'Not bad?' he said, referring to the wine.

'Considering the locale,' I said, 'super!' I took a sizeable draught. I waited while he aimed a few darting glances on either side of my head, not, so far as I could see at anyone in particular or for any reason in particular – perhaps it *was* a nervous tic.

Then he looked at me.

'I haven't read your book on Mrs Wharton, yet, I'm afraid. But I'm going to. I hear it's very good.'

'Thank you.' Encouraged, I said, 'I *have* read your last novel.'

'Oh.' And then sharply, 'And d'you think *it's* good?' The suspicious glance *was* suspicious – and suspicious of me, at that! The young women were all ears. I kept my cool. I said:

'It struck me as truthful, believable, and very funny.'

Obviously the most useful literary quotation I had at my disposal!

'Will your book on Mrs Wharton strike me as truthful, believable, and very funny?' Without a glimmer of expression – and I felt it was not meant one hundred per cent good-naturedly. I said:

'I hope it will strike you as truthful and believable.' And was tempted to the mistake of adding, 'I haven't the gift for being funny.'

I had struck a spark – a darting spark of suspicion, or was it dislike? However he said:

'I'll tell you when I've read it. I'm expecting to enjoy it. I admire her writing. She had many gifts – and many advantages.'

'Advantages?' He couldn't be thinking, as I often was, about the wonderful efflorescence in her sexual life?

'Rich,' he said. 'Well-placed in society. What more could you ask? Apart from great literary talent, which she had as well.'

I didn't say I thought he was ungenerous. He went on without my saying anything.

'She was very, very lucky.' He glanced at the young women while he was saying this.

Even if I'd got to get on with him, I was not prepared to take this kind of conversation lying down.

'I shall be interested to know how you feel when you've read *my* book.' I was surprised by my own provocativeness.

'I'll let you know.'

It was the cue for him to give me a smile. He did not. It was coming to me that in his saying she was very lucky there was a note of envy – with old X Y having just provided me with the quotation of the hour, I couldn't help hoping that Gotham was not going to air a tiresome streak like the old man's of feeling badly-done-to. If I were going to write about Gotham it would be with the presupposition that he had 'got there'. I drank some more of the funeral wine, feeling that I was going to need it.

(Other people round about seemed to be putting it away readily, whether it was in church or not.)

'What did you think of my Address?' (There was singularly little lead-in to his remarks.) There was nothing yielding in his tone of voice – did he sense that I was mildly fed-up with him?

Before I could frame a reply he saved me the necessity of doing so, by going straight on –

'Truthful from my point of view. Pretty unbelievable from the point of view of those bastards. And totally un-funny from any point of view whatsoever.' A spate of darting glances even took in the vaulting above us. 'I have no talent for Addresses, that's for sure, Mr Cole.' He stared at me momentarily. 'I'll never do it again!'

I wondered if other people nearby could hear him. In fact there were several people apparently interested. I said:

'At the back we had an awful job to hear you.'

'That was a dispensation. I lost my touch – if I ever had one.'

'Oh, I don't know,' I said, shrugging my shoulders.

'Did you catch that bit about Cledwyn being called a "self-appointed shuttle diplomat"? That was a mistake for sure. I should never have given them that one.'

He seemed not to care if anyone did overhear him, and to my surprise I felt an impulse to try and cover up for him – a passing change in my situation!

'You only quoted it in order to justify it in a serious, good-willed sense. Right?' (I wasn't sure that I believed it, myself.) With a wary eye on two people who were hovering with intent, I said as ingenuously as I could make it sound, 'I was wondering if it really was a quotation, or perhaps . . . an original invention?'

He suddenly broke an expressionless pause with –

'Ha!'

His young women and I looked at him expectantly.

Ignoring the two bystanders, now patently listening, he said in a biting tone:

– 61 –

'Cledwyn Horsfall – *The Winged Kissinger of Peace!*'

Silence for an instant.

I had nothing to say. The two hovering bystanders had, and they stepped in to say it. Gotham took them up.

There was a sparkle in the eyes of the three young women as I turned away. Did they see the remark as the give-away I took it as – or was it nothing new to them?

The more I thought about it, the more I thought it was the latter.

5

❧ *A Rival on the Scene* ❧

Randa let a couple of days elapse before telephoning me.

'So you haven't gone to Oxford.'

'I should have thought not,' I said, as she was telephoning me at my flat – a tiny basement flat in Doughty Street, found for me by Randa herself, within easy striking distance of Goslett & Goslett's chambers.

'Have you taken up Iris's invitation to drop in for tea?'

'Yes.'

I let her wait a moment. Then, '4 p.m. the day after tomorrow.'

'You must be looking forward to it.'

'I expect I shall find it interesting.'

'*Rewarding*, I should hope, James.'

'That will make everybody happy, won't it?'

'James!' I could hear her laughing.

I started to laugh.

'And how did you get on with Ellis Gotham?'

'We didn't spit in each other's eye.'

'Or fall into each other's arms?'

I treated this with silence.

'All right. We'll be serious. Tell me about Ellis!'

'I didn't find it easy. Partly because his facial expression doesn't give a clue to what he's thinking. Partly because that continually darting glance makes one think he's suspicious of something.'

'I don't think it's suspiciousness. Just nervous tension.'

'And furthermore,' I paused, 'I felt slightly wrong-footed, through being introduced to him by Protheroe, with whom he hasn't been on speaking terms for years – or so he says.'

'It isn't true, you know.'

'It's odd that Protheroe should have told me so.'

'Not really, James. Everybody knows they haven't been close friends with each other for years, though they've both been close friends of Cledwyn's throughout. No. The fact I must break to you, James, if you haven't already discovered it for yourself, is that Protheroe is a great liar.'

'That's very useful to know.'

'It wouldn't have taken you long to find out.'

'It obviously makes my task,' I said ironically, 'just one hundred per cent easier.'

'If you were in *my* profession, James, you'd take it as a matter of course.'

'Everybody lies.'

'That's right.'

'What a *rewarding* conversation this is!' In my qualms about having to cope with living persons I'd so far given little thought to their being lying persons. There was a pause.

'You were telling me about Gotham, James.'

'He regretted saying in his Address that people called Cledwyn a self-appointed shuttle diplomatist.'

'*I* was surprised.'

'Have you heard people call Cledwyn that?'

'No. But it doesn't sound improbable. Why do you ask?'

'Well, something made me suspect it was Gotham's own invention.'

'It's funny enough for Ellis. But what made you suspect?'

'He suddenly came out with an alternative, certainly

his own. "Cledwyn Horsfall – The Winged Kissinger of Peace". How about that?'

Randa laughed. 'That really is good!' She paused. In a different tone of voice –

'Can Ellis be beginning to crack?'

'Crack? What does that mean?'

'Crack in his hero-worship of Cledwyn. Something else you should know, James, is that Ellis was always sold on the greatness of Cledwyn. The absolute greatness of Cledwyn!'

'How extraordinary!' During the conversation I was making notes, of course.

'Not if you realise that Ellis is extraordinarily innocent in some areas.'

'Innocent? What does that mean?'

'He has areas where he's out of touch . . . Out of touch with the world around him. That sort of person often is.'

'What sort of person would you call him, Randa?'

'Come on, James! You know what I mean. He'd usually be called an introverted person, wouldn't he? You noticed, yourself, his lapses in worldliness, in his Address. When he lost touch with his audience, when he offended them, when he gave points to Cledwyn's enemies . . . What do you call that?'

I said, 'H'm!'

I had never heard Randa talk on these lines before. It occurred to me that in her varied legal career she must have had to learn quite a lot about different sorts of person. I didn't know enough to be able to counter her case about Ellis Gotham – if, for that matter, enough existed. Perhaps she was just right.

Looking down at my notes, the phrase 'lapses in worldliness' stood out. A cogent phrase. I could use it to advantage if I ever wrote this book about Horsfall and Gotham and Protheroe. I was impressed by Randa.

'So one of Ellis's areas of innocence encompassed Cledwyn?'

'You can say that again!' A sudden intake of breath was audible over the telephone. I imagined a frown of impatience at my lagging behind in comprehension.

I thought it was probably time I rang off, but Randa went on – as it were spelling it out for me:

'Ellis was completely sold on the greatness of Cledwyn, and on his goodness too. He always seemed to believe that everything Cledwyn did was good and true, if you know what I mean. Really, you know.' She paused and didn't go on.

I said, 'You think Gotham's belief in Cledwyn is finally cracking. Is that it?'

'One must wonder.'

'Are you insinuating that Cledwyn did things that were *not* good and true?'

'I never insinuate, James!'

I was delighted with this response – I recalled that delicious moment in The Gay Hussar when she lowered her eyelids to convey professional discretion. Humbug!

'Of course not, Randa.'

We both paused, each savouring the game the other was playing.

Then Randa said, on a different tack:

'Did you notice that Ellis said practically nothing about Cledwyn's novels?'

'Astonishing. In a service commemorating Cledwyn, nobody quoted a word Cledwyn had written. Very remarkable.' (I already had an underlined note about this.)

'Yes,' said Randa sweetly. 'Yes . . .' I imagined the poise of her head.

'I suppose we're free to think our own thoughts.'

I could see her smiling at the other end of the line –

'There's nothing like the animosity of old friends, is there?'

The conversation ended there.

For a few moments I meditated on the 'innocence' of Gotham. With that consistently darting glance, he hadn't struck me as a particularly innocent-looking man. His absence of facial expression tended to negate his looking like *any* particular sort of man. (In his novels this dead-pan air made his jokes seem all the funnier, *n'est-ce pas?*)

I expected to hear more about him from Iris.

The two days passed and I made my way to the street off Curzon Street. A street of typical late-Georgian terrace houses, houses originally one room wide, two rooms deep, and four storeys high.

The door was opened by an elderly housekeeper.

'Lady Horsfall is expecting you. She'd like you to go straight up to the drawing-room.' She preceded me down the narrow entrance-hall: we passed the door of what must be the dining-room, and at the foot of the stairs she turned into the kitchen and left me to my own devices. Perhaps she had trouble climbing stairs – or perhaps Iris was losing her grip on the staff.

I climbed the narrow staircase. At first blow the house struck me as less luxurious than I'd expected of a man who'd made a fortune – two fortunes actually, one out of playing the stockmarket and the other out of writing books. (Iris must have made a contribution as well.) It wasn't a house that I would say 'smelt of money', though the shabby cream-coloured walls of the staircase were lined two deep with pictures, some of which I guessed must be pretty valuable.

It occurred to me that Iris had been living here alone since Cledwyn's death, and probably alone for a good deal of the time before that, when he was travelling far and wide. I was reminded of her daughter – at the Memorial Service no one had pointed out the daughter to me. *Was she there?*

A small landing and a few more stairs, two doors, one of them open –

'I'm in here!' Iris's voice.

Typically the drawing-room was a double-room, previous front-room and back-room knocked into one. Iris was sitting in an armchair at the far end of the back-room. Again she was wearing the white outfit: I looked more closely this time – it was a white jacket and trousers. Draped round her shoulders was a gauzy scarf whose blue-grey colour matched her eyes. Her hair, neatly waved in Katherine Mansfield style, revealed in the stronger light from a window behind her a blondness much assisted by the hairdresser's art. And although the wornness of complexion in the orbits of her eyes seemed more notice-able here, the eyes themselves were bright with almost youthful vivacity.

'I won't get up.' She held out her hand from where she was sitting. 'Please come and sit down! It's good of you to come.'

I was on the edge of saying It's good of you to ask me. Shyness got the better of me.

'Can you find somewhere to sit down?'

A good question, since there were books everywhere, including on the seats of chairs and sofas. I moved some from the seat of a sofa to the floor beside it, and sat down.

'Tea will be up in a minute.'

I folded one knee over the other, changed my mind and reversed them. Up to now she had not made a single remark to which I could think of a sentient reply.

In the pause we looked at each other, weighing each other up. I noticed again the hunched-look of her shoulders, and now remarked a puffiness of the cheeks and swollen look of the lips – reminding me of someone I knew who suffered from hay-fever. She was breathing noisily.

As the tea didn't make its appearance I glanced ner-vously round the room. More walls like those of the stair-case, which could do with another lick of cream-coloured paint; but a beautiful Persian carpet and luxuriously comfortable – once the books were taken away – sofas and chairs. And almost entirely covering the walls a splendid collection of paintings, contemporary figurative paintings. I recognised a dominating Francis Bacon, a superb Lucian Freud, a couple of Hockneys; and at least three by another artist . . . I hesitated –

'Arthur Boyd,' said Iris.

I felt myself blushing.

'Australian. Cledwyn's favourite. A fine painter.'

I surveyed them. (With a sudden shift of attention I realised that the Lucian Freud was a portrait of Iris herself, a marvellous portrait. The beautiful blue-grey of her eyes . . .)

'Do you like them?'

I said Yes as if it were open to me to say No.

The tea. A housemaid brought in a tray on which there was not only a handsome Georgian teapot, cups and saucers and so on, but also a large plate of sandwiches and a plate with a large cake on it. The maid put down the tray on a low table in front of Iris, who said to me:

'I can manage to pour the tea, but I'm afraid I shall have to ask you to help yourself to sandwiches and cakes.'

'Thank you.' (This brought my total of words uttered to three.)

I got up to take my cup of tea from her.

'Please take a sandwich!'

While she poured the tea her hand was shaking. 'Just managed it!' she said.

'I'm sorry to see you not quite . . . well.'

'It's a damn' nuisance. Emphysema.'

So that was it. 'I'm sorry.'

I took my cup of tea from her. 'Yet you've managed to go on writing.'

'Yes, thank God!'

I took a sandwich. 'That must be encouraging, anyway.'

'It would be if I thought I were going to write anything else.' She looked away, almost angrily. I noticed again the surprising harshness of her voice, though it was not unpleasant.

– 69 –

An excellent cup of tea. A delicious sandwich, cucumber. An English tea-party.

There was a longish pause.

'I've read your book about Mrs Wharton.'

She must have forgotten she told me so after the Memorial Service. Without a pause she went on cheerfully –

'I should like to think somebody will write a book as good as that about me.'

I was not expecting this, and for the moment had nothing to say. Iris said:

'I doubt if they will.'

'I don't agree.'

A new light came into her eyes – pleasure, edged with flirtatiousness? She said:

'The optimism of youth.'

'I don't think so, Lady Horsfall.'

'Please call me Iris! I shall call you James.' Surprisingly she smiled to herself. 'The fashion for calling people by their Christian names the minute you set eyes on them came from America. Better if it had stayed there. I used to call it Instant Familiarity.' She was watching for my response. 'Nowadays everybody does it. I've had to give in.'

'Usage makes perfect.'

She laughed. 'Makes acceptable, anyway.'

'The acceptable *is* perfect.' (I wasn't intending to enter the Oscar Wilde Stakes.)

The blue-grey eyes sparked with fun. 'I like your irony, James.'

'May I have another sandwich, Iris?'

'They're all for you.' She was teasing me. 'And the cake as well.'

I took another sandwich.

'More tea? *You* can pour this time, James.'

I did as I was told and sat down again. I now sat sideways so as to face her. The sofa-cushions billowed round me.

'So you want to write a biography of Cledwyn?'

'Who told you that? Randa?'

'Randa second. Protheroe first.'

Involuntarily – 'Protheroe?'

'Protheroe is the first to tell one everything.' She laughed enigmatically – was it out of friendliness or animosity?

I let her question about the book go.

'For the time being I'm interested. No more than that, Iris. I'm a long way from committing myself finally.'

She said: 'I should have thought Cledwyn offers everything a biographer is looking for. A major novelist and a major world-publicist.' A pause. 'We were very dissatisfied when he didn't get a Nobel.'

In my stupefaction I wondered whether she meant a Nobel Prize for Literature or a Nobel Prize for Peace – perhaps *both*? . . . I should have said I was already conversant with the insatiable desire of writers for praise and prizes: I was faced with crushing evidence that I had still a long way to go.

'Yes,' she said cheerfully.

'I can understand that,' I said, taking refuge in ambiguity – what I actually meant was that I understood that they were dissatisfied.

'I'm glad you agree.' She apparently took it that I meant I understood Cledwyn had a rightful claim. I fingered a coin in my pocket in order to feel if it was on heads or tails – Literature or Peace?

'He put himself up for it. You know you have to put *yourself* up for the Literature Prize.'

'No, I didn't know.'

'You'd be surprised, James, if you knew some of the writers who *have* put themselves up.'

'Really.'

'Of course Cledwyn put himself up. International reputation. Books sell all over the world. We made a few trips to Sweden, talked to people, including members of the Nobel committee. Things seemed to be going well.' She broke off for a moment. 'Did you see in *The Times* that beast Viktor Bergstrom – he's actually one of the judges – saying *in public*, believe it or not! that Graham Greene would get the Prize for Literature over his dead body.'

'As a matter of fact I think I did.' I remembered it well.

'Cledwyn was in the same boat, I'll be bound.'

'Really?' Irrelevantly I imagined Graham Greene and Cledwyn Horsfall sitting together in a sinking dinghy.

'Bergstrom has stopped Greene getting it.' With intense conviction – 'He's stopped Cledwyn.'

'Extraordinary,' was all I could say.

'That's right.'

Iris paused. She was breathing with great difficulty – I couldn't tell if it was emphysema that was impeding her or fury. She said:

'The other thing was an OM.'

To this I could say nothing – other than Christ! which I didn't say.

'He should have been offered a CH at least.' She stopped, clamping her jaw in sheer tension.

Cledwyn Horsfall had died without being admitted to either the Order of Merit of the Companionate of Honour.

'But really it should have been the OM. It *should* have been, James.'

I heard myself saying wimpishly, 'Perhaps he was unlucky.'

'Unlucky!' she cried. 'It must have been some Thatcherite philistine among the Queen's advisers had the last word!'

I was reminded that the OM was in the Sovereign's gift. I nodded my head as if I were agreeing with this peculiar analysis of the situation. She went on.

'These things are important, James. Extremely important if one's hoping to be remembered.'

So – get your OM for immortality! I said, 'Ah! . . .'

'It's no use pretending otherwise,' she added.

'No, I suppose it isn't.'

Something made me think of Protheroe, who might be thought as Sir Frank to have acquired a lesser stake in immortality.

Knighthoods were in the gift of the Prime Minister. Now the Prime Minister was known, had been known for some years, to be given over to monetarism. Frank Protheroe had made his adjustment for immortality. Formerly a neo-Keynesian, he was now, had been for a like number of years, a thoroughly reconstructed monetarist. One might say Trust Protheroe! Yet, and yet . . . In the course of my research I had recently lighted on an article by a professional economist, clearly a committed monetarist, complaining that the Government was abandoning monetarism, and prophesying that by the time a couple of years were up – we were now in 1983 – the Government would be espousing a deplorable intermediate economics, generated (if I understood him correctly) by neo-Keynesianism and neo-classicism *converging* . . . Which made me think again of Protheroe. If a sort of neo-Keynesianism came back, could we rely on Protheroe to *re*-adjust? Knowing him better, now, I felt that Protheroe had won my trust in all such circumstances.

'Why are you smiling, James?' Iris said.

'I didn't know I *was* smiling.'

'Have a piece of cake – you haven't had any yet. It's home-made, all for you. I have a very good cook.'

I got up and helped myself to a slice of cake. (It was excellent cake.) Suddenly Iris said:

'*I* should like you to do a biography of Cledwyn.'

'That's an honour.'

A light in those round blue-grey eyes – they were slightly opaque yet I could imagine them flashing. 'You're a clever young man. And perceptive. And you can *write*.'

Embarrassment and pleasure took away my powers of speech. Praise and prizes. Not *I*, susceptible already?

'I'm speaking as his wife and as a writer. I'm also speaking as a literary executor – I'm one of his literary executors, you know. So is our daughter, Gwendolen. The third is Elly Gotham.'

'I understand.' I was enjoying the cake – she *had* got a good cook.

'I suppose you know Cledwyn sold off batches of his manuscripts, private papers and so on? The bulk of them are now in the New York Public Library, some in the University of Illinois.'

'That's useful to know.'

She gave me a long look.

'There *is* a snag, James.'

'Yes?' It must be the Australian professor who had got in first.

'Have you heard of Barry M'Gann?'

I thought it wisest to say No.

'H'm.' She thought for a moment. Then –

'I'd better tell you the story.' She lit a cigarette. 'I'm not supposed to smoke – you don't smoke, I suppose. Young men don't, nowadays. Only the young women.'

I put down my empty plate and teacup, and sat forward on the sofa.

'Background first.' She paused. 'Cledwyn had a great admiration for Australia and the Australians. Splendid painters – Arthur's Boyd's one.' She gestured towards his paintings. Very dramatic, with a sexual aura – or so they seemed to me. People moving through the air like wedding couples in Chagall's paintings. 'Very splendid,' I said. Iris was going on: 'Splendid writers – Patrick White, Thomas Kenneally and all the rest whom you must know of; and in the past Henry Handel Richardson, for instance – it's incredible she's been forgotten. I don't suppose *you*'ve ever heard of her. Henry Handel Richardson was a woman, you know.' Iris took a breath. 'I think I've just got Roz Curtis to say she'll republish *The Fortunes of Richard Mahoney*.' (I made a mental note.)

Trying to keep up with her I interpolated –

'Playwrights and film-makers as well.'

'Australia has produced artists in numbers out of all proportion to its tiny population.'

I assented.

'Cledwyn was simply crazy about Australia for a time. Crazy about Australians. That's the sort of man he was. He was a Celt. Romantic, if you like. He enjoyed the drama of what he imagined it is to be an Australian. And when he took a fancy to one of them, he saw him or her through rose-coloured spectacles.'

'Was that a fault?'

'On the contrary. It's the way Elly Gotham saw Cledwyn. For a lifetime. That's why Elly is the most devoted and loyal friend Cledwyn ever had.'

'I see.'

'With Cledwyn,' giving me a sidelong look, 'there was a constant succession of people he saw through rose-coloured spectacles. For the time being they were wonderful and could do no wrong. Barry M'Gann was one of those people.'

'For the time being?'

'I'll come to that.' Iris puffed her forbidden cigarette for a moment. 'Out of the blue we were sent a book by an Australian academic about Charles Dickens. Cledwyn read it and was taken with it, decided to review it. He reviewed it very warmly.'

'I used to see some of his reviews.'

'He didn't take on a book for review unless he could review it warmly.'

'What happened then?'

'A letter from M'Gann saying he was going to be in London, could he come and see us?'

'And you said Yes? . . .'

'That's right. And we both took to him. He was cultivated, sympathetic, civilised –'

I interrupted by laughing at the recollection of the Australian academics in a film called *Don's Party*.

'Not macho and drunk?'

'Just the opposite. Very gentlemanly. No Australian accent, of course. One wouldn't know he was Australian if he didn't make self-conscious, rather bad jokes about it from time to time. Couldn't be more cultured and smooth. That is to say we realised he was smooth when the spectacles lost some of their rose-colour. "Too damned smooth!" Cledwyn said, when he began to realise he'd been taken in. But that was much later.'

Iris paused for rather a long time – breathing hard, getting tired . . .

'So M'Gann came to see you?'

'He did. Cultured and smooth and knowledgeable. He knew all Cledwyn's novels inside out – not that there are so many of them: Cledwyn was always trying to do too many other things. I've written more – and Barry knew the most important of them. It was our novels that interested him. He's a Professor of English Literature, so he didn't know a thing about economics, a major part of Cledwyn's life, and didn't seem very inclined to learn about it. But we forgave him that. And he pretended to more interest and understanding of Cledwyn's most recent work for World Détente than we thought he actually had, but he did show signs of proposing to learn, and we thought he was intelligent enough to pick it up. I'm telling you all this in the light of what we came to think about him later, you understand that, James?'

'Yes. But please go on!'

'The fact of the matter is that we all took to each other. In a big way.' She looked at me shrewdly and her eyes began to light up with recollection, amused recollection. 'It was one of those evenings, you know? When we couldn't get him a taxi we put him up here for the night.'

I did know. At dinner in All Souls I supposed that a minor inflow of alcohol produced a major impression on Cledwyn's sobriety. In view of what I'd heard about him from other sources in the meantime, I concluded that he must have had a session with the bottle up in his room before he ever came down. There was a simple explanation of how the first evening together of Cledwyn, Iris and Barry M'Gann ended.

Iris went on. 'M'Gann said he wanted to write Cledwyn's biography. We were all delighted.'

'His official biography?' I asked promptly. *If* I wrote a book about the three old friends it would be very different from an official biography.

'No. Cledwyn was against that. He'd seen too much of official biographies. What's left after the subject's family and friends have had their whack at getting this, that and the other excised . . . He wanted the whole truth to come out.'

'You mean the whole truth as *he* wanted to tell it?'

'As he and Barry M'Gann wanted to tell it, I suppose. I began to be left out of their discussions. The upshot of those was that Cledwyn agreed to give M'Gann a long series of personal interviews, taking him through the most important things in his whole life-history.'

'And that's what happened?'

'Went on over a period of weeks. They used to go up to Cledwyn's study for hours on end. I don't know what they said up there, but Cledwyn used to come down shattered.'

'By the questions that were put to him or by the answers he'd given?'

'I don't know. What worried me was the possible effect of it on Cledwyn's health. I had no idea he was going to die suddenly at the end of it, of course.'

'The sessions were taped?'

'Yes.'

'Where are the tapes now?'

'M'Gann took them back to Australia with him.'

Containing myself with an effort I said: 'They're important, Iris! Terribly important. Do you know what M'Gann is going to do with them?'

'You don't think an operator like M'Gann is going to let anyone else hear them, do you? Before he's extracted every ounce out of them!'

'I suppose he's transcribing them?'

'*He is!* He writes to *me* from time to time, asking me to clarify odd points. His letters to me alternate between the smarmy and the insolent. Don't ask me why!' She stubbed out her cigarette and had an afterthought. 'By every ounce, I mean every ounce. Every ounce of literary réclame, and every ounce of *cash!* He's out for money.'

I felt that my breathlessness had given way to speechlessness. This was my Fate we were talking about! . . .

'Now, James, what about a drink? The whisky's over there, and the ice, and water if you need it. You're looking as if you need the whisky, anyway.' She grinned at me in a tough way. 'I'm not allowed any whisky, so help yourself!'

Whisky – I did need it.

I made myself a pretty small drink all the same – I was self-conscious about staying too long and leaving Iris exhausted. And I was driving back.

I was sitting on the edge of the sofa. Iris looked unwell. It occurred to me that if I were going to write about these people I should have to learn about the symptoms and afflictions of old age.

I was just finishing my drink when a strange thing happened. Iris said:

'Would you like to see Cledwyn's will, James?'

'Well, yes . . .' I felt embarrassed.

'It's in that drawer over there.' She pointed to a desk on the other side of the room. She moved in her chair. 'If you'll help me to get up, I'll find it for you.'

'Are you sure? . . .' I took hold of her elbow to help her, handed her her stick, and stood while she made her way across the room. I really had stayed too long.

Iris opened the drawer and appeared to be searching among the papers in it.

'It doesn't appear to be here, James.' Pause. 'I'm not sure where it is.'

'Never mind.'

Was the will really not there, or had she seen it and changed her mind about showing it to me? The incident was uninterpretable.

'Next time you come, James.'

'Yes.'

We were standing together in the middle of the room.

'It was nice of you to come.' She held up her cheek to be kissed.

I kissed her cheek. 'Thank you, Iris, I've enjoyed it very much . . .'

As I walked down the street I questioned the amount of enjoyment I'd got out of what I'd been told about the Australian professor.

6

❧ *The Deed – and a Will* ❧

Next thing was a letter from Ellis Gotham. Would I meet him for a drink at his club?

Would I *not*? . . .

At five-thirty prompt on the agreed afternoon I presented myself at the club, a large town-house just within walking-distance of where Iris Blackmore lived and where Cledwyn had lived while he was alive. There was a black-and-white flagged entrance hall with a broad staircase to one side, beside the door a glass box with an elderly porter inside it.

'Yes, sir. Mr Gotham, sir. That's right. He's expecting you, sir. You'll find him in The Beargarden, sir. Do you know where that is?'

I hesitated and the porter was out of his box in a trice, showing me round a corner of the hall into a comfortable, middle-sized room where a fire was burning, leather-covered banquettes and chairs arranged in three sides of a rectangle round it.

There was no one else in the room but Ellis Gotham, dressed again in the pale-blue corduroy suit – did he wear it all the time? He levered himself up from the banquette where he was sitting, near to a lamp, reading the *Standard*. The light glistened from his grey head of hair and beard.

We exchanged greetings – I held out my hand and shook his. He winced. I looked down, to see the joints of his hand inflamed and swollen.

'Oh, I'm sorry!'

It was not a good start.

'It's not your fault,' he said.

'It must be an awful nuisance.'

He gave me a quick glance. 'That's right.' And he sat down again.

The newspaper lay between us and I read the headline out of embarrassment.

He followed up his remark. 'It isn't fatal.' His expression gave no clue as to whether he was being ironical. From the way his glance was darting towards me I guessed that he was.

'But it must make living much less endurable,' I said. I smiled at him sympathetically.

'One doesn't live for ever, Mr Cole.'

I felt he was laughing, though it didn't show.

'Do you believe in life after death?' I asked.

'Don't ask silly questions!'

I laughed, myself. Looking at him I was reminded that he was seventy. He had taken off his reading-spectacles. Above the high pale cheek-bones his narrow brown eyes were shining as vigorously as a younger man's.

'What about a drink, Mr Cole?'

I wondered why he'd taken to calling me 'Mr Cole'. 'When you're ready,' I said.

'It would be kind if *you* would go to the bar down there' – he pointed through an open double-doorway to the next room, much bigger than this, where I could see the bar – 'and bring the drinks.'

'There's no hurry,' I said, thinking his complaint might not be suited by alcohol.

'How d'you know *I'm* in no hurry?

'I don't.' I felt myself blushing with embarrassment. 'Are you?'

'No. None at all.'

Crushed, I was silent. So was he. There was a clock on the chimney-piece, ticking.

It was a lofty room with a handsome crystal chandelier glowing over our heads. The plasterwork of the ceiling was gilded and the walls were hung with a Japanese wallpaper resembling fine strips of bamboo. The gas in the mock coal-fire began to hiss quietly.

'For a beargarden,' I said, 'this is exceptionally quiet.'

'For the time being.'

'Why is it called The Beargarden?'

'Years ago some members of the club, ardent Trollopians, christened it that. After the club the Duke of Omnium's sons belonged to.' His darting glances had subsided. 'I believe The Beargarden was originally the nickname for the Great Hall where all the boys used to be taught at Eton.' He paused. 'This Beargarden won't remain peaceful as the club fills up for the evening. You know the convention of this place? Anyone can come up and talk to anyone else, unless they make it obvious they're engaged in private conversation – by hanging out a red flag.' He waited a moment. 'You have been warned.'

'Oh.' I had been under the impression that the two of us were here for extended private conversation.

'Have you been in this club before?'

'I think so.'

'Then I needn't have told you all that.'

I said: 'One doesn't mind being given true information twice.'

He gave me several darting glances. 'Bright young man!' (I was encouraged to think that perhaps I was not doing so badly, after all.) 'You deserve a drink, even if you're not in urgent need of one.' He leaned his grey fuzzy head against the leather back of the banquette. 'Anyway, I want one – a drink sometimes eases this damned pain.'

I stood up. He said, 'I must give you the money' – taking

some out of his pocket – 'as non-members are not allowed to pay.' I went down to the bar.

When I came back he had put his spectacles on, and was reading the *Standard* again. I set down the drinks on a small table in front of us and looked over his shoulder at the newspaper.

'What's the true information the *Standard* is giving us this evening?'

He held it for me to see –

INFLATION DOWN AGAIN

'Do you believe it?'

He was sipping his drink. 'Difficult to answer.' He put down his glass. 'This Government are expert at dickering about with the various indicators – cost of living figures, for one thing.' He paused thoughtfully. 'They've invested a tremendous amount of political capital in monetarism, and they mean to prove it's RIGHT.'

I had started my drink. I said:

'I take it you were a Keynesian, still are a Keynesian?'

He darted a very swift glance at me. 'The difficulty about trying to answer that one is that since 1979 the Conservative Government has operated on monetarist principles claiming great success' – he jabbed his forefinger on the headline – 'with increasing signs of monetarist concepts being integrated as a consequence into previous Keynesian concepts. Strange *mélange* . . . Some people such as Protheroe – who's not an economist and doesn't know what it's all about, anyway – went over to Friedmanism straight away: others are now finding the ground changing under their feet.'

I had another sip of my drink. 'But you and Cledwyn Horsfall weren't converted – to believing Friedmanism is right, I mean.'

'Not I. It will be another ten years before I shall be ready to admit I was wrong.'

'Nor Cledwyn, neither?'

He turned to me in profile, small, bearded profile – and was silent. His glances were darting all round the room but avoiding me.

'You said in your Memorial Address that Cledwyn didn't. Did you not mean that?'

'I told you I lost my touch,' he said violently. 'I was aiming at loyalty, to show Cledwyn at his noblest – though God knows why!' He paused. 'God knows why in view of the fact that it was the *wrong* touch!' Still without letting his glance cover me, he drank a little more. 'There's irony, if you want it.'

I was astonished. I found the conversation difficult to follow. What could he have thought he was doing, in saying what he said in the Address? A dotty action which could only damage both of them. I was reminded of Randa's view of his character . . .

Gotham now turned to me.

'Look here, my friend. You know that Cledwyn held a TV debate with Friedman? Did you see it?'

I shook my head. 'Missed it, I'm afraid.'

'*Cledwyn lost it!* That much was clear to everyone – and it was clear to Cledwyn . . . It shook him. He'd scored some own goals which he could discount to himself. He couldn't discount the major goals that Friedman scored, and they shook him.' At this Gotham did glance at me. 'Cledwyn began to modify his stance from that day on.'

'Did he discuss it with you?'

'He kept out of my way.'

I cogitated over the situation. Sorting this out was going to give me a pretty fair amount of trouble. Gotham interrupted my thoughts by saying:

'Cledwyn was nothing if not a pragmatist.' And he gave a laugh which was not friendly towards Cledwyn.

I resorted to going on with my drink.

Gotham suddenly picked up the *Standard*, folded it, and threw it to the far end of the banquette.

'I didn't bring you here to talk to you about this,' he said. 'It was the last thing I had in mind.'

'It was interesting.'

He gave me a couple of specially darting looks, and I was not surprised.

'Why did you bring me here?' I said helpfully.

He drew a sudden breath between his beard and his moustache, and I saw his chest shaking with spasms of laughter.

I began to laugh myself.

We both drank some more of our drinks. A couple of club members went past the back of one of the other banquettes into the bar.

'I realised, after Iris's wine-party in the church, that I might have seemed a bit off-hand when you were intro-duced to me.'

'By Sir Frank Protheroe,' I said. Would that draw comment?

'By Frank Protheroe. I remember that.' No comment drawn.

'I've wondered about Protheroe's limp,' I said. 'Has he had a stroke?'

'Of course he has.'

'Was it serious?'

'More serious than he admits, according to some of the medicos in this club. *They* know . . . Apparently he's not going the right way about avoiding another. A life-style not conducive to such . . . Another, they say, may well finish him off.'

Unchanging facial expression made his earlier irony seem to me more amusing: it made his present menace seem more frightening – without preventing my appreciat-ing to the full the symmetry of the two old friends' concern for each other's health. Did they know that each foresaw a curtailed lease of life remaining to his old friend?

A pause. Then the sharp brown eyes fixed on me fleet-ingly again –

'I didn't bring you here to talk about Protheroe. I brought you here to tell you I've now read your book.'

'What did you think of it?'

'Do you want to know what I really think of it, or do you want flattery?' – he interrupted himself – 'That isn't an original question of mine – it's what somebody who'd read one of my books once said to me.'

'What did you reply?'

'Why, flattery of course!'

'Do you think artists ever get enough of praise and prizes?'

'Never.'

Silence for a moment or two. We were neglecting our drinks.

'So I'll begin with flattery, of course.'

'Thank you.'

'And then get around to what I really think.' A very meaningful darting glance. 'Does that alarm you?'

'The way you look at me does.' As he was satisfied with that, I went on. 'I don't mind being alarmed, Mr Gotham.'

'It's a very fine book, actually.'

'Thank you.' I had a sip of my drink. He suddenly drank a mouthful of his. He must be in pain.

Thus began some minutes of music to my ears, followed by some minutes of discord, i.e. criticism (which was actually well worth listening to). Then some minutes of discussion. I had no grounds for complaint.

We were still alone in the room. He said:

'I chose this night of the week because there are not usually many people in. Unless I'm on my own, when I want company.' He touched his beard momentarily. 'In the first instance I wanted to have this chat with you about your book. That alone would have been good enough cause for inviting you to come here . . .'

'Did you want to chat about something else, as well?'

Over the rim of his glass, while he was drinking from it, he gave me a glance which was unquestionably suspicious –

'Yes. But there's no hurry.'

'How d'you know *I'm* not in a hurry?' I had decided to meet him on his own ground.

The tense facial expression cracked – into a slackening of the muscles round the eyes which must be a grin.

Grinning in return, I asked him, 'When are you going to tell me what it is?'

'Don't say you can't guess!'

I had no intention of trying.

'I went to see Iris the day after you. I call on her frequently, now that she can't get out, poor thing. She was talking about you. In the highest of terms, I may tell you.'

I picked up my glass. 'I'll drink to that.'

'I think you should. If you win Iris's loyalty, you'll find it very useful.'

'From things I've read about her and Cledwyn, *he* must have won it early.'

'Right from the start. When Iris gives her loyalty, she gives it decisively, on the spot.' He paused. 'Cledwyn was lucky.'

Out of the blue I thought of old X talking about 'help'.

'Their marriage must have been a great help to both of them as writers.'

'Exactly.' He drank another mouthful. 'I'm not necessarily implying that either of them wrote better novels as a consequence, though that's not impossible.' Pause. 'It's a matter of the power with which they projected themselves, on the literary world or on society or whichever way you like to put it. The total power of the two of them in collusion was greater than the sum of its parts separately.'

I made a mental note of 'collusion', said nothing.

'So there you are, James. Iris believes in you. She would like you to write a biography of Cledwyn.'

'Yes, she told me that.'

'What's *your* view?'

'She told me that somebody else is already in the field.'

'Did she tell you who?'

'An Australian professor called Barry M'Gann.'

'That's right.'

'He *is* in the field?'

'Yes.'

'Am I to take that seriously?'

Gotham seemed to hesitate. 'He's not only *in* the field – in some aspects he's in possession of it.'

'What does that mean?'

'It means this.' His glance fixed on me first for an instant, then switched around to the fireplace. 'Since you last saw Iris it has come to light that a legal document was drawn up between Cledwyn and M'Gann, a deed in which Cledwyn recognised M'Gann as his biographer, and virtually handed over to him sole rights to all his, Cledwyn's, private papers and correspondence, together with private information disclosed in confidence –'

'Does this include the tapes of the interviews?'

'I presume so. Everything to M'Gann, and to M'Gann *only* . . . Until such time as M'Gann publishes the biography, or until ten years are up, whichever is the shorter.'

I felt as if I'd been hit on the head. Whether I meant to write the book or not . . .

Another member of the club passed on his way to the bar, but I was completely unaware of what he looked like. The fire seemed to be getting hotter.

'And that's not all, Mr Cole. Cledwyn signed away powers of veto on any parts of the biography by his family, his friends, and – believe it or not! – by *himself!*'

I spent a few moments contemplating my glass, not drinking from it, just thinking . . . It was fantastic. Finally I said:

'I can see why M'Gann would be sold on the idea – it's a biographer's dream. But what on earth was Horsfall getting out of it?'

'Iris will have told you that she and Cledwyn fell for M'Gann hook, line and sinker when they first met him. He played on that to persuade them that Cledwyn's making over these powers to him would make it easier for him to get a publisher who'd really invest money in it, put it across with more confidence, put his heart into hyping it!'

'But what was *Horsfall* getting out of it?' I persisted.

'No money, if that's the first thing you think about. M'Gann paid the lawyers' fees for the deed. Otherwise not a penny changed hands or will change hands. What was Cledwyn getting out of it?' He gave me a sudden piercing glance. 'The certainty in his own mind that the truth about himself would be revealed to posterity.'

'The truth about himself,' I said ill-naturedly, 'as told by *him*?'

'I recommend you not to take that line. His insight into himself, like his insight into other people, was greater than that of any other man I've known.'

(The rose-coloured spectacles, still, in spite of everything!) I said:

'His insight into M'Gann doesn't seem to have been out of this world.'

'It was a stupid, stupid misjudgement!' Suddenly Gotham's pale sharp features seemed to have shrunk with violent emotion: his fingers were clenching and unclenching . . . It took him moments to pull himself together. I waited.

'Iris believes,' I said, 'he only realised when it was too late.'

'After he'd gone to the lawyers and signed himself into M'Gann's hands.'

'Exactly.'

'Had *you* no inkling of this? Weren't you so close to him? Weren't you seeing him all the time?'

'I can't bring myself to discuss it – he told me in a vague sort of way that he was going to let an Australian professor write his biography, that was all.'

'Weren't *you* in the running for writing it – I should have thought you were in a stronger position to write it than anybody else, least of all an Australian professor! You *could*.' (I thought I had better find this out.)

'Absolutely not! I have no intention of writing a biography of him, nor ever had any intention. I told him that years earlier.'

Next I said, 'What about the series of interviews?'

'He told me he was giving the man some interviews, and I should have assumed, if I'd been in the least on the ball, that the interviews were being taped.' Suddenly he stared across the room: his voice came out strangely loud. 'You know what? Well, Cledwyn took me for a sucker!'

'And the deed?'

'D'you think that if he'd told me about that, I shouldn't have told him not to be a cunt?' He broke off momentarily. 'He was concealing it from me. Out of *deceit*.'

It crossed my mind that Horsfall might have been saying things on the tapes about Gotham that he, Gotham, would not like.

'Don't you think, if he suspected that you'd stop him, it was only understandable that he shouldn't tell you?'

'I was used to telling him all the details of *my* life . . . That makes me another cunt.' He broke off again, but again not for long. 'I knew that in the last few years he was telling me less and less about *his* life. I thought it was because he was so distracted and exhausted from travelling round the world.' He drank some of his drink, and banged the glass down on the table. 'It has only dawned on me, since he died, that extent to which I was being kept out of *his* life. When that extent was as big as Salisbury Plain, I noticed it.'

I felt sorry for him, difficult man though he was – difficult if not impossible. I said:

'I've never had the good fortune to know a close relationship like that with any other mortal.' I was speaking the truth. 'If I had, I guess I'd feel as you do.'

'Doesn't say much for *your* sense.' He finished his drink at a gulp. I had another quiet sip of mine.

The thought crossed my mind that on the tapes there was most likely rare information about Protheroe as well as Gotham – and about Cledwyn himself, of course. Horsfall and his Circle! . . .

Someone had come up to our table and was standing over us. Another member –

'Hello, Ellis, how are you?'

Gotham introduced me. 'My guest. James Cole. Adrian Forsyth.'

The other man drew up a chair. 'Let me get you both another drink,' he said. 'Your glasses look as if they need a refill.'

(I had been warned.)

While the other man was away, Gotham told me about him. A nice man, cultivated advertising agent. (I recalled that Gotham spent some years in the advertising industry.) And a long-standing fan of his, Gotham's, novels – and possibly an admirer of *Edith Wharton*.

Forsyth returned with our drinks and sat down with us. He was in his early fifties, I should have said; strongly-built and pleasant-looking. I liked him at sight. There was something about the transparent look in his eyes and the light modulation of his voice that made me think he must have a sense of humour. A few minutes later it turned out that he had actually bought a copy of *Edith Wharton*, on the strength of the reviews. I warmed towards him to an appropriate degree.

He turned to Gotham. 'How's the rheumatism?'

'Bloody.'

'Does that mean you don't feel like dining tonight?'

Gotham said he was going home – which meant that the end of my evening with him was in sight sooner than I'd hoped, though I couldn't complain that I'd been given short measure.

We all drank a little and talked. Then Gotham excused himself and went out.

Forsyth leant forward, a little closer to me. 'Do you know Ellis well?'

'I've only just met him. But I've read his novels.'

'Do you care for them?'

'Very much.'

The other man smiled easily. '*I* think they're better than Cledwyn Horsfall's.'

'I've met other people who think they are.' My favourite literary judgement echoed – 'If they weren't so horribly *hetero*, they'd be *perfect*.' As I doubted if this would be Forsyth's view, I didn't quote. I just smiled easily, too.

'Have you read many of Cledwyn's?' He didn't wait for me to say Yes, but went on – 'Did you know him?'

'Unfortunately not. Unfortunately because I'm now interested in him.'

He looked away for a moment. Then he said:

'Did you hear Ellis's Address at the Memorial Service?' And when I said Yes, he went on very quickly (expecting Gotham to return?), saying, 'What did you think of it?'

'Someone said it displayed the noblest side of Cledwyn's nature.'

'Must have been an enemy.'

I laughed to myself. (It had been Protheroe.)

There was a pause. He looked at me as if he were weighing me up. Then he said slowly, with quiet emphasis:

'I always thought Ellis was very *kind* to Cledwyn.'

I stared at him. Message received! . . .

At that moment we both realised that Ellis was coming back to his place.

There followed a short spell of literary discussion and then Forsyth rose to go back to the bar. He shook hands with me. 'Perhaps we shall meet again.' I hoped we should.

I now glanced at Gotham, to give him the opportunity to say my time was up, though I hoped it wasn't.

'I'm sorry about the interruption, James. One of the hazards of the club.'

'I enjoyed it. It was interesting.'

'Good.'

I said tentatively, 'Actually there was something else I should have liked to ask you.'

Gotham looked at his glass. 'I'm sorry, but I really must go home. Will you grab my arm and help me to get up? I seem to be getting this fucking complaint in all my joints.' He glanced at me sideways. I wondered if I should take absence of facial expressiveness to be compensated for by verbal expressiveness?

He said, 'I'd gladly run you home; but when I'm coming out to drink I don't bring the car.'

'That's exactly my tactics. If you'll let me walk along the street with you till we pick up a couple of taxis, we can go on talking.'

I helped him to get up – he had managed without me a few minutes ago – noticing how light his body was. I could easily have picked him up and carried him. He went into the cloakroom and put on his overcoat.

Outside the club the sky was dark, no moon or stars. The street was narrow and one-way, so the traffic sped past us down it. Gotham said our best bet was to go up to the Square. The night wasn't cold, so we ambled slowly – not that he could have gone any faster – and took up our post on an island at the top of the street.

'Now, James, what is it you wanted to ask me?'

'It's something that happened when I went to tea with Iris,' I began. I told him about her offering to show me Cledwyn's will, looking for it in the drawer, and then saying she couldn't find it. 'It was a very strange incident, very strange to me. I simply don't know how to interpret it. I wondered if *you* . . .'

Gotham was silent, looking down at the ground.

'*Can* you?' I persisted.

'I don't know.' Suddenly he was glancing up at me. 'I can't help thinking I can, you know. Though I've got no grounds but intuition for saying so.'

'After written evidence, intuition's the next best thing.'

'Bright boy!'

(Was he going to be sarcastic every time I made a quip?)

'Well,' I said, all the same.

He took a long breath before speaking. (Out of the corner of my eye I saw a free taxi, but the last thing I meant to do was to hail it at this moment.)

'You can work it out for yourself, that there was something in his will she wanted you to see, something she thought you ought to see, granted you're going to write Cledwyn's biography – which is what she wants you to do.'

(It crossed my mind that so far there had been no mention between him and me of my writing a book about all three of them.) I said:

'And she drew back at the last moment.'

'It's something that isn't public knowledge at present. But it will be . . . She probably wanted to be the person to tell you – a brave gesture if her spirit hadn't failed her.' He paused. 'On the grounds that it *will* be public knowledge, I don't see a great deal of harm in my telling you now, trusting you to keep it to yourself, entirely to yourself, James.' He paused for some seconds. 'Cledwyn left the bulk of his estate to their daughter, Gwendolen –'

'Who wasn't at the Memorial Service.'

'– He left a just adequate bequest to Iris. And a surprising bequest, quite adequate, to someone else. A woman.'

Another Woman! I thought vulgarly. 'Did Iris know in advance?'

'Not a word.'

'Did *you* know?'

'I knew about the other woman, yes.'

For a moment I had nothing to say. A few cars were moving round the Square. Then I asked, 'How long had the affair been going on?'

'Since soon after the War, with a break of a few years after he married Iris.'

'Which was in 1953.' (Ref. *Who's Who*.)

We both paused.

'Do you imagine all this is on the tapes?' I asked.

'It must be. If he wanted to tell everything.'

'To tell everything *for himself.*'

I considered saying we must wait till we heard *how* he told it for himself. Instead I said:

'Nobody has heard the tapes so far but M'Gann.'

'Nor will hear them until M'Gann has written the biography. Remember? The fucking deed!'

'The deed,' I echoed without copying the exact verbal expressiveness.

Gotham went on suddenly. 'I'm forgetting to tell you – in the deed there's a proviso that what's on certain tapes is not to be disclosed until after Iris's death.'

'Shows residual taste.'

Gotham turned his head towards me. 'Do you think you ought to permit yourself that sort of response if you mean to write a serious biography of the man?'

'I'm rebuked.'

'I suppose I must have some residual feeling for the man. You know?'

In the darkness of the poorly-lit Square I tried to see his face – not that I should have been likely to glean much from it. I said:

'But Iris has found out the essential fact from the will?'

'That is so.'

'It's fantastic.'

'You are going to discover that Cledwyn was a fantastic man.'

'Does Iris know now that *you* knew he had another woman all the time?'

'I didn't know all the time. I knew about it at the beginning, but he didn't tell me he was carrying on with the affair during his marriage, not until about ten years ago.' His voice sounded weaker – he was tiring. 'I've avoided finding out if Iris now knows that I knew.'

Gotham turned up the collar of his overcoat, as if he had begun to feel cold. Time had passed without our noticing. The night surrounded us. The Square was temporarily empty.

'I'd be glad if you didn't press me any further now, James. I am in some pain.'

The Square was not empty. 'Here comes a taxi! You take it, Ellis! I'll take the next.'

'Thank you.' I helped him to get in and I heard him tell the driver to take him to his house in Holland Park. Through the window I said to him:

'Can we meet again?'

Against the noise of the taxi starting off I didn't catch his reply.

So I found myself standing alone, waiting for the next taxi. Some minutes went by, giving me time to think . . .

I was in possession of some extraordinary information. It was vital to me. Yet a new emotion crossed the excitement of it. If Iris had jibbed at telling me, I could not help feeling that he ought not to have. *Why*, I wondered, had he?

7

❧ I Make It My Business ❧

I was in Oxford for a few days. One morning a letter from Iris reached me, a poignant note sent on from Doughty Street.

> Will you come round and see me? I can't get out. I doubt if I shall ever get out again.

The handwriting was barely legible.

I jumped to the telephone and got the housekeeper. 'Lady Horsfall is resting, but she said to give you a message if you 'phoned, Mr Cole. Would you come to tea again? That's the best time in her day. She hopes you can come soon.'

I had a premonition of its being urgent.

'I'll come up to London at midday today, and be with Lady Horsfall this afternoon.'

The housekeeper showed me in and on the landing of the narrow staircase up to the sitting-room we passed a woman who was clearly a nurse. I should have liked to ask how Iris was, but shyness suddenly inhibited me.

This time the housekeeper took me as far as the sitting-room doorway, where she hesitated, standing beside me. Iris was sitting in the same armchair, facing the doorway. With her shoulders hunched high, she was breathing with obvious difficulty. Her fair hair was nicely waved as before, her complexion free of make-up: but the telltale hay-feverish puffiness round her nose and mouth seemed to have spread outwards over her face. She was wearing a soft, greyish-blue woollen dress, the colour of her eyes. I took her hand and she offered her cheek to be kissed. I experienced a sudden warmth of feeling – I was being welcomed as a friend. A touching moment. How often was it going to happen again? . . .

'You *will* have some tea, James, *I* can't. Mrs Williams will be *terribly* disappointed if *you* don't.'

I was worried by so many emphases in such a short speech, pressing, anxious . . . 'Of course I will.' The house-keeper smiled at me and went away.

I sat down on the sofa where I had been sitting on the previous occasion, obliquely facing a painting of a bright blue swimming-pool with one naked man swimming in it and another (Hockney himself?) watching him from the side. A pause while Iris caught her breath again.

'James, I wanted you to see this.' She picked up a folded sheet of paper from the table beside her. It couldn't be Cledwyn's will? (It occurred to me that when I was talking to Ellis Gotham the other night in the miserable, un-comfortable darkness of the Square, I had stopped short of asking him the name of the woman who'd been Horsfall's secret mistress throughout all those years; her name must be in the will.) 'I just got it yesterday morning.'

I took the sheet of paper from her – it was headed Monash University, Southern Australia, November 15, 1982.

My dear dear Iris
This is a truly short letter which hopefully will not exhaust too much of your time and energy. My thoughts are constantly with you in your infinitely courageous battle against your emphysema, and my news should, again hopefully, please and encourage you. To keep alive, among his friends and the greater public, the

memory of Cledwyn, whom we both loved so much, I am proposing to publish as soon as possible, naturally with your agreement, the transcripts of our taped conversations, as a stepping-stone on the way to publication of my full biography. In this regard I will be visiting London shortly before Christmas, and will surely get in touch with you the moment I arrive.

Till then fondly

    Barry

'Iris, he can't *write*!'

'Isn't it dreadful? Actually this is one of his worst efforts. He's better in a literary text.'

'When he's not being smarmy and insolent' – I smiled to remind her that I was quoting – 'at one and the same time.'

'Do you think he's ashamed of being smarmy and insolent?'

'I doubt it.'

'So do I.'

'All those terrible adverbs.'

'All that insolent proposal!' Iris cried in a smothered sort of breathlessness. 'Without so much as a by-your-leave!'

'Whose leave does he have to have?'

'Depends on what's *on* those damned tapes.'

We were interrupted by the maid bringing in the tea. She cleared the table in front of me and set down the tray. She glanced at Iris who said, 'Can you look after yourself, James?'

I poured myself some tea and chose a sandwich: Iris appeared to be resting. I was thinking that if M'Gann published transcripts of his tapes, what was on them could be available to *me*.

'Smarmy and insolent,' Iris was muttering.

Smarmy, yes. Insolent – how did that come about? Was it possible that he felt one-up on Iris because *he* knew that Cledwyn had had a mistress for years, while Iris hadn't known, possibly didn't know still? If so, the man was a shit! (As I was not writing about him, I didn't have to be neutral.)

Suddenly Iris seemed to go into a stifling paroxysm. Very alarming. I jumped up from the sofa.

'I'm all right,' she managed to say, and pressed the button of a bell attached to the arm of her chair.

I had no idea what to do, but the nurse came in very quickly, put her arm round Iris's shoulders to support her.

Trying to hold up her hands, Iris said, 'Shall be all right . . . Give me a minute or two! . . .'

I offered to leave.

For a moment all three of us were motionless. The housekeeper appeared in the doorway.

'Keep that letter, James! Show it to Elly for me! . . . I'm sorry . . .' Her paroxysm seemed to be dying away.

'Yes, of course.' I folded the letter and put it in my pocket.

'Come and see me again, James!'

'I will.'

While the nurse went on supporting her, I crossed the room and took Iris's hand. She held up her face. Seen close to, the puffiness and tension seemed to disappear, leaving the image – I couldn't explain it – in *my* eyes of the beautiful woman she once had been.

'Goodbye, my dear.' She was looking up at me.

I kissed her on both cheeks. 'Goodbye, Iris!' Trying to sound cheerful. 'See you soon.'

Feeling depressed and agitated I drove back to Doughty Street, stopping off at a little shop on the way to procure a photocopy of the letter.

Then I telephoned Gotham. His wife answered: he was away for the week in Scotland, talking to literary societies: but he telephoned her most evenings, so she would pass on my message straight away. On the telephone I noticed, as one does, her voice in isolation. Youthful, penetrating, American . . . She must be a young woman of character.

(I wondered what Gotham's first wife had been like.) It was time to settle down to my notes.

In half an hour the telephone was ringing again. Iris's housekeeper. Iris had been taken into hospital.

'Intensive care?'

The housekeeper didn't know. She gave me the name of the hospital and its visiting hours.

This latest news left me more depressed and agitated, and I decided to abandon my notes and go round the corner to see if the pub could still give me anything to eat. (Usually the only food, if any, that local pubs had on offer at night was any sandwiches that happened to be left over from lunchtime.) When I returned to the flat there was a message on my answering machine from Gotham: he would ring to arrange a meeting as soon as he got back from Scotland. I telephoned the hospital, where someone told me Lady Horsfall was as well as could be expected and that it might be possible for her to receive visitors in a few days' time. That suited my plans, as I had to go back again to Oxford for twenty-four hours.

So I sat in my poky basement sitting-room, furnished with bits and pieces from a Habitat sale, two sets of filing-cabinets, one filled with *Edith Wharton*, the other awaiting . . . *The Horsfall Circus*? The sound of traffic in Theobald's Road had died down. Papers strewn on my desk; books stacked on the floor, against one of the walls – books by Horsfall, Gotham, Protheroe and Iris. (Early books by all three of them were no longer in print.) Suddenly I was stricken by a sensation of having let myself become enmeshed in these people's lives. Enmeshed.

It's one thing to read about people who are dead – one can shut the book at any moment: it's another to have them alive and kicking on one's doorstep – making demands on one. For me it was an axiom of my profession that a biographer ought to be free. (That's not quite telling the whole truth, but I'll leave it for the time being.) So far I had tried to respond to these people and to what they were telling me with a strict if friendly neutrality. At this stage it was up to me to listen, and to listen only, to whatever they were telling me, be it absurd, mendacious, serious or truthful; on no account to show surprise, disbelief or shock, and if possible not even to ask questions. No devotee of the I-Am-a-Camera technique when it came to writing the book, I was wholly convinced of the necessity for it when collecting the information beforehand. A cobbler should stick to his last, and that was the last I had defined for myself. So far I'd stuck to it moderately well. The thought of coming unstuck alarmed me. I turned on the radio and listened to the News.

Three days later, in the early evening, I was on my way to see Iris. My previous experience of hospital-visiting was extremely limited, it being the sort of thing I tended to avoid. On the way I'd bought some flowers, bunches of yellow narcissi, the first of the season.

The hospital was in Harrington Gardens, a new private hospital, built of smooth, dark-red brick – I recalled reading a fuss about it in *The Guardian*. In view of the present Government's policy of encouraging the setting-up of private hospitals, with the inevitable reducing of public hospitals. 'The National Health Service,' enunciated the Prime Minister with compelling sincerity from the television screen, 'is safe in our hands.' I was interested to see what a recently set-up private hospital could do. The fuss had arisen from its being very expensive and being very much frequented by people from the Middle East coming to London for the best medical treatment money could buy. *They* had that money.

The lobby made two impressions on me simultaneously: it was less extensive in space than I'd expected, more crowded with people. As was becoming to a modern structure, it had a low ceiling and was divided into living spaces, one of which housed the reception-cum-enquiry desk, another a line of offices-cum-shops where bills could be paid, prescriptions drawn, gift objects purchased in a sort of duty-free atmosphere. And the people? There were families of them, presumably having left their Rolls-Royces and camels in the courtyard outside, now drifting vociferously to and fro between tall potted palms and overgrown monsterias.

I don't know how I managed to get to the front of the throng round the reception desk – it was more like being in a bar than a bus-queue. I enquired for Lady Horsfall. Two classy girls simultaneously consulted a ledger. (There appeared to be no shortage of staff – in numbers, anyway.) The enveloping noise was phenomenal.

'Have you a letter from your doctor?' asked one of the girls, a very pretty creature with spectacles.

'Surely I don't need a letter from my doctor to *visit* Lady Horsfall?' I held up my bunch of flowers.

'Oh!' she giggled uproariously. 'I thought you said you *were* Lady Horsfall!'

I stopped myself asking her if perhaps she thought I'd said I was Una, Lady Troubridge, as she was clearly under sufficient cultural strain already. Instead I merely observed –

'I understand that Lady Horsfall is a patient, and I should like to visit her.' I gave my name.

'I'm sorry. Hang on a minute, please! Gemma!' She called to one of the two girls on another ledger. 'Will you please see to this visitor?'

Gemma was even prettier, and had no spectacles. (I saw with satisfaction that, with or without spectacles, she could read.) She managed to find the appropriate information about Iris. There followed a sotto voce conference with her mate, not quite as pretty. And finally –

'Would you be good enough to go to the waiting-room, Mr Cole? Round to the left and it's the first door on the right. We'll call you in just a moment or two.'

I found the waiting-room, which was rather bare, furnished with slightly worn sofas and easy chairs. There was a beautifully robed lady from Abu Dhabi wearing an eagle mask of leather and beaten gold; two very spruce, overweight gentlemen with moustaches, who looked as if they had just flown in from the Cairo Bourse; a very old man, bearded, sleepy and apparently rather ill; and two or three quite young children running around in dishdashis like nighties.

I sat patiently. In the warmth of the room some of the flowers seemed to be coming out further, opening like small yellow stars, the first of the season, very frail and sweet-scented. I thought of Iris, somewhere in a ward, fighting for breath. Two more men came in and sat down.

From time to time a nurse appeared in the doorway and called out a name. Everyone looked up at her, but nobody identified him- or herself, chiefly because, I thought, the nurse had a striking negative talent for pronouncing Arab names. So far I hadn't seen her collect a single person.

Eventually, to my astonishment, I heard my own name – recognisable, of course. The nurse spoke to me confidentially when we were outside in the corridor.

'I'm afraid Lady Horsfall is not quite well enough for you to go in and see her at the moment. Would you care to leave the flowers and call again in a few days' time? Or 'phone us first of all.'

'I'll 'phone you first of all.'

'Thank you, Mr Cole.' She took the narcissi from me and gave a weak smile. I turned away.

Slightly lost, I hesitated for a moment in the thronging lobby.

'James, what are *you* doing here?'

Frank Protheroe, Sir Frank Protheroe, dark hair curling the back of his neck, light flashing from his thick-lensed spectacles. And the smile . . .

'What are *you*?' I asked, though it was obvious.

'I've been to see Iris.'

'They wouldn't let *me* in to see her.'

'I'd like to see them keep *me* out!' He was standing close to me, only his embonpoint coming between us. Very pleased with himself and no wonder. He glanced round –

'It's like being in the old *souk*, isn't it?'

I thought it less likely to create trouble if I pretended not to have heard. I asked:

'How is Iris?'

The smile suddenly faded. 'In a bad way, I'm afraid, though I've seen her in worse. She wasn't able to talk to me.' He looked up at me. 'Come back with me to my flat, and we'll have a drink. After *that*' – glancing in the direction of the ward he'd just left – 'I need something to restore me.'

'All right.'

With Sir Frank forging ahead, despite his limp, we crossed the courtyard. The sky was black and a cold wind was blowing: behind the picture-windows of the lobby, the throng continued in perpetual motion. I wondered when I should be allowed to see Iris again.

'I live in Eaton Square,' Protheroe was saying. 'On the north side – that's how one gets the sun, you know.' We were now within sight of our cars. 'Drive close behind me!'

I did as I was bidden, the this-year's BMW leading and the clapped-out Citroën following, and we arrived without trouble at Protheroe's house. His flat was on the first floor, with a balcony overlooking the Square. We were let into the flat by a manservant. I was impressed. The manservant's name, it appeared, was Oliver. He took his master's hat and my anorak.

Protheroe led me into a large room. 'This is my sitting-room.' Watching for my response. The walls were hung with a dark red paper, and were lined almost from waist-level to ceiling by a collection of portraits. Even as he spoke I realised what they were –

'Portraits of our monarchs,' he said.

'Fantastic.'

'Reminds visitors of my stock-in-trade.' He laughed. 'They're mostly copies, of course, some of them rather lacking in distinction, not to say verisimilitude. I privately think of them as amusing, though I wouldn't say that to anyone other than you.' He paused. 'That one over there might just at a pinch be after van Dyck.' He moved across the room. 'I want you to see this one.' It was a small drawing. 'This *is* a Holbein.'

'Amazing! How did you come by it?'

'Luck. The owner didn't know its value. *I* did.'

I moved round the room, Protheroe following me.

'Of course,' he said, 'if the Queen comes to see me I shall have to take them all down.'

'Why?'

His pleased-with-himself smile was momentarily tinged with suspicion, but he apparently decided that I was not getting at him. With a sweep of his hand – actually a rather beautiful hand, with the gold ring shining – through the air, he said:

'Just a matter of taste, James. You know? . . .'

The first time I had met him I felt frightened of him: this time I was feeling distinctly tempted to stand up to him. 'Of course' – not caring if he noticed my satirical tone.

'Find somewhere comfortable to sit down,' he said, 'and I'll do something about the drinks.' He paused. 'Would you think it very eccentric if I told Oliver to open a bottle of champagne? He often has one at the ready when I come home. And he knows I'm going out to a very boring dinner-party tonight – given by one of the least exciting worthies at the College of Heralds.'

He went out of the room, and I looked round with wonderment at the gallery of portraits that would have to be taken down if the Queen came. 'Just a matter of taste, you know.' Some of them I recognised, some I didn't – in fact the majority I didn't. I did recognise a very pleasing portrait of Queen Victoria when young, another when middle-aged; beside them, though he was not a monarch, one of Prince Albert, a handsome-looking man. I went on round the gallery.

The room was spacious yet warm and attractive – the red wallpaper helped, especially when one had just come in from a freezing night. There was a row of silver-framed photographs, mostly autographed, on the chimney-piece. Upholstery of sofas and chairs off-white, carpet a dark red like the walls, silky rugs of a subduedly glowing blue, white-shaded lamps – red-white-and-blue! . . . Lots of books, rather less carelessly stacked around than Iris's, infinitely less carelessly stacked around than mine. From the kitchen came the sound of the champagne cork being drawn. Protheroe returned to me. Involuntarily I stood up – and promptly sat down again.

'Do you smoke?'

I shook my head. 'Occasionally I smoke a pipe.'

'I've given it up.' He sat down heavily at the other end of the sofa on which I was sitting, myself. 'The champagne will be here in a moment.'

I asked him to tell me about Iris. He said there wasn't much to tell. They had put her in their intensive-care unit. 'I must make a note to enquire how good it is,' Protheroe said. They didn't expect her to be in it for long.

'That's good news.' I leant my head against the back of the sofa.

'You've fallen for Iris, haven't you?'

I realised that he was looking directly at me.

'I admire her very much.' (I was not going to let Frank Protheroe know my emotions were touched.)

'Cagey,' he said.

'Do *you* "fall for" the subjects of your biographies?'

He now leant his head against the back of the sofa. 'After a fashion, I do.' He paused. 'Are you implying that *you* don't?'

'I think a biographer ought to keep his distance.'

He sat up. There was a silence. 'That's interesting, James.' He paused emphatically, then said with penetrating quietness, 'Are you sure you aren't speaking for your own temperament, rather than your profession?' It was clearly intended to throw me. 'Rather than your art?'

I too sat up. We were staring at each other, without friendliness. He was smiling his smile, damn him!

'Keeping one's distance, James,' he said, 'diminishes one's human warmth.'

I didn't reply. I *was* penetrated. His knack of upsetting my peace-of-mind . . .

At that moment the manservant brought in at last our two glasses and the bottle of champagne in a bucket.

I realised that he'd got me feeling rattled, but I hoped I was concealing it.

We accepted our glasses and the manservant filled them.

'Can we have another log on the fire, Oliver?'

The awkward moment had passed. We drank a little. (It was good champagne.)

'That's better,' Protheroe said. He took off his spectacles and cleaned the thick lenses with a silk handkerchief from his top breast-pocket. He put the spectacles on again –

'What is your opinion of this new move by M'Gann?'

He clearly meant to take me by surprise, so I said, 'Which move?'

'To publish transcriptions of the taped interviews Cledwyn gave him.'

'How did you know that?' (I realised I'd broken my resolution not to ask questions.)

Protheroe replied with an easy-going kind of menace:

'I make it my business, James, to *know* things.'

I was beginning to think he did. He probably was a serious menace to everybody.

Protheroe drank some more champagne. So did I. He said:

'James, let us be friends!'

I muttered, 'Of course, Frank.' And found myself reaching, Randa-like, for some Wildean epigram, such as – 'When a man says Let us be friends! the odds are you'll end up enemies.' Would that do?

The new log in the fireplace blazed up momentarily. 'If he publishes transcripts of the tapes immediately, they must be seen as a positive windfall for you – assuming that your next book is to be about Cledwyn.'

'Is it?'

'Well, is it, James?'

'I haven't decided yet. I have some other subjects in mind.'

'Who?'

I laughed at him. 'That's *my* business, Frank.' I thought, Let's see him make it his business to find *that* out!

Frank laughed, too, and drank a little more champagne. He said:

'Of course that bloody deed cramps your style in doing a book about Cledwyn.'

'As you say, Frank, that bloody deed! Did *you* know Cledwyn was going to do it?'

'I was in Australia at the time.'

'Iris didn't know. Nor did Ellis Gotham. Who did know?'

'Randa Goslett.' His tone was contemptuous. 'His lawyer.'

I said, 'Do you think she ought to be sued by the executors for misadvising him?' I meant it as a joke.

'I gather you read *Private Eye*.'

'She was lucky that he didn't change to some other lawyer after the firm lost that case.'

Frank took his time over making his next remark, then launched it smoothly into the silence –

'It's something one can say in Cledwyn's favour' – a pause – 'that he never entirely relinquished any of his previous lovers.'

'*What?*' I'd allowed myself to show surprise and shock.

Protheroe was now smiling a Welsh cat-like smile.

As I'd fallen from grace in my own eyes, I decided I might as well continue there. I said:

'You mean he had an affair with Randa?'

'It lasted about six months, at its height. Between 1947 and 1948. In those days she was Miranda. And in her twenties. And very beautiful.' He paused. 'I have his letters about it in my archives.'

His archives? . . . Another surprise and shock. The idea

that there was such a thing as Protheroe's archives could be nothing but bad news for me. That was *if* there were such a thing as Protheroe's archives.

There was a long silence while I, for my part, cogitated – in a bout of pretty low spirits. Frank watched the fire burning. Then he got up to re-fill our glasses.

A fresh thought struck me. 'Who, by the way, is M'Gann's lawyer?'

Frank sat down again. And again he took his time over launching, smoothly –

'Jess Goslett.'

'Good God! Is that allowed?'

Protheroe simply leant his balding dark head against the back of the sofa again and held up his glass to the light.

'Is it allowed?' I persisted – my voice was getting louder.

'It has happened, my dear James.'

'Didn't you make it your business to find that out?'

'My dear James, I don't operate sheerly out of curiosity.'

I realised that there was about Frank Protheroe something of what Flaubert called the 'gigantesque'. One could only bow one's head before the colossalness of his remarks. He drank some of his champagne and held out his glass for us to toast each other. I dutifully responded. Then he set the conversation on a different tack.

'I'm glad Iris has taken to you.'

'I think she's a very good person.'

'Yes.' He smiled ironically. 'Cledwyn never ceased to be attached to her.' Then with a surprising change of voice and mood: 'Cledwyn hated me.'

'Hated you? Why?'

'That's another story. Not for now.'

I didn't know whether he was putting me off because he didn't want to tell me or because our time was running out. When he glanced at his watch – a pretty opulent-looking number in two shades of gold – I concluded it was the latter. His dinner-party at the College of Heralds.

'Can't you tell me in brief?'

'In brief, then. Very brief.' He turned his head to look at me. 'It started in our earliest days together. Among the three of us, Elly Gotham, Cledwyn and me,' he paused, 'Cledwyn had to be the universally acknowledged' – he paused again, this time obviously seeking the word he wanted, and found – '*Top-Dog*.' He smiled with obvious amusement. 'An old-fashioned term for a timeless phenomenon.'

'The Americans call it Top-Shit.'

'Top-Dog is the more choice. We say "dog" so much less frequently than Americans say "shit".'

I laughed. He became serious.

'If you're going to write about him, James, the enduring strength of his passion to be Top-Dog is something you must always bear in mind. Top-Dog in all circumstances, in all societies.'

'Seeing his performance in All Souls, one couldn't miss the fact that he was ambitious and vain.' The big barrel of a Welshman, with his Crimean side-whiskers, ringing down the table with his reiterated call, 'This is *goo-ood*, eh?'

'Merely ambitious and vain is not the same thing, James, but we'll let it pass for the moment if you want me to tell the story in brief. Why he hated us, Elly as well as me . . . It will have to be the story in very brief. And to avoid misapprehension, only the story in part . . . You mustn't think you're getting more than that, and even that in brief.' Glancing again at his watch. 'You're shrewd enough to have guessed the gist of the first part already – as Cledwyn got older he was increasingly disappointed in his greatest ambitions.'

I decided it was not the moment to mention the Nobel for Literature and the Nobel for Peace. 'Yes, poor sod . . .'

'He hadn't become Top-Dog in what one might call macro-society. But one's animus against macro-society tends to become dispersed. Not so one's animus against micro-society, in this case old friends, Ellis Gotham and me. When he failed to become Top-Dog among the three of us.' He smiled maliciously.

'Can that be so?' I said in surprise. 'You, for instance, haven't got into the House of Lords.' Hastily adding, '*Yet.*'

'Cledwyn put a stop to that.' He looked at me, his spectacle-lenses reflecting a flash of light, but not distracting from the animus his eyes were projecting.

'What about money, then?'

'Cledwyn made a fortune. So have I.' He saw my look of surprise and I hoped he didn't take it for the disbelief it really was at that time. 'You must understand, James, anything anybody writes about Royalty brings in money. Anything *I* write about Royalty brings in a hell of a lot of money. And Cledwyn wasn't the only one to know how to play the markets – he didn't have a walkover there so far as I was concerned.'

'He must have done where Gotham was concerned.'

'Gotham has never made more than peanuts. But he has written some books that can't be dismissed, especially in competition with Cledwyn's. Haven't you met people who tell you they prefer Gotham's novels to Cledwyn's? Elly's university campus novels, for instance? Even' – he couldn't resist a gibe – '*civic* university campus novels.' He paused. 'We all have – you, yourself, were present when our old friend X said so. There are plenty of people who'd agree with X, you know.' He paused. 'Elly may not have taken them seriously, because he was sold on Cledwyn. But Cledwyn *did.*'

'How odd!'

'It isn't really, if you grasp the fact that Elly was not just sold, he was so totally bemused by the greatness of Cledwyn that he couldn't take any criticism of Cledwyn seriously. Still *is* bemused . . .'

Still? I didn't see fit to comment. 'Ellis is cracking' I seemed to recall.

'Elly's misfortune,' Protheroe went on, 'was that he couldn't believe people thought *his* books were better than Cledwyn's. Cledwyn's misfortune was that he *could*.'

'I see.'

There was a pause. I couldn't help remarking –

'Cledwyn's reputation as a whole was incomparably greater than Gotham's.'

Protheroe shrugged his shoulders. 'Of course it was. But that's beside the point we're discussing.'

'I suppose it is . . .' ('The Winged Kissinger of Peace' ran through my mind.)

'And what we're discussing is only the story in part. Only in part, James. There are other causes as well.' The note of menace again. 'Obviously.'

Protheroe finished his glass of champagne and stood up. 'Let's avoid getting bogged down in more details for the present. That was a sample of them for you.' He was looking at me, smiling. 'Just a sample.'

I replied in similar vein. 'Just the tip of the iceberg, Frank.'

Protheroe laughed. 'You've already established yourself in my eyes as a writer, James, without indulging in extreme flights of metaphor.'

We were both laughing and I finished my drink. Then we stood up, close to the sofa. The fire was burning brightly: around us the portraits of monarchs were gazing down on us. Frank Protheroe looked up at me, no doubt pleased with himself but no longer smiling.

'An iceberg of hatred,' he said dramatically. 'Cledwyn began to hate everybody.' Then he changed his tone of voice to one of gravity and solemnity. 'It was a sad spectacle. Very, very sad.'

He went towards the doorway and I followed him. Suddenly his limp seemed to make him stagger, and I caught hold of his arm to steady him.

'That's all right,' he said crossly.

Have it your own way, I was going to say, but I didn't.

8

❦ *Strong Characters around* ❦
the Place

It was a grey morning – the one after my evening at Eaton
Square – damp and mild, with wisps of fog caught in
the bare branches of trees overhanging the pavement. I
came to the corner of John Street, on my way to the local
shops, and saw, at the opposite side of Theobald's Road,
Randa, walking beside the wall. She had seen me, so I had
to cross over.

'Where are you going?' I asked her before she could ask me.

'Just round the corner – to see someone we're thinking
of taking on as counsel, as a matter of fact.'

'You're looking smashing, Randa.'

She was wearing a trouser-suit which showed off her
long legs and general elongated slenderness. The suit was
made of very dark grey woollen material flecked with light
grey. On her head a beautiful wide-brimmed, black felt
hat. In her hand the slimmest of black leather brief-cases.
So . . . Protheroe's revelations echoed in my imagination
– this woman was once upon a time Cledwyn Horsfall's
mistress. *One* of Cledwyn Horsfall's mistresses. And not
discarded on Horsfall's side when he moved on to another
woman . . . I wondered, Does she hold something against

him after thirty-five years? I wondered because I remembered asking myself, when she pressed on me the Circus as subject for my next biography, Is she hoping for a book which will do the old friends, Cledwyn at the centre of them, down?

'You're looking under the weather, James. Are you taking care of yourself?'

I enjoyed the maternal touch but didn't encourage it. I *was* feeling under the weather, as a matter of fact, after a desperate spell of insomnia last night. Insomnia fortuitously provoked and haunted by Protheroe's speeches probing me. In particular – this really had got under my skin – 'Keeping one's distance diminishes one's human warmth.' Launching me into a fugue of painful self-examination, leading to the most painful of subjects, which I'd by now cultivated quite a skill in avoiding – my marriage . . . Restless hours in the darkness. My obsession with being free – did that go with a diminished human warmth in me? . . . Restless hours in the darkness, of pain, guilt, regret . . . No wonder I looked under the weather this morning!

'I've been thinking, Randa, it's probably time I employed a woman to clean the flat for me.'

'Very good idea, James. But why a *woman* for your menial chores? Why not a man? There are plenty of young men around nowadays who go out to domestic service. Out-of-work actors, for instance.'

'I expect they do the job better, too.'

'James, it's too early in the morning to draw me.'

We both laughed.

'I was going to get in touch with you today,' I said.

'So was I with you.'

We turned to look at each other. 'Who goes first?'

At this moment a huge lorry with at least twelve wheels passed by, pinning us to the wall – the pavement was very narrow – with its roar. Neither of us went first at this moment or at the next.

I tried again. 'I'm in a bit of a state over the deed Horsfall signed with M'Gann.'

'Fire away!' Randa walked unconcernedly on.

I put my questions to her and she gave me reasonable answers. The deed had given M'Gann not sole rights to all Cledwyn's papers etc., but unrestricted access to them for ten years – an important difference from my point of view. As far as Randa knew, Cledwyn had not put any formal restriction on the bulk of them. I began to cheer up. Then came the blow: the interview tapes were M'Gann's *property*. 'There are some that *he* may not publish,' I said. Randa said 'Yes,' so unconcernedly that I wondered if she and M'Gann were in cahoots: I asked if *she* had read the transcripts? 'Yes.' She turned to look at me – 'What else?' And walked on.

I had my question about no persons having right of veto. Randa dealt with it equably. They all had a legal right to protest if they considered the material to be defamatory. She turned to me again. 'In these days Elly is very unreliable.'

'Who in this world isn't?'

'That will be for you to judge,' she said sweetly. 'Isn't that one of a biographer's main problems? Perhaps half the battle.'

'More likely the whole bloody shooting-match!'

Before anything else could be said three Number 45 buses drove past in convoy and we were pinned to the wall again by noise. Afterwards I said:

'I'm forgetting, Randa – what were you going to get in touch with me about?'

'To invite you to a Christmas party at our house on the 17th of December. We're expecting Professor M'Gann to be there. I'm sure you'd like to meet him. He's a charming man.' I couldn't see her face but her tone of voice told all.

'I've heard he's charming.' I added, 'From Iris . . .' which amused me. She was beginning to move ahead of me. I returned to my questions – was it true that the lawyer who acted for the professor was none other than *Jess*?

She gave me a cool affirmative nod without stopping.

'Is that allowed in such a situation?' I demanded.

She stopped at that. For the first time this morning the sleepy, slightly venomous look came to my notice – directed against me!

'My dear James, aren't you acquainted with the expression "at arm's length"?'

'I've heard it, but rarely believed in it.'

'Then you should! You *must!*' She paused and then added calmly, 'It's significant.' At that she turned away from me. I was dismissed.

With an exchange of kisses on the cheek (not facilitated by the brim of the beautiful black hat, of course), we separated.

Well, I'd got some things straighter and on the whole I felt less inclined now to throw in my hand. Nothing could make me feel that way beyond the pitch I had reached during those black hours of last night, the black hours whose shadow I hadn't shaken off . . .

It was daylight now, of course, grey daylight getting lighter. And I had ahead of me the generally assumed-to-be-uplifting experience of 'shopping'. Yet the shadow felt as if it might cling indefinitely. Protheroe was no fool, yet his remarks had got under my skin more deeply than I imagined he intended or knew – on two opposite counts simultaneously, which was curiously bad luck on me. It was obvious that I'd failed to keep my distance where he was concerned: and it was possible I'd lost it where Iris was. And where had I kept it? Frozen in the past of my married life . . .

When I met Lauren I was entranced by her. We got into bed together and it was a wild success – she wanted me to marry her. I did. And then began my discovery that I was failing to keep my distance to a degree that was becoming steadily less easy for my temperament to accommodate itself to. Steadily less bearable; and finally *un*bearable. (This was seeing it from my side: she had her side, which in my saner moments I agreed was perfectly reasonable.) After a year I began to break out. (I was bound to say in my defence that I was much younger then.) And when I was breaking out it seemed to me that the main enmeshing agent was the sexual bond, even though I didn't consider myself to be more than averagely sexed, probably less in fact. I may have been wrong; but I may have been right. For the last six years at All Souls I had lived the life of a bachelor, the sort of bachelor, as I've already observed, who seems to exist stably without any sexual life at all – not, let me say for myself, through impotence or homosexuality, the two commoner causes for bachelor dons living without sex.

Suddenly I couldn't think why I was letting these incredible thoughts pursue me along Doughty Street in broad daylight. And yet, I wondered, how much could one say about what thoughts were pursuing those people walking along the other side of Doughty Street? Human nature is very mysterious, I thought, very unpredictable, and probably – we should have to admit it – pretty ridiculous!

I resolved to concentrate on my further shopping until such time as I got home, when I could turn to any messages left on my recording-machine.

In fact there was, to my surprise, a message left on my machine by the hospital about Iris. Lady Horsfall was recovering satisfactorily: she was still in intensive care and for the time being only members of the family and close friends were advised to visit her.

Members of the family, indeed! Iris's father and mother were long dead: I understood that she had no brothers and sisters; and her only child was Gwendolen, who was working somewhere abroad. Should I masquerade as a close friend? I decided to put off the decision till I'd delivered M'Gann's letter to Ellis Gotham.

I'd no sooner put down the telephone than there was a

call from Gotham, himself, just back in London. He could meet me at teatime in his club this afternoon.

On the dot of 4.15 I presented myself again to the club porter.

'Yes, sir, Mr Gotham, sir. You know where to find him?' The porter had recognised me. 'In The Beargarden, sir.' He had an amazing nose; there was a big hump on the bridge as if it had been bashed with a brick. 'He's told me to order tea and buttered toast for two, sir, when you come. That's if you'd like it, sir.'

I went into The Beargarden. There Ellis Gotham was sitting on a leather-covered banquette beside the fire – in the same place as on the previous occasion. (I thought of Iris always sitting in the big chair opposite the doorway – do people, as they get older, tend to sit always in the same place in a room?) To my surprise Gotham was not wearing his light-blue corduroy suit, but was dressed in a tweed sports jacket – with a light-blue knitted tie. He looked sallower and hairier – and somehow smaller. It was neither kind nor fair to describe him as a little old man, yet the only deterrent factor was whatever struck me in his appearance as simian rather than hominoid – one could imagine him, many years younger, hairy and bright-eyed, jumping lightly, agilely, from chair to chair.

I sat down and handed over M'Gann's letter to Iris. He put on his spectacles, read the letter, looked up at me.

'It's a sod, isn't it?'

I shrugged my shoulders.

'I don't believe Cledwyn for a moment imagined,' he said, 'M'Gann publishing these interviews – fatuous of Cledwyn though that was.' He folded the letter up again and took off his spectacles. 'I must say I'm pretty furious about the position it puts me in, as one of the literary executors. Impotent, I call it! And impotence isn't up my street, James.'

I smiled but Ellis remained furious-faced, so far as his face could be seen for whiskers. He opened a brief-case and handed me a document which turned out to be a copy of the deed. I reported Randa's opinion that it was open to anyone to protest against material that was defamatory. Who was likely to have been defamed? (Privately my list of them was getting longer by the day.)

We were interrupted by a waiter coming in and putting down a tray on the table in front of him. A large pot of tea and jugs of hot water, a plate of hot buttered toast cut in triangular pieces. Ellis served us – clearly with some pain, but rather less pain by the look of it than he had been suffering last time. (How serious was this illness? I thought of Protheroe's ludicrously implying that it was mortal.)

We began to eat. Gotham said:

'I had lunch with Cledwyn's publisher, Jack Heald, just before I went up to Scotland. Cledwyn had been giving him an increasingly hard time, accusing him violently of not doing enough for him – and complaining bitterly about everybody else. According to him, Jack Heald, Cledwyn ended up *hating* everybody.' Gotham bit a piece of toast. (And my thoughts – Protheroe and the 'tip of the iceberg' of hatred.) Gotham went on: 'I'm such a dope that it only occurred to me, after I came away from the lunch, that Jack was trying to tell me that Cledwyn hated *me*.'

'Seems incredible.' I was sure it wasn't incredible.

There was a pause. Then I said:

'By chance I saw Randa in the street this morning. Not so much of a chance, actually – she found somewhere for me to live that's close to where she works, the better to keep an eye on me.' I looked to see how he was reacting: he wasn't. 'M'Gann has sent Goslett & Goslett a copy of the transcribed conversations.'

'Bloody hell, he has!'

'It must be to vet them for libel.'

For the second time I saw his features seem to shrink with violence. 'I'll *say*!'

After a pause I said, trying to calm him:

'I suppose, if he hated everybody . . .'

'Everybody's *in* the fucking things!' He took another piece of toast. 'He hated Protheroe!' He drew a sudden breath and then shouted: 'If there's anything about me, I'll *sue*! . . .'

'And the things about Iris which haven't to be published in her lifetime?' I reminded him. 'He can't have hated *her*.'

'I wouldn't even say that. Considering that every time Iris's illness went into another crisis he began to make arrangements to marry Mollie Tremayna!'

So that was her name. 'Mollie Tremayna,' I said. 'I seem to have heard of her . . .'

'Well-known journalist. Very well-known. Roman Catholic, writes mainly for Roman Catholic publications, in this country and the USA – but by no means exclusively.'

'You know her? You like her?' I was having some small effect in calming him.

'Both. I met her when Cledwyn first began his affair with her, and I've known her ever since – apart from the seven years' intermission when she went to work in the USA because Cledwyn had married Iris. She's a good sort of woman. Too good to be mixed up with a bastard like Cledwyn.' He paused. 'You ought to meet her. I'll arrange for her to come and have supper with us and you must come.'

He drank some tea – it was getting cold.

'Each time Iris's illness went into another crisis,' I repeated incredulously, 'he began to make arrangements to marry Mollie Tremayna? What an incredible man he was!' (And what a subject for a biography!)

'I only found that out quite recently, from a legal friend of Mollie's, whom Cledwyn consulted – about the rules for getting a private licence at short notice. He was sworn not to divulge it to anyone, not even Mollie, at the time. He didn't tell me.'

A pause.

'If he was in such a hurry to marry Mollie Tremayna,' I said, 'hadn't he thought of getting a divorce from Iris?'

'He was in a hurry because he thought he was going to die. Cledwyn had a thing about Death . . . To him the thought of it added to the drama of Life!' The malevolence in the speech was un-missable. 'For some years he was convinced that he had only a short time to live.' A harsh laugh. 'He was right!' Then he went on less violently: 'It's a possible explanation for the marathon dictation of his life's testament to M'Gann.' And now in a reasonable tone. 'He was in haste to marry Mollie before he died.'

'After she'd been his mistress for over thirty years.'

'Just so.'

Gotham poured us a second cup of tea. I took my third triangle of now cool buttered toast – they were very small triangles – and sprinkled a little salt on it.

'Did he think of divorcing Iris, do you know?' (My resolution not to ask questions had gone by the board.)

'He must have.' Gotham looked away for a moment. 'Cledwyn must have weighed up what was best from *his* point of view . . . And decided against divorce.'

'What about Cledwyn's enduring attachment to all the women he'd loved?'

'*Touché* . . . An ungenerous remark. Letting my paranoia get the better of me.'

'If you can prevent it getting the better of you, it can't be morbid.' I smiled at him, but got no smile in return.

'Ungenerous, unjust. You know he didn't leave Iris for more than twenty years after their sexual life was over – and *his* had got into full swing again with Mollie . . . The more charitable explanation is the one *you* just gave – he still remained attached to Iris.' Gotham was thoughtful. 'He was a very emotional man. In some circumstances given to wild swings of emotion, in other circumstances extraordinarily constant. His attachments did endure . . .'

(Just what Protheroe said.) I asked:

'What's the less charitable explanation?'

'He was remaining in alliance with Iris for the better promotion of his career as a writer.'

I recalled – 'the two of them in collusion' . . . And asked: 'Was Cledwyn in love with Iris when he married her?'

'So far as I know, yes. He talked to me about it – I was there when it was going on. Though, now I come to think of it, he didn't call on me for advice.' He turned to look directly at me. 'Who do you think he did call on?' His glance was darting to and fro. *'Mad!'*

'It must have been Protheroe.'

'Right.'

'And what did Protheroe advise?'

'He encouraged Cledwyn to switch from Mollie to Iris. On the grounds of passion, you understand! . . . Protheroe had considerable influence in the making of that marriage.' He paused. 'In due course Mollie found out about it, and she has hated Protheroe ever since. She can't bear him.'

'Yes,' I said quietly.

'Protheroe didn't miss the advantages of the marriage as a literary alliance.'

'Giving Cledwyn further encouragement, I suppose.'

'Of course. Mollie thinks that's where Protheroe threw all the weight of his influence.'

'Which must have been considerable, I should think from what I've seen of him.'

'At the time Protheroe was supposed to be encouraging Cledwyn on the grounds of passion. I'm told that nowadays he says Cledwyn made the choice on the grounds of literary advantage.' After that stroke he said, 'Have some more tea?'

I held out my cup and saucer. 'There are plenty of examples of marriages between writers, and one always speculates, Is the basis mutual passion or mutual promotion?'

He filled my cup. 'Shows how misleading the concept of Either/Or is.' There was no sign of his being amused by his own joke. He simply went on. 'The answer is a bit of both. In some marriages more of one, in some marriages more of the other.'

'It sounds as if Cledwyn's marriage *began* with more of the one and *ended* with more of the other.'

A piercing, darting, brown-eyed glance. 'I'm ready to let it go at that, James, if you are.'

We settled down to finishing our tea – the toast was now somewhat congealed, and fresh hot water didn't really restore the tea. Nevertheless . . .

Gotham started to talk about *Edith Wharton*. Personally I was beginning to feel so overwhelmed by the Circus that Edith Wharton seemed aeons away.

After we left the club Ellis was going to see Iris, so I gave him a lift to the hospital. I had discharged my duty of handing over M'Gann's letter, and I had a copy of the deed in my pocket.

'Let me know how Iris is!' I said as I helped him to struggle out of the car into Harrington Road. 'I want to go and see her.'

To my surprise I heard from him later the same evening. Iris was recuperating well and would like me to go and see her: she sent me her telephone number so that I could arrange it without delay. I did arrange it the following morning – to go and see her that afternoon.

Again holding a bunch of flowers, freesias this time, I confidently threaded my way through the old *souk* to Gemma's station, where this time I projected with success the message of my identity and mission. 'I'll ring for someone to take you to Lady Horsfall's ward,' she said, giving me a pretty smile and pressing a button underneath the shelf which supported her ledger.

'Shall I wait here?' I asked hopefully.

Gemma had met that ruse before. 'Oh no, Mr Cole, in the waiting-room if you please.'

I was duly shown into Iris's room. Being nervous – actually squeamish – about hospitals, and suddenly shy of Iris, I didn't notice much about the room, other than that it was light, shining with medical apparatus which I flinched from looking at (things made of shining chromium

– 124 –

and polished plastic), and adorned by many vases of flowers. Iris was out of bed, sitting in an armchair. I kissed her cheek and gave her the flowers.

'Beautiful freesias. Thank you, James!' she said – and summarily dumped them on the bed.

I sat down in a chair near to her and looked at her.

'I think you look well,' I said.

'You mean better than you expected.'

'Yes, Iris.'

Iris laughed. 'I'm not well, but I think I'm over the worst. I don't expect to be well again, James.'

'There's nothing I can say to that. But I hope . . .'

'Yes.' Her spark of energy seemed to have faded already.

For a moment I said nothing. She was looking pale and old. The colour of her lipstick contrasted unbecomingly with her complexion. She was wearing a white silk quilted dressing-gown, on the pocket of which was embroidered a logo composed of the letters CD.

'What are you thinking, James?'

'You like wearing white, don't you?'

'*Vogue* used to say: White for Blondes.' Her eyes brightened with sarcastic reminiscence. 'I've always had a white dressing-gown.' She looked down at the logo on the pocket. 'I'm not mad about this – when I was a girl the labels on one's garments were meant strictly for the inside. Nowadays everybody wears the labels on the outside. Don't *you* think that's vulgar?' There was more energy in her voice again.

I laughed – sheepishly, because the anorak I was wearing had OLYMPUS written across the left nipple.

'It's a sign of one's devotion to the marketing society, don't you agree, James?'

'Every society demands solidarity.'

Iris laughed but her breath caught and she had to pause.

'That letter from Barry M'Gann, James. Thank you for delivering it to Elly.' She looked at me closely. 'He discussed it with you. And then we discussed it here.' She paused. 'There's not much more to be said at the moment. And probably nothing to be done – nothing, until we know more about what *he's* going to do.'

'I can understand you think he shouldn't publish the transcripts, but it *may* not be embarrassing . . .'

'We shall see. Anyway, we don't want to start crying before we're hurt.'

I grinned. 'Do you expect to get much mileage out of crying after?'

Iris didn't smile. 'We might. Don't be too sure of that!'

I didn't see any reason to argue.

'And "the literary executors" means in effect Ellis Gotham. You can understand that – I'm not going to be well enough, if I'm still here . . . And Gwennie is at the other end of the earth.'

'I know she's working abroad. Where is she?'

'She's got a job with Amnesty International, as a Volunteer in Manila.'

'God! That must be a terrible place.'

'Two civil wars going on at once – one against Muslims in the south, one against Communists in the north. Spread over 5,000 islands . . .' After another breath – 'Anyone who's caught by the opposite side is tortured under interrogation.'

'Doesn't she find it too harrowing?'

'She's a very strong-minded girl. Mad about Human Rights.' Iris momentarily lost her breath again, but she was determined to go on. 'In the league-table of Human Rights, the Philippines are pretty low. Ethiopia's at the bottom, she says. In Ethiopia they just shoot you or put you into slave labour. In the Philippines, if they arrest you, you're there for seventy-two hours and it could be indefinitely. But if they shoot you, as in the case of that man – what's his name? Benigno Aquino – there's an *enquiry*, believe it or not!'

'That's a step up the league-table.'

'That's right.'

A pause which I deliberately prolonged, feeling that Iris was over-talking – I could hear the excitable nervous intensity of the invalid. She was waiting for me to go on with the conversation, all the same.

'I admire your daughter's strength of mind.' It occurred to me that Gwendolen's activities could be seen as complementary to those of her late father for World Peace. At the moment I was so immersed in discovering Cledwyn's infamies that I was losing sight of his admirable actions – and Gwendolen might have inherited Cledwyn's strength of international moral purpose.

'Strength of mind too strong to permit her to come home to be a literary executor,' Iris said tartly.

'Isn't she interested?'

'Not sufficiently. When she inherits Cledwyn's fortune, it wouldn't surprise me if she gives away the bulk of it to benevolent causes.' Iris looked at me obliquely, sharply – 'You know she didn't get on with her father?'

(Was that why she wasn't at the memorial service?) I merely said, 'No.'

'She always said she didn't trust him.'

From what I'd already heard of Cledwyn, it seemed to me that Gwendolen might well have creditable judgement on that score. I tried to imagine Iris's feelings when she spoke of Cledwyn's not being to be trusted, now that she knew that he had deceived her, Iris, for twenty years . . .

'Do you mean politically?' I asked, to try and get out of a difficult spot.

'Politically as well.' Iris stopped for a moment, the subject having been changed. On the new line she said: 'You know he was listening to the SDP? The SDP were after him – they thought they could persuade him to quit the cross-benches.'

'I'm not surprised.'

'They were too small fry for Cledwyn.'

There was a tap on the door and a nurse looked in.

'Your visitor has been here a quarter of an hour, Lady Horsfall.'

'I don't want him to go. Please, let him stay another five minutes, Josephine!'

I said, 'Iris, I really think I ought to go. I'm tiring you.'

'I don't want you to go. Talking to you doesn't tire me. It brings me to life.'

'Life is tiring – by definition.'

I said it for the sake of a quip; and then realised that at the back of my mind there was a correlative thought –

Life tires everybody to death.

I didn't utter that, of course. I was wondering how much longer Iris had of life.

'We were talking about Gwennie, James. *She* won't come back to act as a literary executor; and I'm *hors de combat*. So everything will fall to Elly Gotham to cope with.'

'I'm sure your affairs will be safe in his hands.' I tried to sound a little distant – I didn't want to be drawn into her affairs myself.

'So am I.' She broke off thoughtfully.

'Elly's a dear,' she went on again. 'I'm very fond of him. And so is his wife. Trish is a dear. Since Cledwyn died, Elly and Trish are my closest friends.'

I nodded my head in agreement, while wondering if they really were dears. Gotham, for all his gifts as a writer, didn't strike me in the least as a dear; nor, judged by her voice over the telephone, did Trish strike me as a dear. Perhaps I used the word 'dear' differently.

'Do you know them, James?'

'I don't know Trish yet.' I couldn't say that the name rolled easily off my tongue. American names! . . . (And wasn't it the name of President Nixon's daughter?)

'It's a very happy marriage, James.'

'That's good news.' Trying to conceal envy . . . I thought of saying, It's a second marriage and has only been going five years – it *ought* to be happy. Only five years? *My* marriage had lasted little more than one year.

Iris said, 'It's comforting to be with them.'

'I'm sure it is.' The topic had of a sudden become so painful to me that for a moment I scarcely knew what I was saying.

'You'll see for yourself, James.'

Another tap on the door and the nurse looked in again.

'The five minutes is nearly up, Lady Horsfall.' She smiled encouragingly.

'Thank you, Josephine.'

Iris smiled at me – having no idea what was passing through my mind.

'Goodbye, James. Please come and see me again!' And then on the spur of the moment, 'What about the book, the biography?'

'I'm thinking hard about it.'

9

❧ *The Christmas Party* ❧

As became a big man, Roger Masson, Randa's husband, lived in a big house, in Queen's Gate. Like Randa he was in his fifties, fifty-eight, to be precise. Well over six feet in height, over sixteen stone in weight – the weight deriving, he said, from being unusually heavy-boned rather than grossly over-fleshed. Fair enough; there was nothing gross about him. He had a strong nose and chin, large grey eyes: his hair was thinning at the front and he wore it curling untidily at the back. The general impression his face gave was of thoughtful amiability – not the characteristic I imagined to be most typical of a tycoon. (J Arthur Masson was one of the most powerful pillars of the advertising industry.) He was a cultivated man, and had a practised eye for cultivation. I liked him.

Early for the party, I found Roger standing near the doorway of the main sitting-room, the grand salon, which was on the first floor. I was reminded of Frank Protheroe's sitting-room, with its balustraded balcony overlooking Eaton Square – facing south and getting the sun, of course. This room had a still handsomer balustraded balcony, and, although it was a much handsomer room, 'one', as Protheroe might say, had to admit that it only faced west.

Roger greeted me heartily. 'James, it's months since we saw you here.'

He had a slightly odd voice, full and strong yet curiously high-pitched and hoarse-sounding – natural to him and no indication whatsoever of deficient virility.

'Yes, but I see Randa, you know,' I reminded him. 'We have lunch together at The Gay Hussar. And my flat is so close to Goslett & Goslett's place, that we run into each other in the street.' Out of the corner of my eye I saw Randa further down the room: she had caught sight of me out of the corner of hers. The room was still relatively uncrowded. I accepted a glass of champagne from a waiter.

Roger took hold of my elbow. 'We've got a new painting. Come and see our Schnabel!'

Until now the *pièce de résistance* in the room had been a tryptich by Francis Bacon of strikingly distorted semi-nude males, one of whom appeared to be sitting on the loo. It had been moved to another wall and replaced, I saw, by a huge canvas covered with a very thick impasto in which was embedded broken pieces of crockery.

'It's amazing, isn't it?' said Roger,

'It is.' The glare on the pieces of crockery glistened. I gave it deeper thought. I was wondering what amazing price Roger had paid for it. 'Yes, extremely amazing.' I drank some champagne.

'Now come and see our other acquisition!'

He led me across the room to where, on the floor, a narrow rectangle had been marked out, a foot and a half across and seven feet or so long: and on it had been deposited a layer of jagged stones, about a foot high, painted white.

'Oh yes,' I said. 'I see.'

'Our today equivalent,' said Roger, 'of an eighteenth-century landscape painting.' (He must have got that from some art magazine.)

'It's like looking down on the Himalayas from a low-stationed satellite,' I said, not allowing myself to be outdone. (Not that I had any experience of looking down on the Himalayas from a low-stationed satellite, either.)

'That's *right.*'

We paused in contemplation. I was thinking it was like looking down on something I actually had seen, when visiting in barracks a contemporary who had gone into the Army – all the grassy verges lined with chunks of stone, just like these, that the troops had methodically whitewashed.

'We don't plan on making it as permanent as the Himalayas,' Roger said.

'But it's striking while it lasts.'

'That's right.'

Roger was no fool. Looking at his acquisitions, I thought, If anyone knows how much it pays to advertise, it's Roger.

More people were coming in. 'I must leave you, James. Randa wants to see you, I think.'

I had momentarily lost sight of Randa but I was not perturbed by that. I drank some champagne and enjoyed the look of the crowd which was by now substantial. The Massons' parties were the most fun of any I went to. There was an air of fantasy about them. The guests were mostly drawn from professions around advertising. (What *is* advertising but fantasy?) There were guests of all ages – I watched them go by. Guests of all ages dressed in all manner of party gear. There was something posturing and playful about them – they obviously took it as a matter of course that calling attention to themselves was a duty to themselves, to their chosen profession, and to the public which was waiting on them. They added to the gaiety of life. Elderly men kitted out by Versace for board meetings, Roger being one of them; bizarre-looking young men got up, or rather dressed down, to look like refugees from the Chain Gang; bold, upstanding middle-aged and youngish women in gorgeous evening-dresses, some of them pretty bare at the front; eager very young women in baggy trousers and glitzy tops, bare down to the waist at the back; and a sprinkling of very pretty, very young girls indeed with amusing face-paint and witch-like hair-dos – style of the moment, assimilated *Tatler* punk.

'James, you're looking lost.' It was Randa who had come up beside me, smiling sweetly and showing me her profile.

'Not at all – I'm just waiting to be found.' I'd noticed an attractive girl surveying our today equivalent of an eighteenth-century landscape painting.

'I think that can wait. You must come and meet Barry M'Gann.'

'The hour of glory,' I cried, *'est arrivée!* . . .'

'Do you think so?' Resolute as ever in ignoring my facetiousness.

'Time will tell.'

'Come!' She turned and I followed. She was wearing a stunning blue-black evening-dress that had probably set Roger back a small fortune, her only adornments being just a pair of nice-sized diamond earrings which had certainly set Roger back a small fortune. (Actually her own income must be pretty substantial: she might have paid for them herself.)

She led me towards a group of three people talking to each other: one was Jess, not as tall as Randa and rather wider; one a young woman whom I hadn't previously met but who, I guessed, must be the recently-acquired new partner; the third a large, ginger-haired man who must be the professor from Monash. Randa introduced me first to the young woman, who was dark-haired and dressed in what appeared to be a pink flying-suit, super-neat in cut and ravishing in colour – Yolanda Foley, the newest partner in Goslett & Goslett. Politely I smiled across at Jess.

Then to Professor M'Gann.

So this was the man who charmed Cledwyn and Iris! I didn't know what I was expecting, but I was definitely not expecting a ginger-haired Australian Irishman with the build of a scrum-half. His hair was springy and cut short, his eye-lashes were light. His eyes probably looked smaller than they were because the orbits were fleshy, his face larger and flatter than it was because his nose was blunt and short, his cheeks wide.

'Mr Cole,' he said briskly, while we shook hands. His hand was that of a scrum-half yet its grip was beautifully restrained. 'I've heard so many people speak of you, here in London.' His voice was pitched low. 'You can surely imagine just how grateful I am for this opportunity of meeting you.' He smiled at Randa. 'And grateful to Randa for affording me this opportunity.'

I said, 'Oh good!'

He was smiling at me, wrinkling his eyes attractively. 'Your biography of Mrs Wharton is a marvellous piece of work. You should be proud to have written it.' (When he wrinkled his eyes attractively, it made them look still smaller, of course.)

'I hope that some day I may be,' I said, realising that it was all very well to reach for my rose-coloured spectacles, but there was no need for me to join a public contest for insincerity.

'There speaks a modest man.' He laughed and a pair of vertical lines flashed his pleasure on either side of his wide cheeks.

'I've always suspected modesty of being an ambiguous virtue,' I observed.

At that he gave me a shrewd look.

Randa interrupted me. 'Now that I've brought Barry and James together, I think we ought to leave them to discuss things.'

Before she and Jess and Yolanda Foley could disengage themselves, M'Gann held out his hand towards Jess. 'We'll get together again before you leave, Jess?' he said to her – adding confidentially, 'I need you.' He smiled at her and Jess smiled back. As she turned away he said to me, for the attention of the others:

'There goes one of the best lawyers in the Old Country.'

The others were amused.

It was now open to him to say, Along with the other two. Would he say it? Alas! no. An opportunity missed! For a moment we watched the three lawyers moving into the crowd. Yolanda Foley, I noticed, was small in comparison with Randa and Jess: the ravishing pink flying-suit was wonderfully conspicuous. Jess, lacking Randa's talent for clothes, not to mention her gift of slender figure, was dressed in a shade of brown that made her look older and wider. I recalled the somewhat scandalous rumour that Yolanda Foley had been taken into the firm because she was rather an intimate friend of Jess – 'a feminist crony' somebody had said (not Protheroe!). I got on less well with Jess than with Randa, and was not planning any different approach to Yolanda Foley though she was undeniably attractive.

'Shall we find some place where we can talk, if that's possible?' The professor from Monash took hold of my arm – with gentle firmness. 'I want to have a really private conversation with you, James.'

I spotted an empty corner on the far side of the eighteenth-century landscape – it looked as if the guests were deterred from climbing over it.

'It's *outré*,' said M'Gann, 'yet it's beautiful. So calm, so tranquil.'

We each accepted another glass of champagne *en passant* and sat down on two chairs that had been moved into a corner, at right angles to each other.

M'Gann raised his glass to me. 'To all your literary ventures, past and present, James!'

I drank in return, realising that I now had to call him Barry.

His first move was a series of flattering comments about *Edith Wharton and Her Circle*, which, flattery apart, raised some doubt in my mind over whether he had actually read the book; yet as a performance it was charmingly convincing – had I known nothing about him already I should have been delighted by it. To tell the truth, I actually was delighted by it.

I was being honoured with smarminess for the moment; I wondered when we should get around to insolence.

'Thank you, Barry.' I drank some of my champagne.

I was expecting him to turn next to the subject of biographies of Cledwyn Horsfall. Instead he said:

'I must hear the latest news of Iris, James. *You* must have been to see her recently – *I*'ve only just arrived.'

I told him I'd been to see her in hospital forty-eight hours ago.

'It's extremely upsetting to hear that she's in crisis again,' he said. 'Yet again, this third time.'

'Yes.'

'I know that each time Cledwyn found it extremely upsetting.'

The only words that came into my head were, So extremely upsetting that he rushed off to get a special licence to marry Mollie Tremayna . . . M'Gann must know it was a silly lie, even if he didn't know that I knew. I said nothing.

'She's such a darling lady,' he went on. 'It's a great happiness to me to find that we're always on the same wavelength.' Suddenly he flashed me a shrewd smile – wrinkling his eyes attractively – and added '*Nearly* always.'

He drank some champagne, looking at me over the top of his glass. There was a pause – and an awful lot of noise around us, though we were separated from the crowd by the Himalayas.

Thoughtfully he rested a powerful hand on his knee. (His scrum-half's thigh bulged his trousers.) 'I hope,' he said, 'we're not going to lose her for a long time.'

(Was there anyone in this *galère*, I wondered, who was not contemplating the departure from this life of its other members? On the other hand if we didn't lose Iris for a long time, his full-length biography of Cledwyn would have to wait for a long time, or else come out without the

– 136 –

key material which was to be kept under wrappers while Iris was still alive.)

'I hope so, Barry.'

Another pause. My thoughts were elsewhere. Something had just struck me that had not struck me before – mightn't Cledwyn, in what I'd gathered was his highly emotional way, have genuinely found Iris's going into crisis upsetting, even though he'd been deceiving her for twenty years? *Was* it a silly lie? Or did it happen to be one side of a double-sided truth? . . .

M'Gann said, 'One of my reasons for coming to London now was to see Iris. There are so many things I long to talk to her about.'

'It will depend on whether she's well enough, won't it?'

'And I'm looking forward so much to meeting with Ellis Gotham, whom I haven't met so far.'

'Yes,' I remarked, feeling in no position to promise him a warm welcome. 'And what about Frank Protheroe?'

'Yes, I shall be meeting Frank. Of course I know him already. A fellow-biographer. Most of us know each other, you know.'

Something in his tone of voice made me look at him more closely. It must take considerable stamina, I thought, to keep up this distinguished level of insincerity. I drank a little more champagne thoughtfully.

'And you, James' – he wrinkled his eyes again – 'are a fellow-biographer. Are you going to become, if you'll permit me to express it this way, a *brother-biographer*?' He was looking at me more closely. 'Jess tells me you're collecting material about Cledwyn.'

'Cledwyn is one of two or three potential subjects I'm thinking about,' I said dismissively. I didn't tell him what I was waiting to do at this moment – in spite of a strong impulse to the contrary, I meant to seek out the new member of Goslett & Goslett. The pink flying-suit – I'd been peculiarly allured by the colour, which was brilliant and subtle. How? Why? It must have stirred some memory.

Of what? The only thing I could remember was a lavish bed of geraniums I'd seen somewhere lying open to the sunlight in a public garden. That colour, exactly. Geraniums, of all things!

M'Gann was still talking. 'I want to encourage you to write about Cledwyn. I think you'd do a marvellous job.'

I thought of suggesting 'fair dinkum' but let it stay at 'marvellous'. 'That's kind of you, Barry.'

M'Gann drank a gulp of his champagne. 'James, if you are going to write a biography of Cledwyn, I don't want you to think of us as rivals. We're in this together, James. I want you to think of us as allies.'

'Oh, thank you!'

'I will give you any help within my power. We can share material. Share and share alike – that's fair-dos, isn't it?'

'It is, Barry.'

Smiling – 'Let's shake hands on that, James!'

We shook hands. I shook that large strong hand with the beautifully restrained grip.

We finished our drink and stood up. 'I must go and find Jess,' he said.

I stood still, to let him get away.

He turned back to me with an afterthought. 'I have transcripts of a series of interviews Cledwyn gave me just a few months before he died.' Glancing away. 'Interviews of truly personal revelation.' He paused and then looked at me again. 'One of my reasons for coming to London is to place them with a publisher. In the meantime I should like *you* to see them.'

I was almost too surprised to say Thank you.

'Share and share alike, James.' He grinned. 'I should like to share your critical opinion of them.'

What could he be meaning by that? Was any of this for real? 'Of course,' I said. Had he some doubts about that? 'It's jolly d. of you, Barry.'

'You'll hear from me, James.'

At that he left me finally, left me standing now solitarily

behind the range of whitewashed Himalayas. Where should I look first of all for Yolanda?

I pushed my way through the crowd of people without success for several minutes. Surely she couldn't have left? Had I lost my chance? I came across Jess.

'I'm looking for your new partner. I can't see her.'

'For Yola?' Jess gave me a challenging look. Shorter and wider than her sister, she was by temperament more direct, less smooth and less oblique. 'I don't know where she is, James.' She looked uselessly at the crowd. 'I can't see her.'

She meant that she didn't intend to look, either.

I continued my search on my own. Had Yolanda disappeared like the pursued woman in Romance Literature? Silly idea on my part – on anyone's part, for that matter. I decided to try other rooms, and, half-wedged by the crush in a doorway, I felt somebody take hold of my forearm. I looked down, and saw a shortish, middle-aged man, intelligent and nice-looking –

'We've met,' I said.

'At Ellis Gotham's club. My club. I'm Adrian Forsyth.'

'I remember. I'm James Cole.'

'I know.'

People were struggling to pass us. I said, 'Do you think we should move one way or the other?'

He laughed. 'Yes, this way.' He pointed. 'It may be quieter in Roger's room.'

We collected fresh glasses of champagne, and found Roger's room relatively empty of people – for the simple reason that most of the smaller pieces of furniture from the salon had been moved into it, leaving no space for people. As we came into the room, a couple were leaving: we promptly collared their chairs. There were a few more couples in the room, seemingly engrossed in conversation.

The room had dark walls, on which hung framed posters for some of the best-known manufactured products in the land. Forsyth saw me looking at them –

'Illustrating some of J Arthur Masson's accounts. And

Roger's idea of a joke.' Looking at them – 'He keeps them bang up to date.'

I laughed. 'I remember, Ellis told me you were in the advertising industry yourself.'

'Not the most tactful of openings – my firm is just in the middle of a takeover bid by J Arthur Masson.'

'I'm terribly sorry.' Embarrassed. I was wondering if he would keep his job.

'It doesn't matter. Roger and I get on very well together – though that's somewhat irrelevant.'

'More's the pity! . . .'

He was amused. 'You'd like to cherish a romantic view of business?'

'I know terribly little about business.'

'That's a shame.'

'Shameful, you mean.'

'Why not take a job as a copy-writer and learn?' He was teasing me.

'That's what Ellis did when he came down from Oxford, isn't it?'

'And was successful at it. Several fine writers began as copy-writers. William Trevor's one. Gavin Ewart's another. Fay Weldon's famous for it.'

The conversation had got off the track I'd had in mind – an important track for me.

A pause. A bit more champagne. Forsyth lit a cigarette, offered me one. 'Oh no, I remember you don't. You said so at the club.'

I seized my chance. 'What *I* remember,' I said, feeling nervous lest it might sound too obvious that I was jumping the points in order to get on to my track, 'is that very interesting conversation you and I were having while Ellis had gone out for a pee – it was interrupted when he came back. About Cledwyn Horsfall.'

'Oh yes?' Looking at me oddly, yet I felt sure his attitude towards me was well-disposed.

'You said Ellis was very *kind* to Cledwyn.' I paused.

'Implying, if I'm right, that he was kinder than the circumstances of their relationship warranted.'

Another pause. Against the noise coming from the other rooms Forsyth said, 'Yes, I did mean that.'

'Does it hinge on loyalty to each other?' (Asking questions again!)

'You could put it that way. You know I'm *parti pris* – hundred per cent pro-Ellis.' He shrugged his shoulders. 'Elly was hundred and *twenty* per cent pro-Cledwyn . . .'

I waited.

'What I'm trying to say is that Cledwyn was not always up to a hundred per cent pro-Ellis. Not always. I doubt if ever.' He glanced at me sharply. 'If you're going to write a biography of them, it will be up to you to listen to what we all say, taking account of how we felt about them – then weigh up where you think the truth lies.'

I was amused, having already had my lecture from Randa on this point. What did they *think* a biographer does? . . .

'You're trying to tell me that Cledwyn was not always as loyal to Elly' – in the middle of saying it I realised I was far from certain of it – 'as Elly was to Cledwyn?'

He nodded his head seriously.

'In what circumstances?' I said.

Forsyth drank a little champagne and then thoughtfully drew on his cigarette. 'In the circumstances of getting jobs, for instance.'

'Oh?' I drank some champagne to cover my waiting for an answer. The remaining couples in the room were more or less out of earshot. He was going to open up. We were drawn to each other, I felt.

'Cledwyn and Ellis worked closely together in their days as economists – you know all this. They were known to be close friends ever since Cledwyn took Elly to work with him in the Ministry. That fact and the fact that they had both taken to writing in their available free time led people to associate them with each other. And that remained the case – in a way they came to be identified with each other. That suited Elly all right, but it didn't suit Cledwyn – definitely not! He, Cledwyn, was the greater figure, Gotham the lesser – never the two to be equated with each other.'

'I can see that,' I said, recalling my lecture from Protheroe about Top-Dogs.

Forsyth went on. 'The upshot was that people, when they asked Cledwyn to do some sort of job for them and he turned them down, proposed to ask Ellis as the next best thing.' He paused a moment. 'You know the sort of thing – minor jobs as an economist – Economic Adviser to some unimportant government or other. That was before Ellis went into academic life.'

I thought of Protheroe's reference to 'that *civic* university'.

'And then this began to spill over,' Forsyth wound up, 'into the literary sphere.'

'I suppose the reason for your beginning on all this was to tell me that there were occasions when Gotham didn't get the job that had been referred to Cledwyn.'

'Exactly.'

'How did Cledwyn do it? I'm interested . . .'

Forsyth gave a sour smile. 'He put it about in a Cledwynesque way that there might be dangers . . . Ellis was sharp-tongued, opinionated, *unwise* . . . You know.'

I did know, having seen Gotham revealing himself in the Memorial Address, and on later occasions. If Cledwyn warned people off Gotham as a 'difficult' man, it seemed to me that Cledwyn had a case. Avoiding that issue, I said:

'I'm beginning to see Gotham as unwise if he put all his trust in Cledwyn.'

'You're beginning to get a grasp of it.'

I faced him. 'Adrian, *was* Cledwyn the monster he's beginning to seem to be?'

'Yes.'

I said: 'No man is wholly a monster.'

'Agreed.'

Some people came into the room and went out again. There was still a lot of noise, but it helped to isolate our conversation.

'I'm telling you this, James, because I want the truth to be known about Elly, and I trust you to tell it.' He smiled. 'I like you.'

'It's mutual.' All the same I was beginning to feel that I was landed with rather a lot of people who were intent on having between them a collection of irreconcilable truths told.

We finished our glasses, but we stayed where we were.

'Who else knows about this kind of thing?' I asked.

'Quite a few people, as a matter of fact.' He looked at me straightly. 'Someone who's really hot on this particular aspect is Elly's wife.'

'You mean this second wife, Trish?'

'She's very bright – and she adores Elly.'

I smiled at his seriousness. 'A young woman of character!'

'That's right. And it's something new for Elly. He had no idea what was going on.'

I couldn't believe this. 'Not a man as suspicious as he is?' I said.

'In recent years he's become more so. He has deteriorated.' (I felt this would meet with the approval of Protheroe.) Forsyth continued. 'It didn't take Trish long to rumble what had been going on – and to put a stop to it forthwith. Mind you, she had a blatant example of it pushed under her nose. A literary job, in this case. There was going to be a job for a writer-in-residence at another university – not Virginia Falls. The current holder of the job was a friend of Cledwyn and Ellis, and this chap was commissioned to consult Cledwyn as to whether Ellis would be a good person to succeed him.'

'And Cledwyn said No?'

'I don't expect so – that would be unCledwynesque . . .

But Ellis was never invited.' Forsyth gave me a sardonic grin. 'It happened that Trish had contacts on the faculty of the other university.'

'Well, well . . .'

We now had a long pause – interrupted by a tremendous burst of noise rather like cheering from the other rooms.

'I could do with another drink,' I said. 'I feel I need it.' Forsyth laughed and said he needed one too. 'Let's find one!' But before we got any further we were effectively blocked by the towering bulk of our host. Roger Masson, with a young woman in pink beside him.

'There you are!' Roger's voice, high-pitched and hoarse. 'I wanted to see Adrian before he left.'

Adrian said: 'We were just looking for a drink.'

'Why not?' Roger proposed that he and Adrian should forage for drinks – the waiters seemed to have become rather scarce, though they weren't all supposed to have gone off duty. This left Yolanda Foley and me to sit down and wait.

'I was looking for you,' I said to her.

'I was here.' Cool, friendly enough. Now sitting beside me, almost within touching distance. Touching distance . . . Enveloped in that ravishing colour! I decided to stop thinking about geraniums and begin looking at the woman. Also ravishing, I had to admit, though it went against the grain. That dark hair, those entrancingly-coloured eyes . . . I was being attracted, piercingly attracted – with a sudden shiver I recognised it – towards the verge of something alarming. I hadn't experienced anything like this since that moment in the past when I heard a gentle American voice beside me, saying – obviously to me – 'I'm Lauren' and I looked to see who it was. An irresistibly appealing prelude to . . . ultimate disaster in marriage.

Yolanda Foley was small, fairly small, anyway. She wasn't fragile. The cut of the flying-suit made her look slightly athletic – she probably was slightly athletic, I thought. That was evading the point. It was her face, her eyes, her hair . . . The soft dark hair was cut quite short other than at the front, where it was left, long and fine, to wave in the breeze and fall over her eyes. She brushed it out of the way to look at me.

Her eyes. I couldn't make out what colour they were, even when she *had* brushed the hair out of them. Grey, green, light brown? All three . . .

Cool, friendly enough on her side. On my side a chaos of impulses. And from what followed in the next few minutes, when I looked back on it, I could only conclude that in the chaos I must have lost my sense of direction altogether. My impulses towards her suddenly switched, without an atom of reason, from one opposite to another. From being attracted by a beautiful woman – to colliding with 'a feminist crony'.

Afterwards I could find no excuse for my behaviour, other than that my impulses were in chaos. Nor, I suppose, excuse for her behaviour, other than that I had deliberately scratched hard below the surface of her emotions.

It all began smoothly –

'How are you enjoying the party?' she asked me.

'I think it's brilliant.' (Foolish, voguish word meant to be sarcastic.)

'A marvellous collection of people.' She was watching them, smiling to herself.

'Marvellous people of both sexes,' I said provocatively.

She paused a moment. 'Marvellous women?'

'I'll say! I love those handsome women displaying their breasts, or near enough . . .'

She laughed. 'They have a right to.'

'Because they're obviously successful careerists?' I was aware that ill-nature was taking command of me – I could feel it. And I totally forgot that she, herself, was on the way to being a very successful careerist.

'Is there anything wrong with that? Said truculently.

'Nothing at all. It's just the way they behave when they *are* successful careerists.'

'Yes? . . .' She was provoking me.

'It's the sort of showy, demanding sexuality in which they express it. The second stage of success. They clinch having beaten the men at their own game by then making the men fuck them.'

If she had got up and walked away I should have had no grounds for complaint.

Yolanda did not get up and walk away. On the contrary she sat absolutely still, and said in a cool tone of voice:

'That *is* men's game, isn't it?'

Her tone of voice may have been cool – from her eyes I got a flash of enmity.

In retrospect I couldn't believe I'd said it. I supposed I must have meant it. I supposed she must have meant it.

We were silent for a few moments: with my trying to get back on to an even keel, with Yolanda Foley simply watching me. She said:

'You're looking rather thrown.'

I was too proud to say, By God, I'm feeling thrown – but I was feeling it.

'There's no need,' she said. 'It's the sort of thing men say.'

If I'd looked at her at that moment I guess *she* would have caught a flash of enmity from *my* eyes. I said:

'You sound as if you get it every day of the week.'

'Oh no . . . Only Mondays and Fridays.'

I laughed.

Yolanda laughed.

We were silent again. Incredibly the contretemps seemed, I thought, suddenly to have passed over – or to have sunk below the waves.

'How long is it since you had a drink?' she asked.

'Quite a long time. Why do you ask?'

'Because you look like it?'

Not exactly flattered, I said, 'I've only had about three glasses of champagne all night. What about you?'

'Quite a long time for me as well. And only two glasses

– I don't drink very much.' Her eyes glinted. Grey, green, light brown? 'I've been talking to Roger.'

'I've been talking to Adrian Forsyth.'

'Last time I saw you, you were talking to our Australian professor.'

I turned to look into her eyes, to see if I read sarcasm. 'Is that so?'

'Roger was talking about you.'

'What was he saying?' Why was I always unable to resist asking that question?

'He thinks you're OK.'

'I won't ask you if *you* think I'm OK.' An even stupider thing to say.

'I don't know yet.' Her mouth twitched at the corners. And without an atom of discernible reason, just as before, my impulses switched back again – 'feminist crony' to beautiful woman. A few minutes ago I'd insulted her – now I wanted to kiss her. I glanced towards the doorway – the other two would be back at any moment.

'What does Roger think of our Australian professor?'

'He doesn't know him.'

'What do *you* think?' I looked directly into her face, thinking it would force her to reply.

Silence – apart from the babble coming from the final stages of the party. She was not going to reply.

'Do you know him?' I persisted.

'Not yet. I've only read this manuscript.'

'*This manuscript!*' I cried. 'Do you mean the transcripts of the taped conversations with Cledwyn Horsfall?'

'I mean the transcripts of the taped conversations with Cledwyn Horsfall. He is our client.'

'So you've read them.' I couldn't get over it.

'Why are you so incredulous? Jess handed them to me, to read first.' She touched my hand. 'It's the normal thing to do in the office.'

'What did *you* think of them?'

In the doorway Roger and Adrian Forsyth appeared,

each carrying two glasses of champagne. They were coming towards us.

Yolanda glanced at me quickly. To my utter astonishment, she answered my question. She said:

'I said to him, You can't publish stuff like that.'

Intimations of something shot through my imagination, but I hadn't time to examine what it was before Roger interrupted us.

'Sorry we've been so long. All the waiters seem to have gone home. They do nowadays . . .' He held out the glasses towards us. 'You must be dying for this.'

The intimations? . . . Suddenly identified! They were of this young woman, whether I'd made enemies of us or not, holding the key to problems that were crucially holding me up.

When Roger and Adrian had settled us with our drinks, I said to her sotto voce:

'Will you have dinner with me some time?'

She replied, also sotto voce: 'I want to . . .'

10

❧ *Supper at the Mai Du* ❧

That night I kept seeing a soft waving bush of dark hair springing from above a clear pale forehead and drifting across grey eyes, green eyes, or hazel eyes – which? Dark hair being brushed aside from grey, green or hazel eyes, so that Yolanda Foley could see me.

I knew what was up. No, I said to myself, it won't do. No, I'm not going to!

Next morning I kept hearing what she said when I asked her if she would have supper with me. 'I want to.' Her use of the word 'want' . . .

While I was writing up the notes of my conversation with Adrian Forsyth I kept looking at the telephone. When it did ring, it was Randa, asking me if I'd enjoyed the Christmas party.

'I was pleased to hear that you had a great success with Barry M'Gann.'

'Success never comes amiss, does it?'

'James!'

'What?'

'You're so objective.'

'Which usage do you have in mind? The original one, to mean looking at things impartially, from a distance. Or the current one, to mean having a "goal", an object in view?'

'You know which one I mean.'

'I think I do.'

'I hope you're not going to let me down, James, by not following it up.'

'There you are! A "goal".'

'Barry is willing to help you. I would have thought that might count for a very great deal. He wants you to be allies.'

'Share and share alike. Fair-dos for all . . . I look forward to hearing from him.'

'I'm sure you will hear from him. He's enthusiastic about you.'

I thought of that scrum-half's cultivatedly gentle handshake. 'That's encouraging.' And then I added artlessly: 'Is the old firm having to make a lot of excisions from the transcript of his tapes?'

'You wouldn't expect me to answer that question, would you, James?'

'No, Randa. But I thought there was no harm in trying it on.'

I heard her laugh.

After I had put down the receiver I sat staring at my notes, but I was not seeing them. I was recalling in great strength something else from last night –

'I told him, You can't publish stuff like that!'

Stuff like that.

I absolutely must ring her up and clinch that supper-date.

A date was made for two evenings hence. I asked her if she had any choice of cuisine, any choice of restaurant. She had both: a Chinese restaurant in a street off Shaftesbury Avenue. A woman who knew her own mind – and was ready to make up a man's mind for him.

So it was at the Mai Du that we met. We were both nervous. At least I was.

'I hope you're going to like this place,' she said. 'Jess and I come here. We like it.' She was taking off her overcoat: in place of the pink flying-suit was an ordinary black jumper and skirt. She was smaller than I'd remembered – or perhaps it was being in black that made her look smaller.

A smiling Chinese waiter and smiling little Chinese waitress put away her overcoat and my anorak. 'You see,' she said. 'They know me.'

'It's nice to be known in restaurants. Consoling . . .'

'Do you want consoling?' Dark hair, momentarily brushed aside, she was looking up at me with curiosity – bright eyes, bright grey, green, hazel.

I didn't reply, but looked round the restaurant. We were being led to a table. The restaurant was small and warm – outside was a dreary December night – and pleasant-smelling. The smiling little waitress was standing beside us attentively, ready to hand us the menus. We sat down. On the table was a small vase of paper flowers, pink and orange and white. I looked at Yolanda round the side of my menu-card.

'What are the best things to eat here?'

'Jess and I come often and nowadays we usually let Kam Hseung choose a meal for us from the evening's specialities. She knows what we like.'

This made me smile.

'I suppose I seem to be taking charge,' she said.

'Isn't that a feminist's privilege?'

'We don't say feminist. We say womanist.'

'As you will . . .'

'James!' A clear echo of Randa. 'Surely you know there's only one thing more offensive than male opposition?'

'Male indifference.'

'At least you understand that.'

I put down the menu. 'What are we going to do about this meal? Shall we depute Kam Hseung to choose for us?'

'You agree?'

'I go with the tide.' I glanced at her sideways. 'It would be fun to see Randa's reaction to hearing me say that.'

I couldn't tell if she'd heard the remark. She put down her menu-card on the table. 'Aren't you going to choose one dish?'

'If you think I should. I like those little pancakes on to which they shred bits of roast duck, sprinkle some delicious sauce, and then wrap the thing up.'

'Peking duck.'

The little waitress, listening, nodded her head with renewed smiles and then went away. I ordered some rice-wine from the waiter.

Yolanda and I looked at each other. What about that sudden burst of mutual enmity? . . .

It struck me that she was older than I had been thinking in my fantasies. There were lines at the corners of her eyes. Her eyes at the moment were green, definitely green.

She said: 'Do you like Randa?' So she must have heard my remark.

The same question that Frank Protheroe had asked me. I said:

'Yes and No.'

A big porcelain bowl of soup with a big porcelain ladle in it, together with two baby porcelain bowls with baby porcelain ladles in them, were put on the table. Blue and white-decorated porcelain with semi-transparent little seed-shaped windows.

'Why do you ask?' I said.

We were helping ourselves to soup. 'I wanted to know,' she said.

'Were you satisfied with the answer?'

'I thought I heard more of a No than a Yes.'

We began eating our soup. 'Does it matter?'

'I think it does. Any reason?'

'I feel uneasy with her, or rather not entirely at ease. I'm not sure she's entirely at ease with me, although she tries hard enough.' I paused. 'I suppose I feel she's not entirely at ease with herself.'

'You're wrong there.'

'Then what about her womanism?'

'That's a sign of her having come to be at ease with herself.' Spoken with authority – 'She's now happy with her gender-based rôle.'

'Oh!' Momentarily silenced – gender-based rôle!

She leaned towards me. 'Are you happy with yours?'

'Am I happy with my gender-based rôle?' To answer without irony or facetiousness called for thought, deep thought.

Yolanda was eating her soup. No help from that quarter.

But inspiration came to my rescue. 'Would *you* say I was?' I asked.

She looked at me perfectly seriously. 'I'd say you had some distance to go.'

I turned on her. 'And what about *you*?'

I'd risked reviving that mutual enmity which had sparked up at the Christmas party.

She answered equably. 'I'm well on the way towards it.'

Even at the cost of risking another collision, I wasn't prepared to let it go at that. I said – but mildly:

'Isn't there a fair amount of cant talked about all this?'

Yola put down her blue and white porcelain spoon and laughed at me –

'Of course there is. What would you expect?'

The danger-point was passed. 'I *would* expect,' I said, and laughed back at her.

The mutual enmity must be stilled . . . Suddenly I felt an impulse to stretch out my hand and touch her, touch her face, her hair . . . She was wearing long dangly earrings – her only jewellery – cut from wafers of titanium, rainbow-glistening.

I had put down my spoon and was resting my hand on the table. Suddenly she put her palm lightly over my knuckles. Astonishing! She took her hand away again immediately.

No! It wouldn't do. I wasn't going to!

We finished our soup and the bowls were removed to

make way for the first instalment of what was obviously going to be a tempting array of dishes. I looked at them, trying to identify them. Duck and bass and so on . . . She said:

'You seem pleased so far?'

'It's going to be super.' I tried the wine.

Smiling with Chinese happiness, our waitress disposed the second instalment of dishes.

'Let's start!' We began helping ourselves. Yola glanced at me.

'What's amusing you?' she asked.

'Just how much better with chopsticks you are than me. I'm no good at all.'

'I have an unfair advantage. My father's a business-man in Hong Kong. I used to go back for school-holidays.'

'Ah,' I said, 'mine's a clergyman in Norfolk.'

'You don't use chopsticks very much in Norfolk?'

'Only now and then.' I thought of 'Only on Mondays and Fridays', but thought I'd better wait until the contretemps had sunk further below the waves before I started being funny about it.

'Take heart!' She was teasing me, yet her tone of voice sounded almost tender. She was making up to me. I liked it.

Suddenly I thought of the early days with Lauren. *She* made up to me – in the early days . . . I simply couldn't go through all that again.

I said: 'When I asked you to have supper with me, you said, "I want to." '

'Was that too forthcoming for you?'

'Not in the least. I was glad. It was a bit unexpected. After our . . . collision.' I paused. 'I wondered what was behind it.'

'Behind it?' With a sudden turn of her head she waved the hair out of her eyes and gave me a direct glance. 'There were several things behind it. We were talking about the interviews Cledwyn Horsfall gave M'Gann and the transcripts M'Gann took of them. As you may be going to write about it – it wasn't a typical arrangement, you know – there are some aspects of the case I wanted to put straight with you.'

I noticed her tone of voice was firming up. (She's a lawyer, I thought.)

'Some aspects,' she said, 'as I see them.'

'I can guess one of them.'

'Guess!'

'The deed.'

'That's right.'

'Randa acting for one side,' I said, 'and Jess for the opposite side.'

'I wanted you to know that *I* don't approve.'

'I didn't approve. But Randa inducted me into the significance of "arm's length".'

'Were you convinced?'

'It sounds as if you wouldn't expect me to be.' As she didn't comment, I went on. 'Would *you* call it a lapse in professional conduct?'

'It wasn't technically that. But it was sailing too close to the wind for me to go along with it.'

I thought, More reserves of force! Yolanda went on.

'Jess and I are great friends, you've got to understand that. It was at her instigation – at the time I was immensely grateful for it – that I was offered the partnership in Goslett & Goslett. When that happened the affair of the deed had already gone through.' She gave me a direct look. 'If it hadn't I should have stood out against it.'

'There would have been two of them to one of you.'

'We should have seen what would happen.' Decisively she spooned herself some more fried rice and then skilfully picked off some pieces of flesh from the bass with her chopsticks.

I thought, Professional dissension in the firm! I said:

'I get the impression there's quite a strong element of "spilling the beans" in these interviews.'

– 155 –

'You can say that again.'

'Spilling the beans about other people as well as himself.'

'You can say that again, too!'

'Randa's argument is that Horsfall desperately wanted to spill them. He felt *better* for spilling them.'

'If that's the case he must have felt *very* much better. Some of the other people, though, won't feel better.' Yola smiled maliciously. 'On the other hand M'Gann felt much better for picking them up.'

I was amused, but I went on seriously. (I was pondering 'stuff like that' – which she'd told him he couldn't publish.) I said:

'I presume there must be furore-provoking revelations about sexual affairs?'

'You can presume that again – there's one whole session more or less devoted to them.' She paused. 'M'Gann really does put him through it.'

I recalled Iris telling me that Cledwyn came down from some of the sessions 'shattered'.

It was time to move on to something else. 'Has Randa told you,' I asked, 'that if I write this book, I shall write about the three of them, the three old friends?'

'Sounds a good idea.'

'I don't want to write a massive seven-hundred-page American-style biography, collating every conceivable detail about Horsfall. I'm thinking of something more in the spirit of a novel.' I smiled at her. 'A human document – pardon my flight of metaphor!'

'I love flights of metaphor, especially when they're unfamiliar.'

We seemed to be speaking the same language. 'Horsfall and Gotham and Protheroe, you know?'

'In those interviews you've got your material.' She gave me an oblique cynical grin.

'Furore-provoking material about Protheroe's private life.'

'That's right.'

A pause. We were eating. The smiling little waitress had just shredded the breast of duck on to the little pancakes, sprinkled them with sauce, and folded them up for me. Yola was having them as well. I picked one of them up and bit it. Delicious.

Yolanda said, 'It's interesting, you know. When he's answering M'Gann's questions about Protheroe's private life, Horsfall's attitude is rooted in years ago . . . Maybe the public attitude to being gay hasn't changed very much, even though the law has changed. Of course there's been a shift of fashion in the way people talk about it, don't you agree? Especially where the media are involved. But Horsfall . . . Horsfall was still ruled by the fashion for being totally heavy about it.'

'Really. You surprise me.'

'Do you want an example?' She started to smile to herself. 'Horsfall reports a conversation with Protheroe, where he asks Protheroe if he can explain *why* he's gay. Then he wheels out Protheroe's reply as heavily as if it were the deepest piece of psychology.'

'What *was* Protheroe's reply?'

'He said, "I like cocks".'

I burst into laughter. Yolanda joined in. Then I felt ashamed and pulled myself together. 'Who's to say,' I asked, 'that *isn't* the deepest piece of psychology – for Protheroe?'

'Not I. But you see what I mean about Horsfall?'

'You know, Protheroe once told me he'd lived his life under a shadow. That's a pretty heavy fate for a man. Oughtn't we to treat what he believes to be the cause of his fate with at least some heaviness?'

Yolanda was thoughtful.

'I suppose,' I said, 'you'll excise this illuminating passage before Protheroe's lawyer sees it?'

She nodded her head. 'And other similar pieces about Protheroe. Ditto about the other two.'

'The other *two*!' I exclaimed. 'Who are *they*?'

Equably – 'Gotham and Horsfall.'

'Good grief! . . . Tell me more!'

I had to wait while she ate a little, holding the blue and white bowl below her chin and skilfully conveying grains of rice to her mouth.

'According to Horsfall on the tape,' she said, 'it was in the days when they were young. He says they sort of alternated between gay and straight. They began gay – it comes out in a reply to M'Gann's asking Horsfall about his first sexual experience, and Horsfall says it was with another boy when he was at school. M'Gann latches on to that, and follows it up with one question after another until he's got the whole story.' She shrugged her shoulders. 'M'Gann's very, very inquisitive. And very interested.' She paused to drink some wine. I said:

'Is M'Gann by any chance gay, himself?'

'M'Gann is so two-faced he could be anything. Anything to suit the need of the present.'

'Well, Cledwyn wasn't exactly one-faced, so far as we can gather.'

'You're telling me!'

'Please go on with the story!'

'Horsfall says they each went through this phase of alternating till they finally settled down to women – I mean, himself and Gotham, obviously not Protheroe. They settled down to women and ended in more or less satisfactory marriage.'

'More or less!' I exclaimed, thinking without much generosity of Cledwyn's divagations and Gotham's two essays.

'Well, yes.'

'You're not going to cut all *this* stuff out, are you?'

'We haven't decided yet. Horsfall's is his own responsibility, and there's possible veto objections from his family and friends. Gotham will not be pleased with the stuff about him.'

'I shouldn't have thought he'd care.'

'Gotham may not care about the facts, if facts they are.

It's Horsfall's presentation of them he may not be pleased with.' She picked up her glass again.

'The truth as Horsfall sees it?'

Correcting me – 'The truth as Horsfall wants to tell it.' She paused. 'So far as Gotham is concerned, the form in which he wants to tell it is pretty vicious.'

'I see.' I felt that I did see.

I drank some of my wine, which was not bad. I asked – 'What about the women in Horsfall's life?'

'There's a *series* of *them*.'

'None of whom he could bring himself to relinquish.'

'That's right.' Her expression flickered with amusement. 'You've got that right.'

I considered the source of information which enabled me to get it right. Protheroe – whom Randa said was a terrible liar.

'That's a relief, anyway,' I said, and paused for thought.

Yolanda was watching me with interest.

'I must say,' I remarked, 'that all this is a great help to me.'

'Sexual scandal, you mean?'

'It *is* new material.'

'Sexual scandal isn't the only scandal.'

'What *else* is there? There's *more*?' I couldn't believe my luck in her being so astoundingly lax over professional discretion. Fleetingly I wondered *why*? I had no illusions that she might be doing it for the sake of my *beaux yeux*. Dissension in the firm must be fierce. She must be having a terrible row with Jess. 'What more?'

'Financial scandal,' she said. 'Or near-scandal.'

'*Financial* scandal as well! What did he do?'

'You know he made a lot of money in the early part of his career by financial investment, wily financial manipulation?' She paused. 'In the end he only just missed being caught out.'

'That's no surprise, now. Are you prepared to tell me what it was?'

'There's a third of a tape about it, but it's not absolutely clear. It happened when he was appointed Economic Adviser to the Government – you know?'

'Yes.'

'At that point in time he was expected to declare his interests. And to drop all financial dealing.'

'I expect he didn't.'

'That's where the accusation comes in. He made a great killing on the basis of information that came his way through the official grapevine. *He* says it was innocent – that the deal was in the pipeline *before* his official appointment as Economic Adviser.'

'He got away with it?'

'Scraped home.' She paused. 'He was in favour with the Government.'

'Well, well . . .'

Yolanda shrugged her right shoulder just perceptibly. 'He doesn't conceal the fact that the Treasury and the Bank of England got hot under the collar about it. They sent for him . . . He talked his way out of it.'

'Well,' I said, '*this* is something else.'

'There's a rider to it that will interest you. This comes out on the tape. He had taken Gotham to work with him, and he claims that Gotham knew the deal was already in the pipeline.' She paused. 'But Gotham didn't back him up a hundred per cent.' She shrugged her shoulder again. 'Cledwyn can't forgive that.'

'Gotham wasn't willing to lie?'

'Cledwyn says it wasn't lying. He thinks it was Gotham's envy of his making money . . . He's very bitter against Gotham about it. Still.'

'How in hell is one to sort all this out?'

'I'm sure you will, James.' She was amused by me. She drank some wine.

I said: 'This makes one sexual scandal and one financial scandal.'

'Two excerpts from your book you can be sure *The Sunday Times* will buy.'

'You're too clever.'

She went to work with her chopsticks. 'I'm glad you're enjoying your Chinese meal.'

I was thinking, I've simply got to hear those tapes. I started to eat again. We had been neglecting the food, and like most Chinese food it was getting cold quickly, despite the hot-plates with night-lights burning under them.

'What's M'Gann going to do with the original tapes when he's finished with them?'

'He says he's donating them to an Australian university library – so that he can keep an eye on them, make sure they're kept under wraps.'

'Donating! I bet he's selling them.' I imagined Iris receiving this tasty piece of information.

'You could be right. He thinks he's got his hands on a hot property.'

'Yola' – I looked at her directly – 'we don't like Barry.'

She brushed the hair out of her eyes. 'He's a client of mine.'

I said:

'He offered me a preview of the to-be-published version of the transcripts. I haven't heard a sound since. I think I'm going to ring up and ask for it.'

'The best of British luck to you!'

I put down my chopsticks. She said:

'Are you going to write this book? *Cledwyn Horsfall and His Circle.*' I felt she was laughing at me.

'I haven't decided,' I said. 'The trouble is, there's something I find unpleasant about it. A bad smell . . .'

'Bad smells sell!'

I thought of Randa's contribution to the dictionary of aphorisms – '*It may not be nice . . . but it's amusing.*' I realised that I'd just heard another contribution of immortal verity. '*Bad smells sell.*'

'I can afford to give it till the New Year. *Then* I'll decide.'

There was a pause. Then I said with a sort of mock-playfulness:

'And what about you? How long can you afford to give Goslett & Goslett?' After her behaviour during the last half-hour it seemed a fair question. It sounded as if the row in the firm was terminal. 'Are you thinking of resigning?'

Imitating my mock-playfulness – 'Maybe I'll have to.' She made a gesture with her hand – which I attempted to catch in mid-air.

Kam Hseung and another little smiling Chinese waitress came up with trays to clear the table. I said to Yolanda, 'I've enjoyed this meal, but I've been so absorbed in the conversation I can scarcely remember what I've been eating.'

'Surely you remember the Peking duck you chose?'

'Yes, I do. Really super . . .'

'James . . .'

'I mean to have it *next time* we come.'

We sat quietly for two or three minutes. Kam Hseung came with a large pot of tea and two tea-bowls.

Yola looked at her watch. 'I ought to have told you – I'm afraid I have to leave fairly soon. My children are home from boarding-school.' She raised her eyebrows in amusement. 'You seem surprised.'

'I didn't know you had any children.'

'I have two teenage children.'

'Aged thirteen and fourteen at most.'

She went on looking amused without telling me how old they actually were. Earlier I had concluded she must be over, rather than under, thirty. I now calculated that she must be at least a year or two older than me.

The waving fine straight dark hair had a springiness and a glow. (It constantly reminded me of a shaving-brush.) Through its dark shifting screen the hazel-green eyes scintillated. When she moved her head the rainbow-glistening wafers of titanium seemed to be waving in celebration of something. Time was when I should have been thinking about getting her to bed. That time had gone . . . And for that matter I was still not absolutely sure of where we stood.

'Would you think,' I said, 'it just another example of male chauvinism if I tell you you look very youthful?'

'I should keep my thoughts to myself.' She gave me a look that I could have interpreted as tender. 'I'm thirty-eight.'

The mutal enmity simply must have been stilled . . . We drank some tea.

'Do you have a husband?' I asked.

'We divorced five years ago.'

A moment's pause, and she said:

'What about you? Are you married?'

'Was.'

'Divorced?'

I nodded my head.

'How long ago?'

'Six years ago.'

'How long were *you* married?'

'A year. Just over.'

'Are you willing to talk about it?'

I hesitated.

Then I shook my head.

We drank some more tea.

I changed the subject. 'Have you got a car? If not, I'll run you home.'

'Thanks. I'll take the offer.'

'Where do you live?'

'In Pimlico.'

'That's easy.'

I called the waiter and paid the bill. We stood up while someone brought our coats.

At the door I said, 'Stay here while I bring the car. It will be sodding cold outside.'

'I'll come with you.'

The theatre traffic was not yet out. We seemed to reach St George's Square in no time. I stopped outside the house.

It had a portico, steps up to the door, a balcony on the first floor looking over the square.

Yolanda undid her seat-belt. There was a moment's pause. 'Will you come in?'

I sat still. It wouldn't do. I wasn't going to.

I realised that I'd switched the engine off. I glanced at the clock. Then I undid my seat-belt. 'Thanks.'

We went up several flights of a staircase – the whole place seemed rather dark. Her flat was a maisonette at the top of the house. As we neared the front door we heard sounds of pop-music, sounds which, when she opened the door, turned into a din.

'The boys are home. Not to worry – I'll tell them to turn it down.'

'Will they?'

'Of course. They're well-trained.'

Two children, I was thinking . . .

She took me into a large sitting-room – also rather dark, as there was only one reading-lamp on. I had an impression of books and papers everywhere: books on the walls and in piles on the furniture, papers strewn on the tables and on the floor.

'Move some of the books off that sofa – if you put them on the floor just beside it I shall remember where they are. I work two days a week at home.' She was standing near the door. 'What would you like to drink? I'm afraid I'm out of whisky, so it's either sherry or vodka. Or some wine.'

'Vodka.'

She went out. I moved the books and sat down. The sound of the pop-music suddenly diminished. She came back with a tray on which were a bottle of vodka, glasses, a jug of ice-cubes. She put it down on top of a pile of papers on one of the tables. She poured our drinks. 'When the ice melts it will dilute the vodka.' She removed the books from a nearby armchair and sat down.

We drank to each other. The room was still dark. The

pop-music throbbed in the background. She was looking at me from under the dark hair.

I said lamely, 'This is nice.'

There was a long pause.

She said, 'Would you like a smoke?'

I shook my head.

There was another long pause.

Then she said quietly, 'Are you happy?'

I started. 'Do you mean at this moment? Or always?'

'I don't know. *You* tell *me*! . . .' She smiled.

'At the present moment I'm . . . content. As for always – I should say I'm reconciled.'

'That doesn't sound very happy.'

'It's what I've settled for. The lesser of two evils.'

'And they are? . . .'

Half-jokingly – but only half: 'One's being married, being permanently enmeshed. The other's being monastic, being *free*.'

'Your marriage experience must have been traumatic.'

'It was.' I thought about it. 'Not in the sexual sense – that always went reasonably well. But in the psychological. I began to feel that it was gnawing at me, gnawing at my independence and my freedom, at my singular spirit. (Doesn't that sound pretentious?) I began to chafe. Living intimately with another person. The awful *nearness* it brings . . . I had to get out.'

'Swearing never to get in again?'

'Don't laugh at me!'

'I wasn't.'

Yola came across to me and poured some more vodka into my glass. Before she turned back she touched my hair.

'Tell me what she was like!'

I hesitated. 'I don't know why I'm telling you this much.' I didn't say this was the first time I had let myself go to this extent with anyone for years.

'Please go on. James . . .'

I went on.

'She was small, dark-haired, very lively and attractive. We met at a disco-evening on campus, half-way through my first year at Yale – I was a graduate fellow, she was in her final year. I was hanging about, doing nothing, when someone came up to me out of the blue and said, "I'm Lauren." I looked down at her: she was looking up at me. She asked me to dance with her. I did. She kept looking up at me, dazzlingly – I can remember it now. Something happened.'

Something happened – could anything sound lamer? I had been looking across the room. I saw now that Yola was leaning forward in her chair, listening intently. Yet smiling faintly to herself. (Was she thinking about small, dark-haired, bright-eyed women who made the running?) I went on.

'That's how it began. We went to bed together that night, or rather that next morning. It was wonderful. She moved into my apartment. We were on a high for the rest of the semester. She asked me to give her coaching in English.'

Yola burst into laughter at this. I couldn't help laughing myself at my humourlessness. Coaching in English!

'OK! I enjoyed it and she did an excellent paper in her finals. So there!'

'And then?'

'She said, "Let's get married!"'

'Did you agree straight away?'

'More or less. I've told you we were on a high . . . She introduced me to her parents. Her mother was awful – one of those middle-aged American women who talk perpetually on a harsh, dissatisfied, whining note. I *knew* that. Her Dad was a cipher, reduced to naught by her Mom. I knew *that*, Yola, I *knew* . . .'

'Then why? . . .'

'When you say you're on a high it means you've taken leave of your senses.'

Yola said nothing.

I went on – there was so much more to come . . . 'You won't believe it, but inside a year she had turned into her mother. I don't know if you call that tragi-comedy or just straight farce. She just became insidiously demanding. For consumer goods to begin with. We had to have a new apartment, all fitted out from scratch like the glossy magazine advertisements. I had to have a new car. A video and a bigger TV. And a super music-centre. All the essential features of the American dream.'

'What about sex?'

'She was demanding of that. And *I* couldn't resist the opportunity to oblige. That was the nub of the situation. I was trapped by the sexual bond. That was what I had to break out of to be free, to be my own man. To be my own man, not some woman's. So that's why I've come to stabilise my life without sex. For the person *I* am, this is the solution. I've now lived without it for six years. Independent, Yola, *free* . . .'

Yola stood up and brought across the vodka bottle again. Standing beside my chair, she said gently: 'Why not try an affair that's light and undemanding? No commitments. Just pleasure while it lasts?'

She touched my head again and let her hand rest there.

I must have moved my head away involuntarily.

When she spoke again I could not see her face but I could hear laughter in her voice.

'What's the matter? Am I one of those successful career-women who clinch their success in beating men at their own game by . . .'

'I've regretted saying that.'

'Now I've heard you this evening I can understand better how you came to say it.'

'And there *are* women like that. Have a few days' look round Manhattan!' Hearing an unpleasant sound in my own voice, I climbed down. 'But they're not *all* like that.'

'It doesn't bother me in either case.' She put her hand back on my head. 'Don't let it bother you, James!'

I relaxed. I held out my glass for some more vodka. We had made a peace, a curious peace but, I felt, a lasting one.

Yet that was not the end of it. There was still the thought of an affair that was light and undemanding. She was unspokenly saying, Why not try *me*?

If I were to say No we should have passed a cross-roads to which we could never return, no matter how much either of us – meaning I – wanted to. She was still standing beside my chair. Turning, I put my arms round her hips. It wouldn't do. I wasn't going to! . . . I must stay free.

I heard her breath catch. 'I'm not aiming to de-stabilise you, James!'

I jumped up and held her in my arms. I kissed her – on that mouth I'd been looking at all evening.

She drew away, and took my arms down from her.

'You must go away now,' she said – and then looked up at me. 'And come back!'

I kissed her again. But that was the end of it – till I came back! I said:

'I'm not sure I ought to drive.' We were going together towards the door.

'Shall I call you a taxi?'

'I'll get one in the square. It isn't terribly late.'

And so I found myself out on the pavement in a bitterly cold night. I stood there, half-looking for a taxi, and feeling relief and shame, shame and relief.

'My God, I'm a coward!'

But relief and shame were not all. I couldn't help recognising regret, and *hope* . . .

In a few minutes a taxi came up.

11

❧ *Allies!* ❧

Through Jess I'd located Barry M'Gann. He was staying at one of the clubs in Pall Mall. (He must have talked someone into putting him up as a foreign member.) I decided to telephone him in his room after breakfast.

'This is James Cole.'

'You won't believe this, James – I was just going to 'phone *you*.'

I didn't believe it. 'What a coincidence!'

An urgent note came into his strong, musical voice –

'Unfortunately I've got to go downstairs right away to pick up a typescript that has just been delivered. Can I call you back?'

'Of course.' I gave him my number.

'Brilliant. I'll call you.'

The rest of the day passed. And the next day. No call from the Australian professor. I considered reporting it to Randa, but desisted.

And then I got the call –

'I *must* apologise, James. I *do* want to see you. Will you have breakfast with me at the Savoy tomorrow?'

'Yes.' Nobody had ever asked me to have breakfast at the Savoy before, though I knew it was the thing for certain types to do: its flashiness overlaid by grandeur invited notice from the *Evening Standard*. (Roger Masson probably invited people to breakfast at the Connaught. He had style.)

Looking large and athletic, our professor turned up in a beautifully-fitting light-grey Prince of Wales check suit: he was wearing a dark-red rose in his buttonhole and holding an A4 manila envelope under his arm. He gave me the strong handshake and eye-crinkling smile.

'This is for you.' He handed me the manila envelope. I read –

Face To Face With Cledwyn Horsfall

'In absolute confidence, James.'

'Well, thanks.' I put the envelope down on the table beside where I was going to sit.

'It's just a taster,' he said. 'I couldn't bring the whole thing.'

I wondered Why not? We sat down and waiters came around, flipping open the napkins and laying them in our laps.

'Buck's Fizz for two, Professor M'Gann?'

'Of course,' said the professor, grinning at me.

The drinks came up very rapidly.

I was surprised at the number of people, nearly all men, at the tables all round. A big room: white linen, shining forks and spoons, waiters and commis coming and going; flowers, huge menu-cards . . . There was a clink of china and the subdued buzz of male voices discussing business. Breakfast at the Savoy was obviously popular – especially on expense account.

'What would you like to eat, James?' Barry asked in the manner of a man giving one to understand that the sky was the limit. He really was doing me proud. I wondered where the money was coming from.

'I think I'll have tea and kippers.' (I *liked* tea and kippers for breakfast: at home I had only coffee and cornflakes, so the Savoy could really be said to be elevating my life-style.)

'Kiwi-fruit to start with?' suggested the waiter. 'Mango? . . .'

'Grapefruit, I think.' (I *liked* grapefruit.)

It was Barry's turn. He ordered the same as me. 'Always have tea for breakfast in Ozzie.'

We were left to face each other across the table, finishing our Buck's Fizz.

I glanced down at the manila envelope and decided it would be impolite to open it here and now. At the same time I was puzzled by the whole episode. Why an expensive meal at the Savoy, when he could have handed me the typescript just as easily over a hamburger at McDonald's, or, more simply, over a drink at his club? Was he trying to impress me, to *win* me – and if the latter, win me to what? Actually I was impressed. But rather unlikely to be won.

Our grapefruit arrived.

'You seem to be in high spirits, Barry.'

The smiling vertical lines appeared in his cheeks. His eyes were sparkling.

'This is truly a day to celebrate, James. Iris has formally agreed to the publication of *Face To Face*.'

'Congratulations! You must be very pleased.' And then, 'Has she read them?'

'Not *all* of them.' He failed to suppress what could only have been described as a cynical smile. 'Just a part.'

'Oh yes . . .' I knew which part she had not read.

'Actually she's sick again. I don't think she's well enough to read them in depth.'

'That's sad.' I realised I'd neglected her recently.

'In fact,' he went on, 'the final version that's going to be on offer to publishers now isn't agreed yet. I'm waiting to hear from Jess – we'll have a get-together for deciding at Goslett's. There are a few things on the tapes that have to be pruned out while the persons they refer to are living –'

'Iris, for one?'

'Exactly. You understand these matters, James.

Naturally what can't be published now will remain *available*.' He gave me a shrewd look, narrowing his already narrow eyes. 'I calculate that it will take me at least five years to write the full-length biography.'

'I see your point.' Actually I saw a more cogent calculation, about what might happen within five years. As Protheroe was not yet seventy and Gotham only seventy-one, I was inclined to think it would not. He'd have to wait!

'I'm very confident that I shall be able to publish a highly successful book now. *Face To Face With Cledwyn Horsfall* is brilliant, James.'

Glancing at the manila envelope –

'I look forward to reading it.'

While I was spooning out the last segments of my grapefruit, it dawned on me that the envelope could contain no more than a very small part of *Face To Face*. There was a pause while the tea and kippers were served to us.

'Hopefully the kippers are to your taste, James?'

'I'm sure one can trust the Savoy for kippers. If not for whisky at the bar.'

'What's that?'

'Just a joke. Some years ago the Savoy were fined for adulterating the whisky in the bar. *Private Eye* enjoyed it. But I'm sure they don't do it any more.'

'I'm glad to hear it.'

We began to eat. He had a hearty appetite, and so had I. (Perhaps the Buck's Fizz helped.) For a while he did most of the talking, chiefly about people he knew or had met in London.

'You get around, Barry. I don't know half these people.' He was referring to a string of distinguished writers and publishers by their Christian names – Jack (Cledwyn's and Iris's publisher) and Matthew and Jock and Tom, Harold and Antonia and Michael and Maggie and Anthony, and Melvyn, of course.

'It's the advantage of being a colonial.'

'And an Antipodean . . . There's a lot of Austrophilia about.' Thanks to rose-coloured spectacles in some cases.

'Hopefully there is.'

'Rightly.'

We seemed to be doing well together. I asked, 'What about Protheroe? You told me you were going to see him. You knew him already.'

'That's right.'

'Did you see him?' I had in mind the revelations about Protheroe which he was nurturing on his tapes.

'Yes, I saw him.' He gave me a frank, eye-crinkling smile. 'We had a session of mutual admiration. We biographers . . .'

I should have liked to have heard it. 'And Gotham?'

'A charming man! Really charming, James. He has invited me to a dinner-party at his house. He speaks highly of *you* – and of course of your book about Mrs Wharton and her circle. He's going to introduce *you* to Mollie Tremayna.'

I covered my surprise. 'Has he introduced *you* to Mollie Tremayna?'

'No.' His expression changed. He paused, eating a piece of toast meanwhile. 'No . . .'

I wondered if I were going to hear something approximating to the truth. He went on –

'There's a little local difficulty for us, there, I'm afraid. We're allies, James, you and I. I'm in honour bound to tell you I wrote to her, and she refused to see me. It's a bind . . . She also gave me to understand that I'm not to see Cledwyn's letters to her.' In parenthesis, 'Of course Cledwyn has given me access to *her* letters to *him*.' He went on. 'No reason given, so I don't know how to approach the problem.'

Could the reason be that Mollie Tremayna now shared Cledwyn's final view of him? Since the rose-coloured spectacles came off . . .

'I would truly appreciate help from you, James. It sounds as if she's a difficult woman . . . Wants to keep her little bit of Cledwyn to herself – the sort of thing women do.'

I glanced at him.

'If she agrees to meet you, James, it augurs your being more successful with her than I.' He laughed wryly.

'I shan't be able to tell that till afterwards.'

'Obviously not. If you *are* successful, I would truly appreciate any help you can give *me*.' Suddenly he gave me the top version of his attractive smile, crinkling round the eyes, lines down the cheeks, everything. 'Share and share alike! . . .'

He didn't actually glance at the manila envelope beside my plate on the table, yet somehow its presence became as noticeable as if it were ten times A4 – alternatively, containing the whole of *Face To Face With Cledwyn Horsfall.*

Tact prevented my saying Fair-dos for all. Instead I picked up the envelope with an expression of silent gratitude. As I'd finished my breakfast I didn't need to put it down before it was time for us to leave the restaurant.

We parted cordially. He shook my hand. 'We must keep in closer touch, James. We must meet again.' And with most convincing sincerity, 'I want to hear all about *your* plans. They're of great interest to me.'

'They're still not firm, Barry.'

'Hopefully they will be very soon.'

'Very soon,' I said lyingly.

'Brilliant.'

After that I made for home as quickly as possible and opened the envelope.

A taster. What he had given me, the pledge of his sharing and sharing alike, was some forty pages of a book which must run to three hundred pages.

I read the forty pages immediately – and was fascinated. The timbre of Cledwyn Horsfall's voice, with its element of *hwyl*; the flavour of his devious emotional personality; they came across 'brilliantly'. These pages were free from any scandalous or libellous revelations. They were selected from the tapes in which Horsfall had answered M'Gann's questions about his public life, recounting the part he played personally in high affairs (with no mention of the little hiatus over financial manipulations shortly before – or after – he became Economic Adviser to the Government, that little hiatus caused by the Treasury and the Bank demanding a little chat with him). They were sprinkled with the names of famous people he had associated with. The timbre of his voice, the flavour of his personality, came across so 'brilliantly' that I could hear him, see him – see that large, bald, egg-shaped face with Crimean whiskers, hear that loud sweet voice –

'This is *goo-ood*, eh?'

I read the last page and telephoned Yolanda.

'Thanks for letting us know what he's doing,' she said.

'He gave them to me "in absolute confidence", but there's nothing libellous in them.' I pulled myself up. 'So far as I can see. I know that you –'

'– We've just concluded our cleaning-up operation. He's coming round here to discuss it next week.'

'Will he be displeased?'

'He can console himself that the original tapes are still a hot property. The version of *Face to Face with Cledwyn Horsfall* that we see our way to advising him to publish is on the cool side, I admit.'

'Cautious lawyers.'

'Are *you* complaining about other people being cautious?'

Pause. Stopped in my tracks. She had asked the question good-naturedly, yet . . .

'I suppose not.'

'Can you just give me a list of the extracts?'

'Yes. I've got them here in front of me.' As I went through the pages with her an entirely new thought came into my mind – *we*, Yolanda and I, were the ones who were the allies! An exciting thought.

'Thanks. It's a help to know the detail.'

'In a way they're truly fascinating, as the professor might

say. It's obviously Cledwyn, the real Cledwyn, as he might say, speaking. No messing about.'

'I agree.'

'I want to read the lot. It was a sell, being given only forty pages.'

'He couldn't do that till we've agreed it.'

'I'm glad to see you've put the fear of God into him.'

She laughed. 'Do you think we have?'

I laughed, myself. There was a pause. Then she said:

'Do you think reading the lot will make it more likely that you'll decide to write the book yourself?'

'I need notice of that question. Reading the lot will probably help me to decide one way or the other – help me to assess just how obnoxious they all are. It's too early to say that now . . . There must be quite a lot more water to flow under the bridge, if you see what I mean . . .' I heard her laugh.

It was a delightful laugh, playful yet firm. 'What a metaphorician you are, James!'

'I can't resist appreciation,' I said. 'Let's meet again! How about another supper at the Mai Du?'

'Why not?'

So easy, so simple! What a marvellous woman! I felt excitement springing up at the prospect.

If only I hadn't made that stupid gaffe at the Christmas party! Though I sensed that my offence had somehow been more or less purged, I still hadn't lost the feeling that it was up to me to make some explicit gesture, even if I hadn't been able to make it so far.

On impulse I picked up the telephone again. Now was the time! Holding the receiver in one hand, I furled over the pages of the directory with the other.

Interflora! An order to send roses to Mrs Yolanda Foley . . . How many? A dozen. What colour? Red. And the message, sir?

APOLOGIES   JAMES

12

❧ *A Dotty Dinner-Party* ❧

My invitation to dinner with Gotham, to meet Mollie Tremayna, came early in the early New Year. In the meantime I had a few days in Oxford, where I was urgently telephoned by Gotham.

'James, have you heard about this forty-page extract from *Face To Face With Cledwyn Horsfall?'*

'What!'

'A forty-page extract from *Face To Face With Cledwyn Horsfall.* M'Gann's agent is circulating it round London.'

'Good God!'

'You *have* heard about it?'

I told him the story of my breakfast at the Savoy.

'His agent is circulating the extract to half the publishers in London. Inviting them to an *auction* of the book!'

'That's brilliant!'

'They've sent me a copy as an executor. Iris has got one. I assume they've sent one to Gwennie in Manila – as if that makes any difference.'

'What do you think of it?'

'Awful.'

'Really?'

'We must talk about it when you come to dinner. By then I'll have let Mollie see it.'

Ten days later I was at the house in Holland Park. The night was too dark for me to see much of the outside, apart from its being a modest-sized Victorian house, semi-detached like the rest in the road. It was too cold for me to hang about gratifying my curiosity: further investigation into Gotham's domicile could wait.

Ellis, back in his light-blue corduroy suit, took me into a sitting-room that was much less opulent than Protheroe's, much less run-down than Iris's, much less abandoned to books and papers than Yolanda's. There was a Japanesey spareness about the comfort it proposed – I wondered if this second wife of his came originally from the West Coast. The walls were very light and bare of pictures. On a circular coffee-table there was a vase of pale yellow narcissi – poignant reminder of those I took to Iris in hospital . . .

Ellis's wife came in. Ellis was small, Trish was smaller. She was dark-haired, almost black-haired, with slightly excited-looking dark eyes. Her figure was thin, her body-movements (like her husband's eye-movements) quick and darting. If Ellis had once struck me as simian, Trish now struck me as avian. She was wearing a brightly-coloured Oriental-looking dress which somehow made her look more like a bird, a tropical bird.

'What's your drink, James?'

I said I'd like whisky.

'Sounds a good idea to me.' As she turned away, Ellis caught hold of one of her fingers, saying –

'No, Trish. I'll do the drinks. You sit down with James!'

They exchanged a darting intimate glance, two little people.

'C'me on,' she said. 'I can get around without pain and you can't.'

'Just this once?' He was still holding her finger.

'OK.' Shaking her head she came and sat down opposite me.

Among my Oxford literary acquaintances I'd recently unearthed two or three who'd been to parties at the

Gothams'. Their opinion was that the Gothams' ménage was the most uxorious they had ever encountered, so uxorious that some of Ellis's acquaintances said they found the atmosphere slightly distasteful.

Near to the flowers on the table lay the forty pages. Trish said:

'You've read them, Elly says.'

'The professor gave them to me personally, a sign of special favour.'

'Then you haven't seen the agent's letter? You must – it's a gem!'

With a sharp smile she handed me all the documents, forty pages stapled together with a letter paper-clipped to the cover.

The agent's letter, a round robin to publishers inviting them to the auction, was written with great confidence. It offered the sample in hand as a basis on which to bid for the whole book, which, it told us, contained unusually frank passages not included here. It contrived to insinuate that some of the frank passages were frankly sexy – selling point!

'How's that for a come-on?' Trish's smile was brightly ironic. Her almost black eyes, pink-rimmed and brilliantly glazed in rather shallow orbits, were of the kind that always looked heated to me. (Nothing wrong with that – lucky Ellis!)

'Irresistible, if only for the monumental cheek of it.'

'We had Professor M'Gann here to supper. Ellis hates him.' Her speech was quick and staccato.

'The Gosletts love him,' I said. 'And so do hosts of other people, judging by the way he gets around in London.'

'Brown-nosing like crazy.'

I read the letter again. Ellis came hobbling in with the drinks. I said to him:

'Are publishers expected to bid for a book of which the author is only prepared to let them see forty pages out of three hundred?'

'M'Gann and his agent think so.' He distributed the drinks and sat down.

'Isn't he holding it what's called super-tight to his chest?'

'And why do we think that is?' Rhetorical question from Ellis. 'One: in order to persuade whichever publisher buys it that he's the sole possessor of sensational news. Two: because he hasn't yet got the rest of it finally OK'd by Goslett & Goslett.'

'Do you think it's likely to be sensational?'

'Wild!'

'You haven't read it,' I said, hoping to take him down a bit.

'Personal friend of the author!'

I stuck to my line. 'It may not turn out to be as sensational as M'Gann is trying to make out. If the "frank" passages are libellous, you can take it that Goslett & Goslett will *not* OK them.'

Ellis was sipping his drink – it looked as if his fingers were trembling. (He and Trish were drinking dry Martini and soda.)

'What are you worried about? Wild stories about *you*?' I smiled amiably. 'From what I've heard, I should think there's a fair possibility of the Gosletts having rendered the whole thing innocuous.' (I didn't really believe that.)

Ellis lowered his glass to look at me quickly. He must have thought I'd heard something from Randa. He didn't know about Yola! I drank a little whisky. In an effort to loosen his concern with himself, I said:

'I wish I could think that forty years from now someone will have some wild stories to tell about *me*.'

In the days of the early Ellis Gotham novels, Gotham would have seized on the remark. Now he heard it without a glimmer of interest.

Trish came in with a plate of small round biscuits, made with cheese and still warm from the oven. After eating the first I could have eaten the lot.

A doorbell rang.

'This must be Mollie.' Ellis went out.

A few moments later I was looking at Cledwyn Horsfall's secret mistress of half a lifetime.

I hadn't been expecting Mollie Tremayna to be so tall – she must have been nearly as tall as Cledwyn was. And she must have had a very good figure. She was now well bra'd at the top and cinched in round the middle. (One tends to think of men's mistresses as not being old – Mollie Tremayna was in her sixties.) Her hair must have been brown, was now grey. But the striking thing about her appearance was the high colour of her complexion, a brilliant carmine rose. It was a laughing face, surprisingly soft and amorphous in outline: the muscles were sagging, alas, yet the complexion was youthful. Cledwyn's great love. The famous Roman Catholic journalist. She was wearing a maroon silk blouse and black satin trousers.

I was introduced.

'I know who *you* are,' she said. I found myself looking into hyper-intelligent grey eyes: she was wearing thick-lensed spectacles in tortoiseshell frames.

I just grinned.

'And *you* know who *I* am.' Glancing at my drink she sat down. 'I think I'd like a whisky.'

Ellis was standing behind Trish's chair. 'Darling, I'll get it.' He brushed his hand lightly over the top of her head as he turned away.

Mollie seized the forty pages. 'Have you seen these?' she asked me.

I described how I came to have a copy of my own – stopping short of explaining that it was a *quid pro quo*, the *quo* being anything of interest I could pick up for M'Gann from *her*.

She dumped the typescript back on the table. 'I refuse to meet him. He wrote me a snurgy letter, asking me if I'd give him an interview. Saying he felt he half-knew me

– 181 –

already! . . .' Her eyelids flickered. 'Half? . . . Which half?'

I hadn't heard the word 'snurgy' before: I immediately resolved to use it myself. (I remembered Iris's 'smarmy and insolent'.)

'You may be sure,' said Mollie, 'that the other half stays with me.'

We looked at each other for a moment – the beginning of a rapport?

Ellis came in with her drink. The plate of biscuits went round again. Mollie Tremayna drank a small amount of her whisky, turned down the biscuits, and took out a packet of cigarettes. (I'd gathered that the Gothams did not use cigarettes.) 'Have I time for this?' she said to Trish: 'That's if I'm allowed?'

'Just,' said Trish.

Mollie lit the cigarette and blew out a small cloud of smoke. Then she leant forward in her chair and said to me:

'What do *you* think of this?'

'I thought it was quite interesting. But I know Ellis thinks it's awful.'

I saw the changing expression on her face – an immediate object lesson to anyone tempted to write a biography of living persons. She said:

'It *is* awful. My justification for that judgement is two-fold.' She tapped the typescript as she spoke. '*This* is not characteristic of Cledwyn in the first place, and does him a disservice in the second place.'

'How? . . .'

'In the tone of it, the mood of it. He's in manic, euphoric mood the entire time.'

'Manic, euphoric,' said Ellis on a rising tone. '*Inflated!*'

'And if you want to know,' Mollie went on speaking to me, 'why it does him a great disservice . . . This ridiculously inflated mood encourages all his enemies to *deflate* him. It always did.'

I remembered the sarcastic amusement round the

dinner-table at All Souls after Cledwyn had gone. 'This is goo-ood, eh?'

Ellis picked up the pages. 'Look at this – Wartime passage. Winston Churchill and all that . . . *How I Won the War* by Cledwyn Horsfall!'

I thought Ellis was overdoing it. And I had already accepted Cledwyn as a man given to unrestrained emotion and high drama on occasion. I was surprised that Ellis and Mollie hadn't.

'Elly, don't exaggerate!' Trish was on my side.

'You seem to have forgotten that I was there. And it wasn't like that!'

Trish smiled at him. 'Cledwyn always saw things *larger* than life, didn't he?' She could be surprisingly soothing. 'Honey, *you* see them *smaller*, don't you?' She was smiling at him with her head on one side, bird-like. He did not respond.

'Cledwyn saw them at their largest when he was under the influence of drink!'

Trish glanced at me, her eyebrows lifted.

Ellis addressed himself to me.

'You probably know by now that Cledwyn used to put away the Scotch on a monumental scale, and the effect on him was first of all this sort of inflation. The next stage, a dreadful over-friendliness, confiding, flattering. Final stage, maudlin . . .' He now looked at Mollie – I saw that his face had become white with tension. 'Mollie must have seen all this.' He wanted her support.

Mollie picked up her glass. 'I have been there when it happened.'

'You see!' Ellis said to me. 'I'm not as mad as you think.'

Irrelevantly their discussion of Cledwyn's drinking had reminded me of a story about it that I'd been told just recently. Two stories, actually, one of them comic. Cledwyn and Iris were coming home from a party in a taxi, both of them pissed. At their house Iris managed to climb out and stagger to the door. There was no sign of Cledwyn following. The taxi-driver got out to see what had happened. Cledwyn had slid down to the floor, where he was sitting with his feet braced against the front of the taxi, his knees bent, and his back braced against the seat behind him. He was wedged.

Cledwyn was too heavy for the taxi-driver, who was a little elderly man, to haul him out. At this moment a policeman came by on his beat, a strong fellow who took over the situation. He managed to un-wedge Cledwyn and get him to a sitting position on the pavement. Then he took out his notebook. 'What is the name of this gentleman?' The situation looked ominous for Cledwyn. By this time Iris had opened the front door of the house and was leaning against the lintel. 'He is my husband, Officer. His name is Cledwyn Horsfall.' '*The* Cledwyn Horsfall?' said the policeman. 'Officer, there is no other.'

'Madam, I have admired your husband's books for many years.' The policeman put away his notebook, and bent over the recumbent Cledwyn. 'May I help you to get him indoors.'

Ellis was ranting on to Mollie. 'We've all been there. The question is: Are we going to have everybody there now he's dead?' He dropped the awful forty pages back on the table, where they crashed into Mollie's glass. 'Inviting every political enemy to shoot him down.'

(I recalled Frank Protheroe's 'As a politician he was a failure.') I said:

'Had he serious political enemies?'

'You can't air that sort of bumptious confidence and make mistakes –'

Ellis was interrupted by the sound of a buzzer from the kitchen. Trish rose instantly.

'Will you all come? It's a soufflé.'

Ellis was having difficulty in getting up from his chair. 'El, do you want some help?' A loving look passed between them. 'No, I'm all right.'

I was touched by the loving look. If only his head were

not so bushy and whiskery, if only her profile were not so razor-sharp! What a myth, to associate love with beauty!

On the way to the dining-room I recalled the other story about Cledwyn. Much circulated in gossip, it sounded more like *Private Eye* than the truth. (It crossed my mind that Cledwyn for his sins really had been persecuted.) In the story Cledwyn was taking out his notes for a speech in the Chamber – thus belying the adage he frequently quoted, that 'the worst of speeches delivered extempore is preferable to the best of speeches delivered from notes'. Cledwyn was too drunk to read the notes; fumbling with his spectacles, dropping his notes on the floor, bending down to pick them up – and falling on his face. And being helped up by – of all people! – the Leader of the opposite party. Not good, if true, for a man with political enemies.

Ellis had spoken of 'mistakes'. I wondered what they were. Was one of them that suspected financial peculation at the beginning of his appointment as Economic Adviser – over which Ellis had failed to back him up and so earned Cledwyn's lasting unforgiveness? Ellis must have believed the deal was *not* already in the pipeline – or were Ellis's motives not pure, any more than Cledwyn's? (I privately invented another title for the book: *How I Made a Fortune on the Stock Exchange* by Cledwyn Horsfall.) Ellis was handing round a bottle of wine.

Trish came in carrying the soufflé and we all exclaimed.

'Trish, you're marvellous,' said Mollie, watching her serve it out.

Trish gave her a bright bird-like glance – 'It's quite easy, really.'

It tasted perfect.

Ellis was not diverted from orating his diatribe. He was now going on waspishly about Cledwyn holding forth to M'Gann on the subject of literature. 'Equally inflatedly! . . . *How I Wrote My Masterpieces* by Cledwyn Horsfall. Inviting his literary enemies to shoot him down!'

I thought of those academics whose critical techniques,

Cledwyn said, were unable to cope with *his* novels as well as Dickens's. They couldn't have loved him.

Mollie returned to the conversation. 'You know, James, Cledwyn didn't talk like this when he was sober. He was terribly nervous about these sessions. He was steeling himself to do them. He'd steel himself with Scotch, I'm sure.'

'Aided and abetted by the Australian sod, M'Gann,' Ellis came in again furiously. 'Feeding him with more and more booze so as to get the dirt out of him – sucking up to him meanwhile, telling him the truths he was revealing were getting profounder by the minute. "Your glass is empty, Cledwyn. Just a spot more?" You know?' Gotham's waspishness was sounding more paranoiac by the minute.

'Two-faced,' I said, playing a modest card of my own.

'The most two-faced man in London, I should say,' said Mollie.

'He puts it to the best possible use,' said Gotham. 'Being two-faced means he can suck two bums at once.'

Trish grabbed his hand. 'El!' But it was too late: we had all heard it and laughed. (Sometimes paranoia can be funny.)

'All right.' Ellis began to eat.

'Elly,' Molly Tremayna remarked commandingly, 'what are we going to do about it?' Head-on reference to the main item on the dinner-party's agenda.

'You mean, what am *I* going to do about it?' Ellis took a break from eating hungrily. 'I'm the only literary executor who can. I went to see Iris yesterday. She was too ill to think. As for Gwendolen, she's in the Philippines and won't lift a finger.'

Mollie said, 'They used some material from her in last week's edition of *Human Rights World Wide* on TV. Did you see it? She did a first-rate job.' She glanced at me. 'I happen to know quite a bit about the Philippines.' I took it to be a reference to the Philippines being a Roman Catholic country.

'I saw it, too,' said Trish. 'I agree.'

She and Mollie now exchanged glances – I thought they were going to try jointly to get Elly back on the rails.

'That,' said Ellis, 'doesn't affect the issue so far as I'm concerned.' He lifted his face to look at us – a face white and distorted. I didn't like the look of things. 'Gwennie,' he said, 'hated her father's guts!'

'Elly!' Trish grasped his hand again: he freed it and used it to help himself to more wine.

'What about the others?' Trish said calmly. 'Their glasses are empty.' She took the bottle from him and came round the table with it. Meanwhile Ellis stared at Mollie fixedly –

'Well, Mollie, are we going to let this damned book go through without a fight, or are we not?'

'With a fight of course.' Mollie looked round at Trish and me. 'I,' she said, 'have had a different idea, a new line of attack. Is there cause for stopping *Face to Face* being published on the grounds that Cledwyn never intended the interviews for publication when he gave them? They were intended strictly for use in the compiling of the biography.'

I recalled Gotham's saying that Cledwyn must have been a fool if he didn't foresee a possibility of transcripts being published.

'There's no reference to the tapes in the deed,' Mollie said with emphasis. She clearly thought she was on to something. I didn't – and furthermore I was beginning to be seriously bored with the whole affair.

'That's a point on which we can take legal advice,' said Ellis. Which at least meant that it could be dropped for the time being.

I said, for a change of subject, 'Will Cledwyn's publisher have views on all this?'

'Jack Heald? He certainly will. His office has got a copy of the "auction catalogue", but Jack's away on holiday and hasn't read *Face to Face* yet. I've got an appointment to see him next Monday.'

Mollie: 'Do let me know what he says!'

'I propose you and I meet immediately afterwards and go into conference.'

I wondered if I was going to be invited to attend. I was not invited.

A pause during which we finished our soufflé.

The sound of the buzzer in the kitchen.

'There's another soufflé. A smaller one. In case anyone would like some more.' Trish looking bright-eyed and bird-like, and also pleased with her timing.

'Brilliant!' said Mollie. It was obvious that we were all going to have some more.

Trish went to the kitchen. Ellis decided to fetch another bottle of wine. Mollie and I were left together, facing each other across the table. Her rose-coloured complexion had a certain charm . . .

'I'm glad you're going to write a book about Cledwyn,' she said.

'It'll be better than M'Gann's, if I do.'

'Cledwyn fell for M'Gann's book about Dickens – *I* thought it was poor.' She grinned at me in a friendly way. 'Yours will be better. As you say.'

'Are *you* going to write about Cledwyn?'

'I'm a journalist and journalists write about everything that comes their way.' She checked herself. 'To be serious, James, the answer is Yes. But it will be sheerly a personal memoir. Cledwyn as I knew him. Not a biography.'

'If I do write a biography, I trust it will read less like a biography and more like a novel.'

'I like the sound of that. And Cledwyn would have liked it, too.'

I was touched.

Trish came in with the small soufflé and Ellis had opened the second bottle of wine. We began the second round of the meal.

I had one of those sudden moments I have from time to time, when I saw myself as if from a distance – What am

I doing here with these people? Enmeshed. I must be mad!

Mollie was on a fresh line. 'I have all Cledwyn's letters to *me*,' she was saying. '*My* letters to him are in the New York Public Library, and I'm going to get a stop put on anyone using them till I've finished with them. Which Professor M'Gann should know won't be very far this side of the grave.'

I couldn't resist joining in.

'He's very miffed,' I said, 'because you won't let him see Cledwyn's letters to you.'

'What impertinence!'

'He tried to recruit me into bringing persuasion to bear on you.'

'Oh!' She had been just going to drink some wine: she spluttered and had to dry her lips with her napkin. 'Oh!' she said again. But then she asked in a relatively calm tone of voice:

'Did he tell you what he's going to write about me in the biography?'

'I don't think he's got beyond coping with his tapes yet.'

'Cledwyn told me there's not much about me on the tapes.'

I nodded my head as if in agreement. If there was a whole tape which wasn't to be used while Iris was still alive, I was wondering if Cledwyn had told her, Mollie, the whole truth.

At that I suddenly wondered if Cledwyn had ever told anybody at all the whole truth. Ellis said:

'It looks as if I'm going to be the only one who *isn't* going to write about Cledwyn.'

Trish smiled at him across the table. 'Are you sure?'

Mollie said, 'You'll have to. To straighten all this out.'

I contributed, 'It's fairly clear that Frank Protheroe's going to.'

'Protheroe!' Mollie looked at me. 'Of course you know Protheroe. What do you think of him?'

'I haven't made up my mind.'

'Protheroe is *malevolent*.'

I glanced at Trish and Ellis.

'Protheroe is the most malevolent person I've ever known.' Mollie was speaking with tremendous ill-feeling. 'I have cause to know that, James.'

I fiddled with my wine-glass. 'Yes . . .' (In her eyes Protheroe had diverted Cledwyn from marrying *her*.)

'Has Protheroe told you,' Ellis said to me, 'that he's going to write about Cledwyn?'

'To be accurate, he only told me that he has this, that and the other in his archives.'

'Then we can only hope,' said Mollie, 'that a second stroke will carry him off before he can use them!' She took a second breath and went on. 'Protheroe is a liar!' (There she was in agreement with Randa!) 'Protheroe will tell lies about Cledwyn, James; he *hated* Cledwyn. He hated Cledwyn when he ought to have been grateful to him. For all the things Cledwyn did to help him.'

'Isn't that not uncommon? You bite the hand that feeds you . . . What's called "only human" . . .'

Ellis said, 'I hear that Protheroe's gone to Australia.'

'Australia?'

'He won't get anything out of the professor here. He may be hoping to ferret something out in the Antipodes.'

I recalled that M'Gann was supposed to have donated the original tapes to his Australian university.

Ellis and Trish were now collecting the dishes. Mollie said to me:

'Cledwyn has been much maligned and much misjudged. He was an extraordinary man.'

'Life must have been hard on you . . .' I watched her anxiously lest I'd overstepped the mark. Our rapport appeared to hold.

'My religion didn't make it easy, but I got over that.' Mollie was speaking easily. 'I knew that he wanted to marry me, and would have done if he could. And

I didn't let it cut my social life and professional life to pieces.'

I said nothing.

We had both finished our glasses of wine. Ellis came back and re-filled our glasses. And then Trish brought in the pudding.

'A pavlova!' cried Mollie in rapture.

'It's the In-thing,' said Trish with amusement.

A pavlova with raspberries.

'Elly's favourite fruit,' said Trish, giving him an indulgent smile.

The evening became for the time being less fraught. We began talking about books, reviews, current fashions in literature. And then, as if spurred by having had *The Sunday Times* and In-things as subjects of conversation, we went on to feminism, Thatcherism, and suchlike. Mollie praised Germaine Greer; nobody praised Mrs Thatcher.

We had come to the end of the meal. Mollie lit a cigarette. I had a new idea, addressed myself to Ellis.

'Everyone's badgering *me* about the book I'm supposed to be going to write. What are *you* writing?'

Gotham looked around at us, the pale sharp features of his face peering from the undergrowth of hair. Actually the wine had brought the faintest colour into the said pale sharp features – without easing the tension in them . . .

'What am I writing? Another novel, I expect.' There was something evasive in his tone of voice.

'What sort of novel?' Mollie.

Without a glimmer of change in facial expression – 'One that will combine high art with high success.'

'Congratulations!' said Mollie.

'Thank you.'

'So what's it about, Elly?'

'A Woman, of course. In this glorious year of 1983, what else?'

'Yes. Go on!'

'She's a lesbian, of course.'

'Oh!'

'An unmarried mother.'

We began to laugh.

'And black!'

Trish, presumably having heard all this before and consequently not being momentarily shocked, as Mollie and I were, out of a sense of taste, once again grasped Ellis's wrist.

Ellis was looking at us in turn –

'You see a truly beautiful metaphor,' he said, 'for England.'

'It's got everything a journalist could want,' said Mollie. She was amused.

'That's right,' said Ellis. He paused. 'But now you've got to think about Art. What's required for Art? *Magic!*' He nodded his head as if agreeing with himself. 'For Art it must have Magic, Fantasy . . . Well, I have that crowning touch of magic ready for my creation – she'll have a short prehensile tail. Can't you imagine the magical realism of the moment when she swings by it from a magnificent chandelier?' He paused. 'And the magical aptness of the appendage when she beds her mate?'

'Elly, that's enough!' Trish no longer restrained herself. She was grasping his wrist so hard that her knuckles had turned white.

'Please!' Ellis begged her. 'Let me finish! Let me explain how I'm going to establish a final reputation as Thoroughly Post-Modern Elly. The story will flash-back and flash-forward in Time, flash upward, flash downward, flash inside-out . . . Parts of it will be written as Film-Script – very important . . . You'll have Narrative Play, not to mention Fore-Play, and every other kind of Play. I'll give you Parody and Pastiche.' His narrow eyes were sending out brilliant darting glances in all directions. 'I'm expecting to scoop every prize of the season, every praise of academe.'

We were reduced to silence, as if the vibrance of dottiness in the air were overpowering.

'All right,' Ellis said. 'I'll make some coffee for you all.' He got up with difficulty – Trish did not attempt to stop him – and went out of the room.

When he closed the door Trish said quietly:

'If only Elly wouldn't do that sort of thing! Sure, among his friends it's OK. But not among folks outside. They take him seriously and hate it – and hate *him*!'

This suddenly took me back to my first sight of him, at the Memorial Service for Cledwyn less than half a year ago, my first being aware of – and perturbed by – signs of rashness, unwisdom . . .

Mollie was saying something to comfort Trish.

Ellis looked in at the door. 'Coffee in the sitting-room.'

We moved into the sitting-room and Ellis brought in a tray with coffee things on it. Trish said to him:

'You must sit down, honey, really must. I'll do the rest.'

The earlier tinge of colour in his complexion had vanished: instead of its usual white it was now a strangely dead grey. All evening he had not said a word about being in desperate pain. I had a feeling of nameless apprehension.

Trish handed us each a small cup of black coffee. Sugar. Mollie said, 'Have you by any chance got any cream?'

'Of course.' Trish went out to fetch it.

There was a momentary silence. Then we heard a telephone ring. Ellis cocked his head: Trish was answering it. Then silence again.

Trish appeared in the doorway, fluttering, her face white. To Ellis –

'It's Iris . . .'

Ellis tried to jump up and hobble towards her. 'She's dead?'

Trish's mouth opened and said Yes, although no sound came out; Ellis put his arms round her. She loosened them. 'You come and speak – the nurse is still on the 'phone.'

They both went out.

Mollie and I were left alone.

Not knowing what to do or say, I drank some coffee.

Then I happened to look across at Mollie.

Tears were rolling down her cheeks.

She saw my distress.

'Don't worry, James! I'm not weeping over Iris's death.'

'No? . . .'

A short dreadful pause –

'I'm weeping over *my* life.'

13

❧ *The Mole* ❧

Low-spiritedly I was gazing through the window at a
heavy January sky from which rain was falling steadily
on the roof-tops. It was the day before Iris's funeral.

The window was on the fourth floor, one of the biography floors, of the London Library, and I was sitting un-
comfortably on a low window-sill which was made of metal
with the central heating radiator running just below it – as
the radiator was hot, I had folded my anorak under me as
insulation. The narrow alleys between the racks of books
were deserted. Bare electric light bulbs shone at intervals:
very occasionally there was the ringing sound of somebody's tread on one of the metal-grating floors, either this
floor or one of the floors below it. I had a reference book,
which I had just taken from the shelf, open in my lap. I
was thinking that I ought to have seen Iris again before
she died.

When I wrote about Mrs Wharton and her circle it had
troubled me not at all – I had not given a thought to it –
that all the characters were dead. Perhaps it was because
they were long-dead. With Cledwyn Horsfall and his circle
death was happening in the present: they were dying off
while I was there. Cledwyn and Iris were gone: Gotham
and Protheroe still to go . . . I resented feeling low-spirited.

Why had I allowed myself to get enmeshed with *these* people?

For a little while I let my gaze dwell on the roofscape, wondering whether a painter's eye could make anything of it. The library was in the middle of a jumble of buildings of about the same height; the nearest, some twenty yards away and built of dark greyish yellow brick interspersed with white-framed sash-windows, was noticeable for its unusually steep and deep mansard roof, skilfully slated. Immediately opposite where I was sitting there was a top-storey parapet which someone had converted into a roof-garden: two white summer chairs and a solitary cypress, desolate in the rain. And beyond the roofscape the top half of *The Economist* building rose – a thing of no great beauty, and, if it was of a piece with most of the tall buildings in London, nevertheless unlikely to be a joy for as long as all that.

The view was dotted with lights burning in offices. The afternoon was darkening visibly while I sat there.

I was distracted by ringing sounds at the far end of my nearest alley. It was one of the staff with a trolley-load of books which he was putting back on the shelves. I returned to reading the reference book I had taken down for myself.

A voice behind me said in a powerful whisper, 'James!' I turned, startled.

Frank Protheroe! I thought he was in Australia. Here he was, looming at my elbow in a dark London suit.

'What are *you* doing here?'

'What are *you*?'

We grinned at each other.

'Two supererogatory questions,' he said. (We were conversing in whispers.)

'Positively otiose.'

He tried to sit down beside me on the window-sill. 'Too narrow and too hot,' he said crossly.

I began to spread out my anorak for him, but he was

– 196 –

standing up again. He picked up a book I had set down beside me to take away. 'What are you reading?'

He opened the book. Anthony Hope's *A Servant of the Public*.

'Is he someone you're thinking of writing a book about, if you don't write one about Cledwyn?'

I found myself looking up at the supremely pleased-with-himself smile – I had refused to tell him previously.

'Perhaps,' I said.

'Surely you can find someone better than him?'

'First of all, there's an opening for me. He's a minor writer but nobody has written seriously about him so far. I'm simply not interested in writing about someone about whom fifteen biographies have been written already.' I took a breath. 'Secondly, he's much better than you appear to think. I suppose you only know *The Prisoner of Zenda* and *Rupert of Hentzau* – which of their kind happen to be pretty accomplished.'

Protheroe was not pleased. 'My dear James . . .'

'Have you read *Quisanté*, for instance?'

'It has its merits.'

Even if I hadn't known him for a liar, I should have been pretty sure he'd never set eyes on it. I said, 'Or, by the way, *The Dolly Dialogues*?'

'Years ago.'

'I wouldn't be surprised if Ellis Gotham learnt something from *The Dolly Dialogues* when he began writing that super dialogue in his first novels. I must ask him sometime.'

Protheroe shrugged his shoulders. 'Are you seeing much of Ellis?' His interest in Anthony Hope had totally faded.

'Oh, occasionally . . .'

He showed signs of sitting down. 'How is he these days?'

I re-folded my anorak so that he could sit on it beside me. Our conversation continued in low voices – we were not supposed to talk in the place at all.

He turned the upper part of his substantial body so as

to be at 45° to mine. 'I suppose he's finding it increasingly painful to get about, poor devil! Has he taken to a wheel-chair yet?'

'No,' I said firmly. 'When I last saw him he was much as usual.'

'When was that?' He adjusted his horn-rimmed spectacles.

'Last week. I was at his house the night we heard that Iris had died.'

'Poor Iris . . . Very sad news. That was the night I got back from Australia.'

There was a pause.

'Are you going to the funeral tomorrow?' I asked.

'I saw a notice of it in *The Times*, but I haven't received an invitation.'

'In the absence of Gwendolen it's being organised by Ellis.'

'Perhaps that's why I haven't received an invitation.' His serene smile was touched with sarcasm.

I noticed that the member of the staff with his trolley had moved out of sight. The place appeared to be deserted.

Suddenly to the surprise of myself, I said:

'You never told me, Frank, why you and Ellis Gotham have scarcely been on speaking terms for God knows how many years – God knows how many decades.'

He looked at me. 'There's no reason why I shouldn't tell *you*, James.' Through the lenses his eyes looked sharp and intent, and inquisitive. I recognised the emphasis on 'you' with distaste. He glanced round and then back to me.

'It's absurdly simple, really,' he said. 'I seduced a boy Ellis was in love with. It didn't mean anything to me, just all in a day's work.' He smirked. 'But Ellis turned paranoiac about it.' His supremely pleased-with-himself smile shone reminiscently. 'A very unsophisticated boy . . . I had to show him the ropes.'

Reading in my face astonishment, he added as a stroke of corroboration:

– 198 –

'It's all on the original tapes.'

The original tapes!

'How? –' I began. And did not finish. There was a loud peremptory 'Sh-sh-sh!' and storming out of the next alley came a tall, stringy, elderly woman member of the library. She was dressed in a tweed coat and skirt, country shoes and a tricorne hat. 'Please be quiet, you gentlemen! It's most disturbing!'

Instantly Protheroe jumped up. 'I'm so sorry. *So* sorry . . .' Bowing and scraping. '*So* sorry . . .'

I stood beside him.

The lady nodded curtly in receipt of his apologies and retired to the alley from which she had emerged.

Protheroe and I stared at each other. Then I grabbed my anorak and my book. 'Come on, we'd better go.'

Protheroe stood for a moment, looking in the direction where our visitant had disappeared. Then he whispered:

'I think that was Mrs Pankhurst.'

I took him by the elbow. 'Come on!' I steered him expeditiously by the nearest way to the lift. (I felt his limp more pronounced than it had been.)

When the doors of the lift closed behind us and we began to move down, I said:

'*How* do you know what's on the original tapes?'

Frank turned his smile, now super-pleased-with-himself, to bear me down in triumph.

'I have a mole.'

There was no one else in the lift. He paused.

We had reached the bottom and the lift-doors opened.

I registered the book by Anthony Hope that I was taking out of the library. Frank collected his overcoat and brief-case from the cubicle by the front door.

We faced each other on the threshold. 'When are you going to tell me, Frank? Now?'

'If you so wish.'

I looked at my watch. 'It's a question of where. There are two quite nice pubs nearby, but alas! they won't be open.'

'I don't do my drinking in public, James.'

'Then what about tea? Tea at Fortnum's? Tea at the Ritz?'

We stood looking at the rain. 'Tea at my club, I think,' he said. And he called a passing taxi.

His club was no distance away but the taxi had to go into orbit to get there. I noticed with pleasure the club's appropriateness to Frank – rather grander than Ellis Gotham's. We went up to a beautiful spacious drawing-room on the first floor, where a row of tall Georgian windows looked out on to the rain and, through the rain, on to the façade of another rather grand club across the street.

There was no one else in the room. I sat down on a sofa before the fire, a real fire. Frank switched on a couple of lamps and rang for our tea. He looked around him.

'It *is* a beautiful room,' he said in a soupy voice. 'This is my period, James.' He glanced at me and I realised that he was laughing at himself. He sat down at the other end of the sofa.

'You have a lot to tell me,' I said.

He nodded his large balding dark head. 'Yes, indeed.' He took off his spectacles and cleaned them. Without them he looked different, as if he were blind. I noticed at the same time that his face looked heavier than I recalled, and oddly blotchy. His travels had worsened his health.

'I have a lot to tell *you.*'

He put back his spectacles and again I found him giving me the look that was intent and sharp, and inquisitive . . . Every time we met this kind of inquisitiveness was in the air, this insinuating of a probe into – I had no doubt *what* it was into – my sexual nature. In the first place I was deeply resistant to having my sexual nature probed by anyone: in the second place I could see myself getting intolerably bored with having it constantly mis-diagnosed by Protheroe. '*You* will understand this . . .' 'Of course I can tell *you* . . .' As well as intolerably boring, it was faintly sickening.

A waiter came in and Frank ordered tea. Something

made me think of Oliver and his bottle of champagne 'at the ready'.

Frank rested his head against the back of the sofa and said:

'I take it that you know all about the forthcoming auction? Of *Face to Face with Cledwyn Horsfall*.'

'I've seen the extract that M'Gann's agent has circulated.'

'What do you think of it?'

'Interesting. And the accompanying letter is very artful.'

Protheroe laughed. 'The promise of scandalous revelations?'

'Exactly.'

'Publishers with their tongues hanging out and the Sunday newspapers queueing up?'

'That seems to be the aim.'

'Well, it won't happen!'

'Really . . .'

Frank sat up and looked sideways at me. 'There aren't going to be any scandalous revelations, my boy. Not about me, anyway.'

'No?'

'I told you I've got a damned good libel lawyer. He's put the fear of God into those Virago sisters.'

'Well, well . . .'

'Actually the book's being handled by that lesbian attachment of Jess Goslett, Yvonne something or other.'

'Her name isn't Yvonne.' I could have added, And in *my* experience she isn't lesbian either. However I thought better of provoking him. 'Her name is Yolanda,' I said. 'Yolanda Foley.' I felt a spurt of private pleasure in uttering her name in public, and I drew back from letting Protheroe know that I was more than well-acquainted with her – he was capable of putting two and two together and deducing that *I* might have a mole!

'My lawyer says she's quite bright. Let's hope she is.' He laughed brutally. 'If she slips up, the Virago sisters are in for trouble.'

'Deep trouble? . . .' (Quoting him to himself.)

With reluctant amusement he paused an instant. 'All right, James . . .' Then he went on:

'In my opinion *Face To Face With Cledwyn Horsfall* – though M'Gann doesn't know it yet – is going to be a damp squib. A very, very damp squib. Take my word for it!'

I thought Protheroe's word for it was not to be sneezed at. I said:

'Although publishers are expected to bid on the strength of a forty-page extract and an artful letter, they must know that Goslett & Goslett will have gone quite a way towards cleaning the book up – that's assuming the scandal was there in the first place.'

'You may assume the scandal *was* there in the first place, my dear James.'

('He can't publish that stuff!' – Yola.)

'I must take your word for it, Frank.'

'I've told you I make it my business to know things.'

'And now you definitely do know.'

'Definitely.'

'Thanks to your mole.' It amused me to say that.

'Thanks to my mole.'

The waiter came in with a tray on which was our tea. He put it down on a long table between our sofa and the fireplace.

'It will be Lapsang,' said Frank.

'Suits me, Frank,' said I.

He poured it for us.

'Explain about your mole,' I said.

'It so happens that someone who has heard the tapes – legitimately, within the restrictions M'Gann has imposed – happens to be a friend of mine.'

'You seem to have friends everywhere.' (He could not know that in my mind I was spelling 'friends', after old X, with a capital F.)

'I have in most places,' he said with satisfaction.

'I can believe it.'

We tasted the temperature of our tea. As yet it was too hot for us to drink.

'You didn't actually get to hear the original tapes,' I said, 'or read the unexpurgated transcripts?'

'No, no. I couldn't get near the tapes – M'Gann has made a very thorough job of his restrictions. And keeps the unexpurgated transcripts in his personal possession. I wouldn't be surprised if he keeps them under his pillow.' He paused. 'My friend listened to the tapes several times and made notes of things that might interest my lawyer.' He grinned. 'Or might interest *me.*'

'Were there many things?'

'More than enough, James.'

There was a pause. The room was quiet, apart from the faint crackling of the fire and the splashing of the raindrops against the windows. He said:

'Cledwyn really hated me.'

'Did he give away a lot of detail about your private life?'

'Everything he knew, that's all.' He corrected himself. 'Everything he knew and too much that he invented.' He smiled maliciously. 'It doesn't seem to be generally recognised that' – he paused for emphasis – 'Cledwyn Horsfall was a liar.'

I laughed – at the private thought of pot and kettle.

'I'm not having it, James. I'm simply not having it.'

'What sort of thing did he say?'

Frank put down his cup and saucer and looked at me with amusement and menace.

'That's *my* business.'

'Posterity has an interest. You know?'

'I'm sure it has. But if that story, or any part of that story is to be told, James, it's going to be told by me. Not by Cledwyn Horsfall or Ellis Gotham or anyone else. Especially not by Cledwyn Horsfall and Ellis Gotham.'

I thought What about me? but I said:

'Are you going to write *your* autobiography, then?'

'I reserve my position.'

'You mentioned Ellis Gotham. Do you think he's going to write about you?'

'If he does, he won't do it very well.' A leisurely gesture with his well-kept hand. 'Actually I doubt if he'll write anything else. I think he's extinct.'

'Does *he* hate you?'

'Are you joking?'

I drank some tea.

Protheroe went on. 'If Ellis *is* going to write about me, it's time he started. In fact he may have left it too late already.' He paused. 'As you can see for yourself, he's not a good life – far from it.'

'I'm not an expert in these matters.'

'You can be assured that *I* shall enter the field last.'

I said 'Yes,' but I could not help recalling Ellis Gotham's malevolent wish, playful or not, that another stroke might carry Protheroe off first. Suddenly it seemed to me certain that Gotham *was* going to write.

Each of them was counting on entering the field last. Old friends . . .

For a little while Protheroe was silent; and I had something on which to reflect.

'Some more tea?'

I held out my cup and saucer. 'I was thinking about your mole, Frank. Didn't you have more to tell me?'

He filled up my cup again. 'Nothing I didn't expect. But it was useful to see my expectations actually expressed.'

I waited.

'A certain amount about my sexual orientation, of course – but not too much. You know? He had his reasons for holding back there . . .'

Before I could ask him what he meant by that, he went on.

'It's what he put on record about my political orientation that's what I expected and that's what's completely untrue. Untrue, and, as a matter of course, out to damage my reputation.' He paused. 'He claims that I changed my political orientation in order to strengthen my chances of following him into the House of Lords.'

I remained silent. I felt we were entering into the realms of fantasy.

His pleased-with-himself expression had changed into a glare. 'I was convinced of the rightness of the Friedmanite case *before* the Government definitely took it up.'

In this case, it seemed to me, he might for once be telling the truth.

'What did Cledwyn say to that?' I asked.

'Of course he was opposed to it – told me I should turn out to be wrong.'

'What is it on the tape that you object to?'

'What do I object to?' His voice rose in pitch. 'On the tape he says that for my own good he *encouraged* me!'

'To strengthen your chances?' I said.

'That's what he says. That's a lie to begin with. He follows it up with a more grotesque lie. An incredible lie. He says that wherever he had the opportunity he assured people who mattered, in the Government – and elsewhere – that I could be relied on for unqualified political support. What the Prime Minister refers to as "one of us". That's what he says on the tape.'

'Yes? . . .'

'I know for a fact – from several sources – that he was going around saying the *opposite*! Dishing any chances I might have had.'

I remembered his having told me this before. I had doubted, then, that he stood a chance of following Cledwyn into the House of Lords: learning a bit more about it in the meantime had led me to think it was utterly unrealistic. I kept quiet.

Protheroe said: 'He establishes me as venal.' He paused. 'And he establishes himself as a bloody liar!'

I nodded my head to signify that I had heard (not that I believed).

The blotchiness of his complexion seemed to be exacerbated by emotion. Passionately he said:

'*The opposite of the truth!*'

Again I nodded my head and, in an effort to shift the line of conversation, said:

'Do you think it was deliberate, calculated?'

'Cledwyn was one of the most devious and calculating of men.'

'*You* must know, Frank . . .'

'The trouble was' – Protheroe suddenly laughed harshly – 'that like many such men, he often got his calculations wrong.' He paused. 'People always assume that calculating men get their calculations right. They often get them wrong.'

I said: 'Did Ellis Gotham play any part in this?'

'I don't know. One supposes he was in Cledwyn's confidence at the time.' His tone of voice changed. 'There's some doubt about this. I gather that there's very little reference to it on the tapes. Or reference to Ellis's being in Cledwyn's confidence about anything else – such as their work in Whitehall!' A dramatic moment.

'Really?' I was recalling Gotham's memorial address.

'Even I am surprised.' His tone of voice was now reasonable. 'According to my mole Ellis is given practically no credit for anything, on the tapes. After all those years of loyalty . . . You know, James, I feel almost sorry for Gotham. Almost!'

I said ironically, 'Gotham gets *dis*-credit all round?'

Protheroe laughed coarsely. 'In several forms, I gather, public and private.'

'Does Cledwyn volunteer it, do you know? Or is it wormed out of him by M'Gann?'

I was answered by a confident, knowing look. 'Cledwyn was capable of not letting M'Gann worm things out of him that he didn't intend to be wormed out. Believe me! . . .'

'All the same Iris said he came down from the sessions "shattered".'

'It's interesting. There's a pretty example – of how far Cledwyn permitted the worming to go. On the tape he tells M'Gann about his friendship with Owen David. You know who Owen David was?'

'An Oxford poet who was killed in the War.'

'A very good poet.'

'I agree from the little I've read.'

'A very good poet, and a very attractive young man. Very attractive to Cledwyn. Cledwyn tells M'Gann about this friendship. How devoted he was to Owen David. How much he loved him.' Protheroe paused. Then delivered his coup –

'Cledwyn doesn't tell M'Gann that in 1943 he offered Owen David marriage.'

'*What!*'

Protheroe contented himself with an eloquent gesture with his hand. The gold ring swept elegantly through the air.

I was too taken aback to ask how on earth he, Protheroe, knew. Or to ask myself how much truth there might be in the story. And also not too taken aback to feel there was something ridiculous about it.

There was a long pause.

'Some more tea, James?'

'Thank you.'

As he handed me the cup and saucer, he said: 'You look as if you might prefer a little brandy. Would you?'

'No.'

The tea was getting cold.

'You said,' Frank went on, 'that Owen David was killed in the War. He was killed during the War when he was home on leave, killed in a motor-cycle accident. It was *said* to be accidental – he ran his motor-bike into a tree. But one wonders. Cledwyn . . .' He shrugged his shoulders. 'Anyway, the coroner found it was accidental.' He paused. 'It was a great loss. Cledwyn was deeply upset. So was Xavier.'

'X?'

'Of course. Owen David was another of his boys. Before Cledwyn took him away.' His tone of voice became silkily smooth. 'If you want to check up on it, you can ask X. I'm sure he'll tell *you*.'

I set down my cup and saucer. We had come to the point I had foreseen: having disliked having my sexual nature continually probed by this monstrous fellow, I had reached an intolerable pitch of boredom with having it continually mis-diagnosed. I was absolutely sick of it.

'Why are you laughing?' Protheroe looked at me with slight incredulity.

'It's a choice, Frank. Either I laugh at you; or I pick up one of these cushions and stuff your face with it! Having the *impertinence* to insinuate that *I'm* one of old Yeo's boys! Or' – I made myself clear by emphasis – 'anything of the kind.'

The pleased-with-himself smile for once vanished – and was replaced by a furious-with-me glare.

'You're talking balls, Protheroe,' I said. 'Sheer *balls*!'

He was speechless. It was obvious that he was entirely unused to being challenged, let alone told he was wrong, by someone thirty years younger than himself. Possibly, at his present eminence, by anyone at all. But no sooner had I done it myself than I wondered what sort of a fool I had been.

'Young man!' His face reddened terribly – I imagined his blood-pressure going off the top of the scale. 'You would be ill-advised to quarrel with *me*!'

The way he said '*me*' was frightening. I heard myself saying:

'I suppose I should.' (I didn't want him to have another stroke in my presence.)

There was another long pause. His smile was coming back, half-pleased-with-himself and half-sarcastic.

'You still have a great deal to learn from me.'

I looked down at my teacup, in tentative relief that

the storm might be blowing over, superficially at least. I considered that I still had a good deal to hear from him if I were going to write about the Circus. *If . . .* It struck me that I was beginning to find them all intolerable.

He said: 'We have much in common.'

I thought it would be compounding my unwisdom to point out that there was much ground that we didn't have in common. I was afraid I might have made an enemy of him. It was all very well for me to feel reassured for the moment, here and now; but that was no guarantee whatsoever of what he would be saying behind my back to other people in the future. (In fact to think of such a thing as a guarantee was pretty absurd.) It was the opening to make amends.

'We both think Cledwyn was a very good writer. And possibly a very useful contributor to World Détente.' (I didn't know if he would admit the latter.)

'That's right,' he said. His tone of voice was almost friendly. He must be attempting to make amends. 'We are both trying to understand Cledwyn in . . . his totality.'

'In his totality . . .' I couldn't help feeling seduced – 'in their totality' was just how I wanted to understand the people I was writing about and to represent them to the people who read my books. How they lived in their inner selves and how they lived in their web of relationships with other selves; both woven into a seamless totality. This had nothing to do, of course, with the extent to which what Protheroe was telling me bore any resemblance to the truth.

The waiter came in to remove the tea-things. Frank said:

'Would you think it to be a good idea if we had a drink before you leave?'

I thought it would. He ordered drinks for us.

The drawing-room was darker. The embers of the fire were still glowing and the rain was still splashing against the windows. The lamps seemed brighter. I glanced round at the early nineteenth-century paintings and furniture – and at Protheroe. 'This is *my* period.'

I said: 'Why do you think Cledwyn did this? Why did he give these tapes with all these somewhat incredible revelations on them?'

Protheroe was thoughtful.

'I think he wanted to leave behind him material that would make his biography one of the most remarkable of memorials. He was disappointed with the prospects of the books he had written himself: he thought they had failed. And of his posture on the world-stage, he was doubtful. Setting down on tape all this –'

'All this stuff . . .'

'Setting down on tape all this stuff was his last throw. Stuff that will be remembered. You know?' He paused. 'Immortality at any price.'

'You may be right.'

'I *am* right.' Frank snorted with amusement and self-approval.

The waiter brought in our drinks. Frank had ordered champagne. He said:

'It's not my usual time of day, but it's my usual drink.'

The waiter stirred the embers so that they blazed up.

The fire of Frank's malevolence seemed, I thought, to have dimmed for the time being. He was sitting quietly, relaxed, his large head, with dark luxuriant curls clustering at the neck, resting again against the back of the sofa. He was drinking very slowly.

'Tomorrow,' he said reflectively, 'we have Iris's funeral. Poor Iris . . . She always wanted Cledwyn.'

'In a sense she kept him. He didn't leave her.'

'He didn't leave home, you mean.'

I said, 'Do you think she knew about Mollie Tremayna?'

'People can know things and *not* know things.' He raised his head to look at me.

'I suppose,' I said, 'one could equally say Poor Mollie.

She always wanted Cledwyn. Over a lifetime, against such odds . . .'

'Yes.' Frank sat up and drank a little champagne. 'It's very George Eliotesque – *Waiting For Death* . . . Iris dies too late for Mollie. Mollie must be thinking every hour of the day, If only! . . .'

'It's an extraordinary story. I wonder what Mollie's attraction was for Cledwyn. Over a lifetime, against such odds . . .'

Frank turned to look at me powerfully. (Did I think his fire had dimmed?)

'I've always assumed,' he said, 'it was correction.'

'Correction?'

Smirking, supremely pleased with himself –

'He went to her for "correction". You know?'

I drank some champagne and tried not to choke on it.

Malevolent and mendacious – Protheroe was also mad!

14

❧ *Sandwiches and* ❧
Home-Made Cake

From Golders Green the funeral party came back to Iris's house off Curzon Street, a strangely constituted party – Ellis and Trish; Iris's housekeeper and nurse; Iris and Cledwyn's publisher, Jack Heald; Randa and myself; Randa had brought Yola with her; and at the last moment Gwendolen had flown home from Manila, with the intention of catching the first flight back. (Frank Protheroe was at the crematorium but had not come to the house. Barry M'Gann had not put in an appearance at all.)

We stood round in the drawing-room where I had sat with Iris. All the Boyds and Hockneys on the walls, in the centre of them the compelling portrait of Iris by Lucian Freud, opposite to it the Francis Bacon; the sumptuously plump cushions on the sofas and chairs, the silky Persian carpet underfoot – familiar and sad . . . The armchair facing the door had been tactfully moved away. We stood drinking an indifferent wine and eating sandwiches and home-made cake served by the housekeeper – I recognised funeral baked meats.

I introduced myself to Gwendolen and politely enquired about her journey home. Her face lit with animation. She had had a succession of routine travel vicissitudes: she began a lively description of her responses to the first one. Then of her responses to the second one. Then a *third* . . . Her interest was in how each one struck her and how she responded to it. Then began a *fourth* . . . I realised what I had let myself in for. Lively, clever, witty though some of them were, they began to pall on me. For Gwendolen it was apparent that they were a perpetual source of excitement because they had happened to *her*. From time to time she gave me a sharp glance to make sure that I was giving proper attention.

Gwendolen was an unusually tall young woman, still wearing her travel-gear – it looked as if she had brought no other – of old jeans, navy jumper, clean shirt and worn-out hush-puppies. What I was not prepared for in advance, nor properly accommodated to here and now, was that she was an exceptionally beautiful woman. Really exceptionally beautiful!

Yet while before me stood one of the most beautiful women I had ever met, I realised that out of the corner of my eye I was trying to glimpse Yolanda across the room. I paid attention to the travel stories. Gwendolen was about thirty, I supposed. She must be almost as tall as Cledwyn was: the jersey and jeans revealed – uncalculatedly, I was sure – a long, lithe body, fairly narrow in the shoulders, small round the waist, and beginning to bloom at the hips. Her hair was fair, and cropped off in bits as if she had done it herself with a pair of nail-scissors – most inappropriately punky-looking. A lovely face: eyes pale blue, like Cledwyn's only more deeply-set and not bulging; delicate arched eyebrows like Cledwyn's; and a perfect, faintly-tanned complexion.

Absolutely beautiful, and yet – I admitted to myself that it must be due to some quirk in my own nature – she scarcely attracted me at all. Perhaps it was the unusually high degree of her concern with herself, which some men might feel lured to try and penetrate, which had the opposite effect on me. The conversation continued with little sign of exhausting itself, or rather of exhausting Gwendolen. Incidentally it was of no help to me so far as I had my own axe to grind: I was learning nothing at all about what she felt towards Cledwyn and Iris, apart from any deductions I was at liberty to make from the fact that she never mentioned either of them: I began to understand why she had not come home to Cledwyn's funeral and was merely putting in a formal appearance at Iris's.

Iris had given me a clue. Gwendolen's concern with herself had somehow become enclosed by her work for the Third World: she was standing before me in her mother's sitting-room, making conversation that interested her; while her inner self was locked in Manila. She was rich and she was going to be richer. If movements within that self-absorbed inner self impelled her into deciding to hand over her riches to Amnesty or some other deserving human cause, she would hand them over. External criticism would make no impression on Gwendolen where self-criticism told her she was right.

What a beautiful woman!

We were joined by Ellis and Trish. Trish began by asking her politely what sort of a flight she'd had . . . Ellis took me away, introduced me to Jack Heald and left me to talk to him.

Heald was a tall, elongated man, dressed in a double-breasted navy-blue pin-striped suit: he grew wings of smooth grey hair on either side of his head. Ellis had told him who I was, so he soon began to talk about Cledwyn – in a clipped style of speech that contrasted amusingly with his elegant, slightly languid posture. His manner was unbuttoned and informal.

In a little while I had my opening. 'What do you think,' I asked, 'about *Face To Face With Cledwyn Horsfall*?'

'From what I have seen of it, it's a very silly book.'

I thought that was definite enough to encourage me to my next question. 'Are you going to bid for it?'

'No, indeed.'

This answer seemed to me so definite as to bring the conversation to an end. I was silent.

'Have you met our Australian p-p-professor?' he said.

'Yes. Have *you*?'

'Yes. He came to see me. *He*'s a smoothie . . .'

'I know someone who thinks he's the most two-faced man in London.'

'I like that.'

'You know what Ellis says to that? It means he can suck two bums at the same time.'

Heald laughed. 'Good for Ellis!'

Our conversation continued for a little while on a friendly note. He sounded me about my plans for doing a biography of Cledwyn. 'I should like you to come and see me. If you would.'

I said I would. A further step down the road of commitment . . .

As I left him I found Yola beside me. She was wearing the same black jumper and skirt, without the dangly rainbow earrings that she had been wearing at the Chinest restaurant. It occurred to me that her wardrobe was probably scanty – which was not surprising when she had two boys to keep at boarding-school and a large flat to run. A large flat, a large dark flat full of books and papers . . . I found myself visualising it with emotion – and suddenly realised that I was seeing myself living in it!

She smiled up at me. 'I saw you making an impression on Jack Heald.'

'It sounds as if he wants me to write about Cledwyn.'

'So do I.'

'What *I* want to know is this: which is it they're all so crazy about – me for myself, or me rather than Barry M'Gann?'

She brushed the hair out of her eyes. 'You rather than Barry M'Gann.'

I grinned. 'I suppose I asked for that.'

'Aren't you often asking for things?'

'I avoid asking for anything.' I was not smiling.

She put her hand on my forearm and looked up into my face again. 'You avoid accepting anything.'

Thrown, I spent a moment trying to pull myself together. 'Perhaps not always,' I managed to say.

She laughed. 'Will you have supper again with me at that Chinese restaurant?'

'I accept on the spot.'

Her hand was still lying on my forearm and was manifestly noticed by Randa, who was just joining us. Yola removed her hand. Randa smiled imperturbably: her eyelids swiftly dropped and rose.

'I'm glad to see you here, James.'

I felt she wasn't glad to see Yola's hand on my arm. I said: 'And I'm always glad to give gladness.'

Randa looked at Yola. 'Do *you* find James terribly facetious?'

'Yes.'

'I do apologise for it,' I said. 'It's my only failing.'

The housekeeper was passing and I accepted another sandwich from her.

'All set for the auction?' I said to Randa.

'That's more in Jess's province than in mine.' She turned smoothly to Yola. 'And Yolanda's, of course.' Back to me. 'Yola's been editing the manuscript.'

'I remember asking you if you had to excise very much.'

'And I was unable to tell you, James.'

'Can you tell me now?'

Yola said: 'We've had to excise as much as you'd expect.'

Randa looked at her with concealed disapproval, smiling. Smiling at independence, if not rebellion in the firm.

'How is the professor taking it?' I asked.

Looking away, Randa raised her wine-glass to her lips. Her profile rose smoothly from her throat.

Yola said: 'I hope he recognises that he hasn't any alternative.'

I said: 'A pity! It's what you excise that makes it a hot property.'

Randa looked at me. 'Why do you say that? How do you know?'

I said: 'I don't know for a fact. M'Gann promised to let me see the manuscript. You remember? "Share and share alike." You were there when he said it. He sent me the same extract that his agent has since circulated to all the publishers, and I'm still waiting for the rest. I can only infer that he wants to keep certain things under wraps.'

'And they're the things you think we've excised?'

'The dirt, as one might say.'

'I might *not* say!'

'Merely by imputation from the agent's letter, Randa.' I was careful not to let myself look at Yola.

'I regret that you're taking this line, James.' Randa gave me a shrewd glance. 'I hope you are not being affected by Ellis.'

'What makes you think that, Randa?' Ellis – her client!

She said: 'Surely you see that it's to your advantage to be on the friendly terms that Barry offered? I think he's a little disappointed in you.'

'I'm sorry about that.' (M'Gann must be a little disappointed in my not meeting him to report on Mollie Tremayna, for instance.)

'He's very busy with preliminary promotion.'

'I should have thought he might have managed to find his way into here today. Preliminary promotion.'

Randa ignored the remark. She said: 'Ellis wouldn't have him on the list. Barry's hurt at not being here – he was very devoted to Iris.'

The idea of Barry M'Gann having a tender hide was new to me. I said:

'He could have gone to the ceremony at Golders Green

without coming on here. Like Frank Protheroe.' I kept my eye on Randa's face.

'Frank Protheroe!' She smiled her characteristic smile – a shade less sleepy-looking, perhaps a shade more venomous. 'Barry and Protheroe are on bad terms. Protheroe has done everything possible to emasculate the book.'

'Has he succeeded?'

'You can take it the book would not be leaving our hands if it contained any material that might be the basis for legal action.'

'So you *have* cleaned it up!'

'I didn't express it in those terms.'

'If you have, it becomes all the more important for me to see the material that's been cut out.' I was enjoying the conversation. 'If I'm to write the truth about Cledwyn, it's imperative. The truth he tells about himself.'

Randa was not enjoying the conversation. She smiled silkily. 'You're not in serious mood today, James.'

Yola said to me: 'The final version, as it leaves the firm, will not be libellous in any way. *I* can vouch for that personally.'

Yola was looking at me: Randa cast a darting glance at her. 'Yes,' Randa said. 'Yola has done splendid work on it. Jess has every confidence in the final version.'

'In that case I simply have to take my own steps to see the unexpurgated transcripts. Either break into M'Gann's rooms or employ a mole in your office.'

Randa touched the knot of hair at the back of her long fragile head.

'I don't think you can do either, James,' she said. 'That's why I think you should repair your fences with Barry. I know that you can.'

At that Randa moved across to Gwendolen. I moved closer to Yola. We were interrupted. Ellis joined us. In his light-blue corduroy suit. He looked dartingly from Yola to me and from me to Yola, and then all round the room.

'What are you two up to?' he said.

'Discussing the topic of the month,' I replied.

'It won't be long before we know the worst. Or the best. The auction is next week.'

'Jack Heald says he's not going to bid.'

'A very silly book.' Ellis mimicked Heald's clipped speech.

'More silly than it's dangerous to Cledwyn's reputation? . . .'

'No. It's dangerous to Cledwyn's reputation because he, Cledwyn, is being so silly.'

I felt disinclined to argue and looked to Yola for support.

'That was not our concern,' she said. She gave Ellis a sparkling glance. 'Our concern was libellousness. The law has no concern with silliness.'

'How right you are!' said Ellis fiercely. 'If the law had any concern for silliness, half the novels that do get published wouldn't get published.'

Yola played up to him. 'Think of the fortunes that would be lost!'

I heard the sound of Ellis's bees buzzing. Pacifyingly I said:

'Oh well, the professor may not persuade anyone to publish it.' By now I was feeling thoroughly fed-up with the whole topic.

'May not?' cried Ellis. 'May not, with his outstanding gift, his double-gift!'

Yola recognised the allusion and laughed.

'He *will* get it published!' Ellis cried.

I tried again, though I couldn't think why I was taking the trouble. I said:

'Well, if he does, nobody may take any notice.'

'That's a thought,' said Ellis, disbelievingly though less paranoiacally.

I said: 'When *is* the auction?'

'Next Tuesday. Jack Heald will be finding out who bids. He'll be letting me know the result straight away. I'll let you know.' He paused. 'In fact Mollie is coming round to our house to be there when we hear. Will you come?'

I said I would and we discussed the arrangements. I had a fresh idea.

'What about Gwendolen? I suppose you've now had a chance to discuss the book with her. What line does she take?'

'She compares the magnitude of our problems here and of hers there. In the Philippines, trying to do something to stop hundreds of people being arrested and imprisoned or tortured and shot every month of the year . . .'

I was silenced.

'I tried to get her interested. She just said, "Ellis, I'm afraid I can't *see* it."'

I thought Good for her! Ellis went on.

'I tried to get her interested, and I got nowhere. So I'm on my own – with the support of Mollie and Jack, but they have no official standing. I mean the standing I have as literary executor.'

'I don't think that's important,' said Yola.

'And Protheroe?' I asked.

'It's interesting you should mention him,' Ellis said. 'He made a point of talking to me this morning, when we were hanging about in the Garden of Remembrance. He seems very pleased with himself. That's nothing new. And he speaks as if he knows things that nobody else knows, and that's nothing new, either.'

'What does he know that nobody else knows?' Yola asked.

'That there's a load of scandalous and damaging revelations about himself. One can't say his way of life hasn't provided a basis for them. *But*, his lawyer has been on to the Gosletts' – Ellis looked hard at Yola – '*and*, he says, has put the fear of God into them. He seems to be satisfied that the danger to him is averted so far as he's concerned. Then, with typical insidiousness, he says there are scandalous and damaging revelations about me. Cledwyn has been a sod to *me* . . . Protheroe's a liar and five years ago

I wouldn't have believed it. Now I do believe it.' The tension that alarmed me had come into the muscles round his eyes, which had begun to burn unnaturally. 'That was very stupid of Cledwyn. He's been a sod to me. *I* can be a sod to *him*!'

'Have you put your lawyer on to Goslett & Goslett?' I said thoughtlessly.

Ellis glanced across the room to where Randa was talking to Jack Heald. I realised the mistake I'd made.

'Randa Goslett is *my* lawyer.' He paused. 'She's supposed to be on my side. While her sister, an equal partner in the same firm, is on the side of the enemy. What do you think of that?'

Yola intervened. 'Ellis, please! . . .' Her voice was gentle and appealing as she repeated what she had said to me in Randa's presence. 'The final version of this book, as it leaves the firm, is clear of libel.' With a simple gesture she took hold of his arm.

I said: 'You don't have to worry, Ellis . . .' I was not so sure, of course. M'Gann could restore anything he wanted to restore at his own risk. Furthermore there could be stuff which was pretty nasty from his point of view while not being actionable – nasty when blazoned in the Sunday newspapers.

Iris's nurse came up with a bottle of wine and filled our glasses. The housekeeper offered us more sandwiches.

'What else did Frank Protheroe say?' I asked.

Ellis without any change in facial expression managed to convey a slight relaxation. 'He was extremely solicitous about my state of health, rather as if he were expecting me to pop off fairly soon. Expecting *me* to pop off before *he* does. Which will leave the way open for him to write anything he wants to write about me.' He uttered a sort of laugh. 'Well, he needn't be too sure. I thought he didn't look too good himself. In fact not good to any degree. His face looks heavy and a bad colour. His face tells the story – he's overdoing it.' The paranoiac look on his own face was reappearing. 'Well, he may not see me off as easily as he thinks!' His eyes were burning opaquely again. 'He who pops off last writes loudest!'

Yola and I laughed. It was funny – crazy . . .

'You *are* going to write?' I said.

'I see no alternative. I must have my say. This silly book may be cleaned up, but the original tapes exist for M'Gann to use at will if he waits long enough. It will take him six or seven years to write his biography of Cledwyn, he says. He can get in last if he wants to.' Ellis transfixed me with his burning glare. 'And so can you, James.'

'If I decide to do a book about Cledwyn.'

'Haven't you decided yet?'

'No.' I covered my powerful conviction against writing about all these people in their Circus, by saying: 'I said I'd give it till the New Year.'

'We're in the New Year now.'

'Then my decision is imminent.'

Ellis turned away. 'I must make a last attempt to get a response from Gwendolen.'

Yola and I glanced at each other. It would soon be time to leave. I had drawn her into a corner away from the others. From it we could look through a window into a little paved back-yard, uncared-for.

'Is the decision imminent?' she said.

'It just has to be. I can't go on like this, arguing it over with myself incessantly and coming to no decision. The processes of the mind aren't getting me anywhere . . .'

'You've painted yourself into a corner.'

'Exactly. My only hope, so far as I can see, is something outside the processes of the mind.' I resorted to facetiousness. 'A movement of the soul, perhaps. An all-change in the unconscious . . .'

'There are such things.'

'Possibly the voice of God.'

'You don't believe in God.'

'And I'm no lover of metaphor, either.'

I suddenly was aware of how the intimacy between us had grown. I wanted to move nearer to her. She was looking up at me, the hair falling away from her eyes, the shape of her mouth at once firm and gentle.

'I can't decide between wanting and not wanting to write a book about Cledwyn and his circle. In the meantime I'm bogged down in these present goings-on. It's just what I wanted to avoid – I saw it at the start. Instead of *observing* these people I'm *enmeshed* with them. I'm beginning to feel claustrophobic – hemmed in by animosity on all sides . . . I want to get *out!*'

'Why not take a vacation from them?'

'What do I come back to afterwards?'

'You could write a fantastic book about them. They've had fascinating lives. They weren't always like this. And they've written fascinating books.'

'Fascinating lives which end in them all hating each other, lying about each other, doing each other down in the face of history. What a demeaning spectacle!' I paused. 'To me it almost seems demeaning to human nature in general. When Randa first put me on to the idea of the book I thought she was looking for a book by me that would do all three men down. "The animosity of old friends". I accommodated myself to the idea because she made me see it as funny.' I paused again. 'My first instinct was right.'

'Don't you feel any sympathy for them?'

'How could one help it? This last throw of Cledwyn's is a shocker. Yet, poor sod, one can see it's a final outburst of pain at believing all his ambitions had failed.'

'When we're in pain ourselves, don't we sometimes turn and inflict pain on the people around us, sometimes on our nearest and dearest?'

I looked down at her, moved by deep emotion. *Here* was someone . . .

'That is so,' I said.

We were both silent for a moment.

'It has to be written about,' she said.

'Everything has to be written about. But it doesn't follow that it has to be written about by *me*!'

She smiled. 'You could write a fantastic book about them.'

'You've said that before. The question is – Could I spend five, six years of my life on a book which I could see at the start was going to end like this? Which was ultimately going to go against the grain?' I took hold of her hand. 'Against the grain of my feelings *au fond* . . .'

'Really so?'

'Yes. *Animosity is hateful!*'

We were interrupted by the nurse offering us some more wine.

'That's why my only hope,' I went on, 'is a movement of the soul, an all-change in the unconscious –'

'Or the voice of God.'

We had both begun to smile.

'I'm *waiting* for it.'

'Let us hope you don't have to wait long.' The grey-green hazel eyes suddenly sparkled. 'Or you'll be over the top.'

'Well, shit!' I said.

We were standing very close to each other. Then we realised that the party was breaking up. It was time to say our goodbyes and make for the door. When I came to Randa she said:

'Yola and I will be going back together.'

And so it came about that I found myself momentarily left alone on the threshold. An odd thing happened.

Trish came up to speak to me before I could go. Below her almost black hair her face – she wore no other make-up than a pale lipstick – looked terribly white.

'James . . .' She pitched her voice low. She was so small and bird-like that I had to stoop to hear what she was saying. It seemed that she didn't want the others to hear.

'It's about Elly. He's under awful strain . . . If *you* can do anything to ease it, will you?'

'Of course.'

Her fluttering manner dropped away – she was appealing to me from a steady concern for Ellis, a steady love. And although she was so much younger than Ellis, that steady love was impressive.

'You probably don't know,' she whispered. 'He's had another . . . episode. He doesn't want anyone to know.' She paused and I was afraid tears were coming into her eyes. 'And that's not all . . .' She glanced round. 'He seems . . . somehow unstable. He's thrown by all this hatred.'

I said: 'I understand. I'll keep a friendly eye on him.' And then I added: 'I shall be coming round to you next Tuesday.'

'I'm so glad. Thank you, James.'

She went back towards Ellis and I turned to go downstairs, downstairs in this old house of Cledwyn's and Iris's, for the last time.

But I hadn't reached the bottom of the stairs when I heard footsteps behind me – Ellis. He put his hand on my shoulder so that I had to pause. Standing one step above me, he said:

'I'm not going to let Protheroe affect my confidence by a hair's breadth. I don't give a damn what Cledwyn's said about me – it can't amount to a row of beans. In this book or any other book that M'Gann may run up from his fucking tapes.'

'I'm glad about that, Ellis. You *must* be right.'

'And if *this* book is going to be more damaging to Cledwyn than it is to me, then why should *I* worry?' He paused dramatically. 'I'm not sure I shan't let it go through without a fight. I haven't said this to the others, James.' He stopped for a moment. 'Don't be surprised if I throw in my hand!'

'That really will be a surprise. A welcome surprise . . .'

'Listen to me, James. I'll tell you the truth.' His small sharp brown eyes were darting glances all over the place, but some of them caught me. 'The truth is very simple and very final. I've *had* Cledwyn!'

Turning quickly he clutched the bannisters and scrambled back up the stairs to Trish.

I walked down into Curzon Street in a turmoil of ideas which hadn't settled down by the following Tuesday evening when I went to the house in Holland Park.

In the light sparse drawing-room I sat on edge, as did the others, while he waited for Jack Heald's call. In fact we did not have to wait long. The telephone rang. Trish ran out to answer: Ellis hobbled after her.

Mollie and I sat motionless until Ellis and Trish came back. Ellis gave us the news.

'*Nobody* has bid for it!'

Trish came in with a bottle of champagne.

The evening was transformed. Mollie's rose-coloured face was radiant, her transparent grey eyes sparkling through her spectacles. Trish's attention was fixed on Ellis.

Some of my attention also was fixed on Ellis – was he going to announce his defection? It appeared that he was *not*.

There was obviously a great deal they meant to discuss between themselves. I'd had enough of them for a while, and after we'd shared the bottle of champagne, I found an excuse to leave.

For me, however, the evening had not come to the end of its surprises.

When I got home, I found a bouquet of flowers left on the doorstep (improperly by some delivery-service). Extraordinary. I opened it.

A bunch of yellow roses. And a card –

NEVER EXPLAIN NEVER APOLOGISE   YOLA

15

❧ *Yes – No* ❧

A large flat, a large dark flat full of books and papers
. . . It looked exactly the same. In the living-room
Yola switched on a lamp and I sat down on the sofa.

We had come back after a second supper at the Chinese
restaurant. A curiously relaxed supper, harmonious . . .
Had our exchange of roses, the red and the yellow, contributed? I was inclined to think it had. It had made something
plain . . .

Yola stood poised, beside the lighted lamp. Wearing the
geranium-pink flying-suit. Brushing the dark hair out of
her eyes. She said:

'This time I have some whisky.'

'Have you got any vodka?'

'Yes . . . But I thought your drink was whisky.'

'It is. But it depends . . .'

'On what?'

'I haven't forgotten the vodka last time.'

'OK,' she said, lingering softly over the 'O'. 'Give me
time to open a fresh bottle.'

'No hurry.'

She went out of the room, and I sat back on the sofa,
thinking.

It was ten days since the evening in Holland Park when

we heard that nobody had bid for M'Gann's book. In those ten days Ellis and Mollie had got together with Jack Heald to decide on their next move. (There was still no sign of Gotham's intention to defect.) Each of them thought M'Gann would in the end find a publisher: neither of them wanted the book to come out. Heald had consulted his firm's lawyer, and they had decided to take counsel's preliminary opinion on whether the book could be stopped on the grounds of Mollie's idea, that Cledwyn had given the interviews on the unquestioned understanding – which Mollie and Ellis were prepared to swear to – that the material was for use only in the biography and not to be published verbatim in transcript.

To my non-legal mind, and to Yolanda's legal mind, they hadn't much hope. Once they were in the witness-box it would not be difficult for M'Gann's counsel to elicit the fact that each of them had, aside from their impartial evidence as to Cledwyn's intentions, personal reasons for trying to stop the book's appearance. The more I heard of it, the more convinced was I that Ellis would defect in the end. 'That would show sense,' said Yola. 'I should admire him for it.'

In the meantime I had quietly withdrawn myself from their disputations. When I was not completing work on my notes and files, I had made a start on reading Ada Leverson as well as Anthony Hope. It was like coming out into the sunshine – with a brief spell of being pulled back into the shade, though he was unaware of it, by Jack Heald. The day after the auction fell through he telephoned me to go and see him. I agreed partly out of curiosity and partly out of encouragement by my agent, who opined that I'd nothing to lose. (The publisher of *Edith Wharton* had a loose option on my next book, but 'nothing to worry about'.)

Jack Heald had risen like a heron from his desk – a big desk in a small office – when I came in: tall and elongated, he looked even taller and more elongated in a white polo-necked jumper, the collar of it rising to his chin and the bottom of it sliding down his narrow hips. The wings of hair above his ears, smooth and grey, looked as if they had been freshly combed, though I imagined they always looked like that: he was that sort of man.

'Welcome!' Shaking my hand in a gesture that combined decisiveness with elegance, he had sat me in a single big easy chair and returned to behind his desk. 'I'm not taking you to the Board Room,' he said. 'We can be cosy here. Some coffee?' He spoke in bursts, so staccato that they sounded almost like a stammer. He actually had a slight stammer.

I'd said Thank you and he'd called his secretary – a pretty young woman, lady-like and lively.

'I've a great admiration,' he said, 'for your *Edith Wharton*. I didn't get a chance to say so the other day – a funeral wake for Iris was hardly the occasion.'

I shrugged my shoulders and he obviously read that to mean 'I don't see why not,' even if I didn't say it.

'Actually I wanted a p-p-private chat with you.'

I murmured something to signify friendly acquiescence.

At that moment his secretary brought in the coffee, a single cup for me.

'I don't drink coffee,' he said, by way of explanation.

It needed a Managing Director to explain – it was a cup of Nescafé. (I wondered if he had other dietary fads besides coffee – he was so slender, if not thin, that he might well not eat much at all.)

'Now,' he said. His long pale face was bright with energy. 'Let's get down to it! If that suits you.'

'Very well.'

'This b-b-iography of Cledwyn Horsfall and his circle.'

'I ought to say that I've not finally decided to write it.' I felt the shadows coming up.

'That's for your d-d-decision.'

I laughed ironically.

'I've read your *Edith Wharton* with great care,' he said.

'And I talked to Iris at length. *I* should like you to write about Cledwyn.'

I'd smiled though my spirits sank. Someone else wanting me to write it . . . 'That's encouraging,' I said, while feeling the reverse.

'And if I got the chance,' he said, 'I should like to publish it.' He gave me a shrewd look. 'I presume you've got a contract with your present publisher. That's not my business. At the moment.'

I took the opportunity to drink some of his disgusting Nescafé. (If he didn't drink it himself, he couldn't know what it tasted like.)

'You must be wondering,' he'd said, 'what my business *is*. Asking you here. I'll tell you in a few words.' He paused. 'I'm concerned with keeping Cledwyn Horsfall's books alive.'

'You think they're in for a spell of neglect?'

'That's pretty certain. I'm saying this in confidence to you.'

'He's one of your major writers?'

'I'm in b-b-business, Mr Cole.'

'I understand that.' Dim remark.

'I'm a great believer in Horsfall's books. They *ought* to be kept alive, non-fiction and fiction equally. And I want *us* to d-d-do it!'

'Is there going to be some difficulty in that?'

'He's probably in for a spell of neglect like all writers when they die. But I have a more serious worry beyond that. Cledwyn didn't improve his chances of survival by quarrelling with academe.'

That modern academe, I thought, whose techniques he said couldn't cope with *his* novels as well as Dickens's –

'He did that all right.'

'Times have passed when a writer could afford to buck academe.'

'I suppose so.'

'Times have come when academe has an increasing say

in setting writers up while they're alive, and massaging their reputation when they're d-d-dead. Academe has become very powerful – there's now a hell of a lot of them!' A smile swept the troubled look from his face. 'You know Ellis's aphorism? *Eng. Lit. has got a strangehold on English letters.*'

'An exaggeration!' Typical Gotham, I thought. But funny.

'Aren't all aphorisms? That's what m-m-makes them aphorisms.' He was pleased with his joke. I was beginning to like him. There was a pause.

'I'm not Gore Vidal's publisher,' he said. 'But if I were, I should be even more worried about his future than I am about Cledwyn's. *He*'s going down the same road as Cledwyn – only further and faster!'

'That interview where he said academe really hates imagination!'

'More especially his biting remarks about their eliminating literature from their courses and replacing it with literary theory.'

'I suppose there's something in that.' I couldn't help laughing.

'Of course there is! That's why they'll make him pay for it. Vidal will suffer for it more than academe will. They'll see to it that he doesn't survive.' He looked troubled again. 'It's got to be my t-t-task to see that the same fate doesn't overtake Cledwyn over here. If that's p-p-possible.' He picked up a gold-plated pencil from the desk-top. 'The right sort of biography coming out in four or five years' time might help to turn the tide. A biography written by y-y-you, of course.'

I'd said nothing. He'd come on to the scene too late. Horsfall must have been a remarkable man on the *sum* of many counts; but on the *literary count alone* not remarkable enough, in my eyes, to justify asking me to spend years on writing about him and his circle, whose behaviour towards each other I'd come to abhor.

'Will you think it over?' He'd inscribed some sort of doodle with his gold pencil. Looking down – 'I'd make it worth your while.'

I'd said I would, and shortly afterwards I'd left his office.

By now, though, sitting in Yola's sitting-room after eating a splendid Chinese meal with her in an atmosphere of rising harmony, I had pulled out of the shadow of my meeting with Heald.

'Sorry I took so long,' she said, as she came in with the fresh bottle of vodka, glasses and a jug of ice-cubes.

'I'm happy.'

She poured the drinks and handed me mine. Then she sat down on a chair near to me. 'Cheers!'

We drank and were quiet for a little while.

'Do you want a smoke?'

I shook my head.

'You look so much less nervous than you did when you were here last time.'

'I'll say . . .'

'You seem different. You've seemed different all evening.'

'How?'

'Happier. Easier . . .'

'I'm both of those things.'

'Then something has happened. You've been keeping it from me.'

'Only till now.'

'Is it about writing the book?'

'It is.'

'The sign you've been waiting for?' She had begun to smile.

'The sign I've been waiting for.' I began to smile in return. 'The movement of the soul, the shake-up of the unconscious, the metaphor's immaterial . . . *it's happened*! I don't know how or why it's happened: it just has. My dilemma is solved. An open and shut case, if that's the correct term.'

'It isn't. But tell me – what did the voice of God say? No, don't tell me – I can read it in your face. It's No.'

'A definite unequivocal No.'

'Oh, James! . . .'

'I didn't tell you I've been having sleepless nights over that beastly book, that bloody book! But I have. Awakening to this same grisly state of Yes – No night after night. I woke up to it again, or thought I had, last night. And then – this is where you'll never believe it – I suddenly was aware that I *hadn't* wakened up to it again. Something was happening, had already happened. I knew it the way you know things in a dream. I knew it. I heard it. NO!' I sipped the vodka. 'So there you are. The deal's off. I'm free of it. Free, can you imagine? The relief of it! I feel calm and composed and unfettered. I don't have to write that bloody book about those people being bloody to each other. I've had an all-change of the spirit – I'm a new man!'

'It's fantastic.'

'Are you glad?'

'Of course I am! I want you to be happier and easier.'

I finished my vodka.

'Why not?'

She stood up and took my glass. I said:

'I like you in this pink flying-suit or boiler-suit or whatever it is. It's smashing. Smashes me, anyway.'

She looked at me over her shoulder and grinned. When she gave back the glass I said:

'When I was here last time there was pop-music in the background.'

'That's because the boys were home from school.'

'Oh . . .'

She was amused. 'Do you want me to put some on now?'

'Why not? I thought the throbbing sound in the distance was . . .'

She laughed at me. 'OK. I'll go and do it.'

She went out and for a minute or so the room was silent,

and dark, lit only by the single lamp. It was the sort of room one could sink into. I shifted myself for comfort among the cushions on the sofa. The music started up in the distance. Yola came back.

'That's nice,' I said. 'I was waiting for you.'

She looked surprised.

'I feel a new man.'

She came over and put her hand on my head. I felt her fingers in my hair.

'I'm so glad for you,' she said.

'I'm so glad for *you*.' I put down my glass.

'What does that mean?'

I took hold of her hand and drew her down to sit beside me.

'The shake-up in my unconscious has settled my other dilemma. You know? . . .'

'James!' She was laughing.

I stretched out my hand and brushed back the hair from her forehead. (It did remind me of a shaving-brush.) Then I quietly joined my mouth to hers. Afterwards she said:

'This doesn't sound like a definite unequivocal No.'

'You've forgotten the all-change in the spirit! It's a definite unequivocal Yes . . . Well, a fairly unequivocal, fairly definite Yes.' I paused. 'I felt terrible when I left you last time. A coward, to be precise. I knew I was determined never again to be locked into marriage. You were offering me something much easier, do you remember? I remember the exact words. "Why not try an affair that's light and undemanding? No commitment. Just pleasure while it lasts." Do you wonder I remember it exactly?'

She moved her head away so as to look at me.

'Is that what you're saying Yes to?'

Faintly abashed I said: 'Yes.'

She laughed again. 'You don't have to look like that, James. That's the offer that stands. What was it? An affair that's light and undemanding . . .'

'No commitment.'

'Just pleasure while it lasts.'

We looked at each other. I picked up our glasses, handed hers to her; and we drank an unspoken toast. Then we lay back on the sofa, leaning against each other. Gradually we folded our arms round each other. The music was throbbing in the next room.

'This is so pleasant,' she said.

I was thinking of this all-change in the unconscious. After a monastic life for six years it was pretty radical. I didn't feel calm and composed. I was feeling expectant and excited, on the edge of change.

The minutes passed. 'It *is* so pleasant,' I said.

After a little while she said, without moving: 'When are you going to make love to me?'

'Now.'

After another little while she detached herself from me. 'Are you going to stay here overnight?'

'That's what I had in mind.'

She nodded her head and said quietly:

'That's the best idea.'

Slowly we rose from the sofa.